Prepare fo. S0-BXX-331
visions of today's darkest
dream-weavers . . .

A nightmare train on a journey to one man's ultimate doom.

The seductive embrace of Death in the flesh.

An antique mirror plagued by hideous reflections of a childish monster.

Human hearts bound in a relentless puzzle of desire, despair, and death . . .

Night Visions: The Hellbound Heart

"*Required reading for anyone ready for 'the good stuff' in short horror fiction. You won't find these great stories anywhere else!*"　　—*Fangoria*

Coming soon:　Dean R. Koontz, Robert McCammon, Dennis Etchison and Stephen King.

Edited by:　Douglas E. Winter, Alan Ryan and Clive Barker.

The NIGHT VISIONS series
published by Berkley

NIGHT VISIONS: DEAD IMAGE
edited by Charles L. Grant

NIGHT VISIONS: THE HELLBOUND HEART
edited by George R.R. Martin

◄NIGHT VISIONS►

THE HELLBOUND HEART

ALL ORIGINAL STORIES BY

CLIVE BARKER
RAMSEY CAMPBELL
LISA TUTTLE

Edited by George R. R. Martin

B

BERKLEY BOOKS, NEW YORK

NIGHT VISIONS: THE HELLBOUND HEART

A Berkley Book/published by arrangement with
the editor

PRINTING HISTORY
Dark Harvest edition/October 1986
Berkley edition/March 1988

ISBN: 0-425-10707-8

For Kirby and Kay,
agents and friends,
with love and appreciation.

GEORGE R.R. MARTIN

RAMSEY CAMPBELL

LISA TUTTLE

CLIVE BARKER

Introduction
The Horror, the Horror

WE CALL THEM horror stories.

There are fools out there who really do think that clothes make the man, and that labels define the literature. Most of them don't read horror stories. Why should they? The term itself condemns the genre as surely as a cheap off-the-rack polyester suit condemns the man who wears it. Great literature should concern itself with life in all its infinite variety, with love and death and birth and hope and lust and transcendence, with all the experiences and emotions that make up the human condition. A sort of story that by its very name proclaims its obsessive interest in only one emotion, that exists solely to evoke fear in its readers, well, that's obviously second-rate stuff, hardly worthy of attention. The closest analogue is pornography, which like horror fiction is dedicated to a single emotion and exists only to evoke lust in its readers. Besides, that packaging— nothing worth reading ever hit the racks wearing a glossy black cover with dripping-blood typography.

Those who hold to these views also tend to think that science fiction is about science, that the mystery is the most important thing in a Raymond Chandler mystery novel, and that Madison Square Garden sits somewhere near Madison Square with all its shrubs and flowers.

We who know better still call them horror stories, but it *is* an off-the-rack sort of label, and sometimes we quibble about it and devise more respectable terms. Horror, we say with indignation; no, no, I'm not after *horror*, I'm interested in *terror*, I'm interested in *fear*. Terror tales? Fear fiction? It will never fly, Wilbur.

Ghost stories, now that has a nice ring to it, very tweedy and dignified and conservative, something that Russell Kirk and Sheridan LeFanu might be comfortable in, lots of tradition there, like an old school tie. If we write ghost stories, we could join all the exclusive clubs and sip cognac from snifters while wearing our smoking jackets. No one would dare sneer at the authors of *ghost stories*. Too bad there are so few ghosts to be found in the pages behind those slick black covers.

How about *supernatural stories*? That has a nice ring to it, and we can pretend that we're not related to those screenwriters who seem so obsessed with psychotic teenagers, baby-sitters, and kitchen implements.

Or maybe *dark fantasy*—now there's an uptown sort of phrase. I'll just hop into my Porsche and zoom right past that 7-Eleven with its tacky racks of horror paperbacks, head straight for my favorite reading boutique to buy a dark fantasy. And on Tuesday morning the sanitation engineers will come and cart my trash off to the sanitary landfill, too.

Ultimately, the efforts to give horror a more fashionable name are as doomed and pointless as the sporadic attempts to rename science fiction, and just as unlikely to convert the heathen. No matter what we call it, there will still be those out there who insist in judging a book by its cover, and a genre by its worst examples.

And since we're speaking frankly here, let us own up to it—horror has given its enemies a lot of worst examples in recent years. Speak to me not of teenage slasher movies and the novelizations thereof, of all the endless rehashes of last year's best-sellers, of violence and gore for the sake of violence and gore, of a thousand thin, derivative, pointless stories told in a prose as melodic as nails on a blackboard and peopled by bloodless vampires, cardboard cops, possessed demon-brats, moronic heroes, and long marching columns of faceless minor characters who exist solely and entirely so that the rats can eat out their eyes. During our recent "horror boom," too many publishers and too many writers seemed to feel that all they really needed was a glossy black cover, a short title spelled out in dripping blood, and a blurb comparing the author to Stephen King, and never mind that nothing fresh or unexpected ever happened inside those pages, that the plots were devoid of sense, that the characters were seldom any more human than the monsters.

Horror can be more than that.

Which brings us, in a roundabout way, to *Night Visions*.

This is a showcase anthology, conceived by Paul Mikol and the folks at Dark Harvest Press. The concept is simple. Three writers, one guest editor. Each writer contributes 30,000 words of original, never-before-published horror fiction. A dozen short stories, a trio of novelettes, a single novella—it doesn't matter; we want the stories the writer wants to tell, at the length he wants to tell them. Everyone is paid a pittance, so it's clear from the start that no one's in it for the money. These are labors of love. Instead of money, the writers are given freedom and the challenge of producing the very best work of which they are capable. Given the caliber of the typical *Night Visions* contributor, the result is an anthology that shows what horror stories are like at their best, what the genre can be, should be and sometimes is.

Night Visions: The Hellbound Heart features work by Ramsey Campbell, Lisa Tuttle and Clive Barker. This might be considered to be the British invasion volume of *Night Visions*—Campbell and Barker are both British, and

Tuttle is a Texan living in London. The British were writing bloody good horror stories long before anyone ever thought of embossing a cover, and Barker, Campbell and even Tuttle are a part of that tradition. They are three very different writers, but they share something as well, and it's more than just a fondness for fish and chips. It has a lot to do with why we read fiction, and horror fiction in particular.

Those who claim that we read horror stories for the same reasons we ride roller coasters are missing the point. At the best of times we come away from a roller coaster with a simple adrenaline high, and that's not what fiction is about. Like a roller coaster, a really bad horror story can perhaps make us sick, but that's as far as the comparison extends. We go to fiction for things beyond those to be found in amusement parks.

A good horror story will frighten us, yes. It will keep us awake at night, it will make our flesh crawl, it will creep into our dreams and give new meaning to the darkness. Fear, terror, horror; call it what you will, it drinks from all those cups. But, please, don't confuse the feelings with simple vertigo. The great stories, the ones that linger in our memories and change our lives, are never really about the things that they're about.

Bad horror stories concern themselves with six ways to kill a vampire, and graphic accounts of how the rats ate Billy's genitalia. Good horror stories are about larger things. About hope and despair. About love and hatred, lust and jealousy. About friendship and adolescence and sexuality and rage, loneliness and alienation and psychosis, courage and cowardice, the human mind and body and spirit under stress and in agony, the human heart in unending conflict with itself. Good horror stories make us look at our reflections in dark distorting mirrors, where we glimpse things that disturb us, things that we did not really want to look at. Horror looks into the shadows of the human soul, at the fears and rages that live within us all.

But darkness is meaningless without light, and horror is

pointless without beauty. The best horror stories are stories first and horror second, and however much they scare us, they do more than that as well. They have room in them for laughter as well as screams, for triumph and tenderness as well as tragedy. They concern themselves not simply with fear, but with life in all its infinite variety, with love and death and birth and hope and lust and transcendence, with the whole range of experiences and emotions that make up the human condition. Their characters are people, people who linger in our imagination, people like those around us, people who do not exist solely to be the objects of violent slaughter in chapter four.

The best horror stories tell us truths.

Clive Barker, Ramsey Campbell and Lisa Tuttle are among the very finest writers in the field, and in the pages that follow you're about to sample each of them at the top of their form. All the usual editorial promises apply; these are stories that will give you nightmares, that will make your heart pound in your chest, your hair stand up, your palms sweat, your flesh crawl. Don't start this book late at night, and if you do, leave the lights on, and so on, and so forth.

But let me add this. When *Night Visions: The Hellbound Heart* is back on the shelf, when your flesh has ceased crawling and your hair has fallen back into place and your palms have dried off, when the sunlight is pouring through your kitchen window . . . you will still remember these stories, these people, these experiences-you-never-had. You will think about these stories, because there are things in them that bear thinking about. And you will come away not merely horrified (for if the truth be told, being scary is the *easy* part), but also disturbed, and moved, and maybe . . . just maybe . . . a little bit changed.

George R.R. Martin

RAMSEY
CAMPBELL

In the Trees

THRELFALL SAW THE aftermath of the crash as he slowed for the detour. Beyond the police cars and their orange barrier, smoke veined with flames smudged the grey sky. Braking, he thought of matches a child had been playing with, matches spilled from a box. They were telephone poles that had fallen from a lorry, blocking both westbound lanes of the motorway and smashing a car. He hoped the driver had got out before the car caught fire, hoped the police hadn't recorded his own speed before he'd seen them. He cruised past them off the motorway, off his planned route.

He was already late for the next town, the next load of unpopular books. He stopped in a parking area with a padlocked toilet and a bin surrounded by litter, and dug out his road atlas from among the week's newspapers. It looked as if the most direct route was through the green blotch on the map and the horizon: pines.

He swung onto the road with a screech of gravel. The road ploughed through the flat landscape, past stubbly fields relieved only by a couple of derelict farmhouses and rusty scraps of cars, and the forest seemed no easier to reach than the blob of sun in the sky. When at last he came to the forest, he had to drive alongside for miles, until he began to suspect that the road through was closed. No, here it was, and he braked fiercely as he turned.

The trees cut off the sunlight, such as it was, at once. He hadn't realized the road would be so gloomy. He might have felt the trees were closing their ranks against him and his vanload of books, pulped wood on the way to be pulped again, books returned by the bookshops because they were too late for the fads they'd been written to cater to. Still, he didn't suppose butchers felt uneasy driving meat past animals. He switched on his headlights and was picking up speed when the children walked into the road.

The sight of the coach parked by the road must have alerted him, for he was braking almost before he saw them—luckily for them, since they dawdled on the road as if he weren't there or had no right to be. They were boys in their early teens, a classful of them accompanied by a disheveled teacher whose long legs seemed bent on tripping him up as he scurried after his class. "Hurry up," he cried. "Stop talking. Leave him alone, Selwyn. On the bus, all of you. Double quick."

He saw Threlfall's car and held up one hand. "Could you let them cross?" he shouted. "Would you mind?" Perhaps it made him feel less ineffectual. He turned on the boys behind him. "Leave that, Wood," he cried.

Or it might have been "Leave that wood," for the three boys who were arguing about how many fish and chips they could afford were dragging what looked like a branch. They stared blankly at him and dropped it. "Not in the road, you chump," he yelled and flung it toward the trees.

It wasn't just a branch, it was carved. Threlfall could see that much before he got out of the car. He felt entitled to be outraged by the boys, who'd piled onto the bus and were opening the windows so as to throw out the wrappers of chocolate bars, and by their teacher—all the more so when he saw that the carving at the thick end of the branch was a face. Why, it must have taken days of careful work, more than you could say for too many of the books in the van. "You aren't just leaving that there," he protested.

The teacher thumped on the window nearest the culprits. "Do you hear? You were told to leave those things alone. They weren't rubbish at all." To Threlfall he said apologetically, "You can't tell them anything these days. I'd make them put it back, but we're already late."

"Sodding right we are." The coach driver climbed down, hands on hips, and glared at Threlfall. "He isn't a ranger, he's just interfering. Make up your mind if you're coming. Put it back yourself if you like it round here," he growled at Threlfall, and pushed the teacher up the steps.

The bus roared away, its headlights slashing at the dim trees, its windows spilling litter and the clamour of the schoolboys, three of them still arguing over two fish and three lots of chips, no, let's have three chips and two fish . . . Threlfall went back to the car, started the engine, stared at the dashboard clock, then abruptly he parked off the road and went to pick up the carved branch.

He didn't much care for it now that he looked at it closely. The eyes bulged like knots in the wood; the face looked tormented, struggling to open its mouth. At least someone had felt something while it was being made, not like the hacks whose failures filled the back of the van. It didn't matter that he didn't care for it, he still had a duty to save it: anything else was vandalism.

The overcast was tattering. Sudden sunlight picked out the trail the branch had made as it had been dragged through the pine needles, beyond a map carved on a board at the side of the road, a map of woodland walks distinguished by markers of different colours. He memorized the positions of the walks before hefting the branch and starting down the slope.

The nearest path was marked by a yellow post. The trail of the branch crossed the path and led under the trees. He had to slow down once the dimness closed in, chill as water. When his eyes adjusted, he saw how he appeared to be surrounded by paths, a maze of spaces between the trees. Most of the apparent paths led into long waterlogged hollows. More than once the branch had been dragged through hollows, and he had to jump across.

Soon the trail crossed another marked path. It should be marked red, and when he peered along it, past the glare of sunlight on its stony surface, he could just make out that it was. Now he could hardly see the trail, even when he was among the trees and the glare had drained from his eyes. The piny smell made him think of a hospital—long, dim, deserted corridors that led nowhere. He stumbled under the weight of the branch and slithered into a hollow, ankle-deep in mud. He could no longer see the trail, either in front of him or behind him, but wasn't there a stony path between the trees ahead? He had to stagger onto it before he was sure there was.

What was more, it led to a building. He could see a corner of the wall beyond the farthest bend in the path. Even if the building wasn't where the carving had come from, whoever was there could take it—Threlfall had spent too much time already in the woods. Which path was this? It ought to be the green one, as he recalled, and soon he passed a post that looked green, though with moss. Whoever was in the building would confirm the way back to the road.

He rounded the bend nearest the building, and nearly dropped the branch for throwing up his hands in frustration. The hut was in ruins: not a wall was left intact, and there was no roof. All the same, the interior looked crowded with figures, too still to be people. He went forward, trees whispering behind him, the face with its knotted eyes lurching in his arms.

The hut had no floor. The earth between the walls was planted with carved sticks that looked as if they were growing there, not sticks but stunted trees with atrophied branches. All had faces; some had more than one. All the faces gave the impression of being not so much carved as straining to free themselves from the wood.

He stepped through a gap between two walls. Tall grass snapped beneath his feet. If he couldn't find the spot where the branch had been stolen from, he would have to leave it wherever there was room. He held it above his head and shivered with the chill that was sharper than under the trees. Perhaps he was shivering a little at the tortured faces too. Of course the carver must have based them on shapes in the wood, that was why they gave the impression of growing. No wonder they were so grotesque, especially the one that looked like a mother whose child's face was growing on her cheek.

He turned away and frowned, realizing that there was no space within the hut where the faces could have been carved. Something else was odd: seen from inside, the hut seemed less ruined than partly built and then overgrown. One side of the hut might almost have been a bush that had grown into the shape of a wall. Weren't those its roots in the grass? But he was wasting time. He'd grasped his stick in order to lay it down when the voice said, "What do you think you're doing?"

At first he didn't realize that it was a voice. He thought it was a crow that had made him start and glance round, or a chainsaw, or even a frog croaking close to his ear, especially since he could see no one. "Where are you?" he demanded.

"You'll find out, I promise you."

Perhaps the speaker thought Threlfall hadn't asked where but who. Was the voice coming from the wall that looked most like a bush? "I'm putting this back," Threlfall said.

"Putting it back now, are you? Too late."

"I didn't take it," Threlfall said, resisting a nervous urge to tell the speaker to show himself. "Some children stole it. I brought it back."

Himself or herself—with such a voice one couldn't tell. "You'll do," it said.

Threlfall felt obscurely threatened. He had a sudden unpleasant notion that someone was about to lift one of the carved faces above the wall, a face with its jaw moving. "Look, I'm leaving this here and I'm going," he said sharply, shivering. He laid the branch down carefully, then he fought his way through the grass between the carvings to the gap in the walls.

Nobody had appeared. Nobody was in sight when he looked back from the bend in the path. It wasn't worth trying to retrace his route through the trees; it wasn't worth the risk—he couldn't locate the trail he'd followed—and in any case the green path would soon join the red and so lead him back to the road. He turned the third bend and found that the green path petered out in undergrowth.

On the map the green had crossed the red twice. He could only go back, staring fiercely at the hut as he passed, doing his best to shake off the impression that a face was watching him from among the crowd of carvings. Perhaps one was, he hadn't time to see. He was glad when a bend intervened.

The deserted path wound on. Was there anyone in the woods beside himself and the unpleasant carver? The creaking that made him glance round must be wind in the trees. He hurried on, searching for a junction to interrupt the endless silent parade of trees, trees beyond counting on either side of him, trees massing away beneath their canopy until they merged into impenetrably secret dimness. There—a marker post in the distance, a reason for him to run—but when he reached it and stood panting he found that it didn't mark a junction, only the path he was on, and it was painted orange.

It must have been red until it was weathered. He was sure there hadn't been an orange path on the map. He must have walked at least a mile from the hut by now; surely he had to be near the road—and yes, he could hear voices ahead, where a dog was sitting patiently beside the path. It took him five minutes of running, giving way frequently to jogging, before he was close enough to be certain of what he was seeing. The dog was a tree stump with a root for a tail.

Then the voices had been wind in the trees. If he let himself, he could imagine that he was still hearing them farther down the path, laughing or sobbing. Movement in the trees beside him made him turn sharply, but it was a display of inverted trees in a pond, intermittently illuminated as the clouds parted and closed again. He hurried on, past the sound that wasn't voices. Whatever was making that sound in the murk beneath the trees, he hadn't time to look.

The road couldn't be much farther. Wasn't that a car passing in the distance ahead, not a wind? He was walking as fast as he could without running, his feet throbbing from the stony path. It must be the sound of traffic, and there at last was the junction with the yellow path. Nevertheless he hesitated, for the sound had seemed to come from directly ahead, beyond the next bend in the orange path that must once have been red.

He shouldn't turn now. Not only was he sure where the road was, but he could see shadows moving on the path where it curved back into sight for a few yards beyond the bend, shadows of people among the unmoving shadows of trees. Thank God that's over, he thought vaguely, and almost called out to the people round the bend—had his mouth open to speak as he rounded the curve and saw that the shadows were of bushes, so grotesquely shaped they looked deliberately sculpted.

They weren't shaped like people. He hadn't time to decide what they were shaped like, even if he wanted to, nor how their shadows could have appeared to be moving. It must have been a trick of the light, but it wasn't important, especially when he looked away from the bushes. A few hundred yards beyond them, the path came to a dead end.

He ran to it, not thinking, and stared into the endless

maze of trees, then he took a deep breath and ran back to
the yellow path. That had to be the way, though the paths
seemed to have nothing to do with the map. He ran, lungs
aching, round a curve and then another, between the trees
that he could almost believe his run was multiplying, and
let out a gasp so fierce it momentarily blinded him—a gasp
of relief. There ahead, where a car swept round the dim
curve past a filling station, was the road.

Thank God for the filling station too. He could ask his
way back to the map and his car: he didn't trust himself to
judge which direction to take along the road. He looked
both ways before crossing to the forecourt, though the
curve prevented him from seeing very far along the silent
road. He could see someone moving beyond the grimy
window of the office. For a moment he'd been near to
panic as he realized that the pumps were rusty, the filling
station obviously disused.

He grasped the shaky handle of the office door, and
cursed. The office was bare and deserted. What he'd taken
to be someone was a torn poster, in fact several layers of
posters, flapping restlessly on the office wall. He caught
sight of a telephone on the crippled table that was the only
remaining item of furniture, and he was struggling to open
the door in case, miraculously, the telephone might still be
working when he saw that it was nothing but a knotted
stick. Were they posters on the wall? Now he peered
through the dusty glass, the figure looked more like layers
of bark, and all at once Threlfall was walking away, round
the bend in the road, which led to a few sawn logs and a
forester's hard hat. The sawn logs would have been blocking the road if there were a road, but beyond them were
pathless trees and growing darkness.

It was still a road, he told himself desperately. It must
be a forester's road—that explained the vehicle he'd seen
passing. It had to lead somewhere; it was preferable to the
paths, at least it was wider. He ran back past the disused
filling station, and there, surely, was a forester, presum-

ably the one who'd left his hat. Certainly someone was standing in a thicket by the road and watching Threlfall through the dark green leaves.

Threlfall turned his back and waited for the man to finish relieving himself. Thank God for someone who would know the way out of the woods. He waited until he began to wonder if the man had been watching after all. Perhaps he hadn't seen Threlfall, but then why was he taking so long in there? Either he was breathing heavily or that was wind in the trees.

Threlfall cleared his throat loudly before turning. The man hadn't moved. "Excuse me," Threlfall said: still no response. He walked around the thicket, making as much noise on the pine needles as he could, without being able to catch sight of the man's face. "Excuse me, are you all right?" The unresponsive silence dismayed him so much that it took more effort to step forward than to force his way through the bushes.

Twigs scraped his skin, the touch of dank leaves on his face made him shiver. Twigs hindered him as he gasped and struggled backward out of the thicket, which felt all at once like a trap. He hadn't seen the body of the figure, only its face grinning at him, the eyes bulging like sap. He hadn't time before he recoiled to be sure, and couldn't make himself go back to determine, that the carved face bore a distorted almost mocking resemblance to his own.

He ran stumbling along the road, which gave out after a few hundred yards. He peered wildly into the depths of the trees until they seemed to step forward, then he fled back past the figure in the thicket, past the filling station where the figure on the wall was still moving, onto the yellow path. Why him? he thought distractedly, over and over. Why not the schoolboys, the teacher, the coach driver, the hack writers, the publishers, the booksellers, the bookseller who'd given him back the study of English forests with the comment, "I thought this would be different from his other mystical rubbish"? If only Threlfall had that book now, with its maps of walks! But it was in the van, wherever that was.

He had to stay on the yellow path, it was the only one he knew. There must be a junction he'd missed, there must be a route that didn't lead back to the hut and the tortured faces and, presumably, their torturer. The trees or the darkness between them closed in, urging him faster along the path, yet he felt as if he were still in the darkening thicket, not running, not moving at all. He'd mistaken several trees or roots beside the path for marker posts or figures waiting for him when a crumpled piece of paper came scraping toward him around a bend, along the path.

He couldn't have said what made him pick it up: certainly not tidiness—perhaps that it seemed infinitely more human than anything else in the woods. He unfolded it and stared, for the moment past comprehending. It was a map, a tracing of the carved map of the walks. It seemed a vicious joke, since he couldn't locate himself on it in order to find his way. He was preparing dully to throw it away when he rounded the bend and started, seeing where the map had come from. A man was leaning on a stick at the side of the path.

He had a long brown weathered face that hardly moved, a twisted nose, large ears. Threlfall stumbled up to him and handed him the map while he struggled to be able to ask the way, to speak. The man took the paper and displayed it to him, his cracked brown thumb tapping the paper to show where they were, then tracing a route: right here, left, turn back on yourself . . . He handed it back to Threlfall, nodding stiffly, having spoken not a word.

Something about his eyes made Threlfall mutter a hasty thanks and hurry away—something about the way the man was supported by the stick. The route seemed more like the solution to a puzzle, and Threlfall wasn't even sure that he remembered it correctly as the dark welled between the trees, the wind snatched at the map until the paper tore, a croaking in the trees behind him began to sound

like words as it came closer, first "Give that here" and
then, almost at his back, "Look at me." That was the last
thing he would do; he couldn't even have looked back at
the man with the twisted nose once he'd realized how alike
in appearance the stick and the man's weathered skin had
been. Here was a junction where he could see no coloured
markers, and he had no idea which way to go. A wind
took him unawares and carried the map away down one
path, and a last instinct made him flee along the other, up a
slope that seemed to be growing steeper, actually tilting,
as he caught sight of the road beyond it, and his van. He
almost dropped his keys as he reached the van, almost lost
them again as he locked himself in. As he started the
engine, he thought that something like sticks clambered
swiftly onto the road beside the carved map, croaking.

All the same, as soon as he was out of the woods he
stopped the van. The bookshops he was supposed to fit in
today would have to wait until tomorrow. He unlocked the
back of the van and rummaged through the cartons, where
eventually he found the book on English forests—published
posthumously, he saw now. It said little about the woods
he had escaped except that they weren't worth visiting;
perhaps the author had felt that to say more might attract
the curious. Threlfall closed the cartons and locked the
back of the van and slipped the book into his pocket, then
he let out the deep breath he'd had to take before turning
to the photograph of the author. This was one book he
wouldn't see destroyed, that he would always keep. He
climbed into the driving seat and drove away, still seeing
the photograph he'd already known was there: the long
weathered face, the large ears, the twisted nose.

This Time

As CROSBY EMERGED from the dentist's he almost tripped over a dog, which vanished behind the bushes. He took more care while crossing the road to the park, for he felt unreal, dreamy. He tongued the hole in his stony jaw and tried to recall what he'd dreamed.

People were walking dogs in Birkenhead Park, or being run by them. A man was training an Alsatian called Winston. On the fish pond the white ducks looked molded out of the reflections of clouds. He had been counting backward from thirty; he'd reached fourteen before the anesthetic worked, and then he'd seemed to begin counting an altogether different set of numbers backward, on and on into the dark. He felt he had arrived eventually, but where?

He walked through the shortcut from the pond to his street. On the playing field beside him, rugby posts were panting in the August heat: H H H. As he opened his front door, pushing back a couple of letters, spacious echoes greeted him.

His face no longer felt stony. The gap in his jaw was plugged with an ache. He was glad he'd drawn today's stint before he had gone to the dentist's—but nevertheless he was anxious not to lose the impressions he'd gathered in the waiting-room: a mother holding her child like a ventriloquist's dummy from which she was determined to coax a brave smile, a teenager who had tried to pretend that the bulge in his cheek was nothing worth noticing, just a sweet. Perhaps Crosby could sketch something for his exhibition.

He gazed across his drawing board, out of the window. Beyond the long garden, the pond blazed among the trees. The head of the little girl next door kept popping over the seven-foot hedge like a jack-in-the box; the seat of her swing was concealed by the hedge. She made him feel all the more unreal, and incapable of sketching the impressions he wanted to fix. When at last he began to sketch, he was hardly aware of doing so.

Ten minutes later he had finished. The man's face stared up at him. It was hairless, and looked smooth as a baby's face, as though it had never been spoiled. Was it a face or a mask? It looked too good to be true, especially the eyes.

Was it even worth preserving? It meant nothing at all to him—yet that was why he filed it away, in the hope that he would remember where the impression had come from. His thoughts were dodging aimlessly about his mind, like the echoes in the house.

Never mind: he was visiting Giulia. He would have waited for her in the art gallery, except that he might disturb her at work. Instead he wandered about the park before catching the train, then strolled through Port Sunlight for a while. Along the vistas of the Causeway and the Diamond, the trees were dark and velvety, unrolling their long shadows on the plots of grass. Everything was steeped in evening light: the columns and domes of the Lady Lever Gallery, the half-timbered cottages that looked outlined and latticed in charcoal, their gardens trim as carpet tiles. Even the factories beyond the estate looked to be pouring forth gold smoke, like a lyrical advertisement for cigarettes.

Giulia was wearing her grandmother's apron. "How do you feel?" she said.

"Cut off from everything."

She gave him a wry smile. "That's hardly new, is it?"

He followed her into the kitchen of the cottage; he'd found that he wanted to talk. "I hope you'll be able to eat," she said anxiously.

"Certainly." She was making several of his favourite dishes. They were too old, and had known each other for too long, to express their affection in words.

She emerged from the pantry bearing spices. "So may I take it that your air of gloom is an aftereffect of the surgery?"

"No, not really. My book has been out for a month, without a single review. What makes it worse is the trash that gets reviewed—three notices this week for a collection of pornographic comics."

"That's exactly why you shouldn't mind that they don't appreciate you. Few things of any worth are appreciated in their own time, I've told you that before." She frowned exaggeratedly at him. "Now, Thom, you just enjoy being depressed. Some of your work satisfies you, doesn't it? That's all that any genuine artist can hope for."

"I suppose so." He sighed, to make her chide him further. "I wish I had more time to do something special for the exhibition. Instead I'll be wasting a day on this damn television show."

"You'll be reaching a new audience direct rather than via the reviewers. How can that be wasted time?" She said almost wistfully, "If I had a television I'd watch you."

They ate in the kitchen, then carried the rest of the wine into the parlour and played chess. One of Crosby's sketches hung above the mantelpiece: an enormous man whose round head resembled a pudding balanced on a larger, and who was devouring a pudding that looked like him. Secretly he felt that Giulia's appreciation was worth all the gushing of reviewers.

When each of them had won a game, they stood close together in the small porch, not quite touching, and lingered over their good-byes. The rocking of the dim train lulled him, made him feel he might be able to meet all his commitments, after all. As he reached home, close to midnight, someone was walking an off-white dog in the park.

He woke convinced that he had been counting backward. The series of numbers had seemed very long. He felt frustrated by his inability to concentrate or to trust himself to his intuition; he had no time now to add to the exhibition, when the private view was only two days hence.

But perhaps— He retrieved the sketch of the smooth-faced man from the file and pored over it. Had he dreamed that face too? The enigma annoyed him, but there was another feeling which, if defined, might help him complete the picture. Usually he regarded his subjects with detached yet affectionate humor, like a father or a historian— but he was sure that whatever he felt for the smooth face, it wasn't affection.

The sound of applause, which he thought at first was a flock of birds starting from the trees, roused him. Down by the fish pond, fishermen appeared to be presenting one another with awards. They were blurred, for Crosby's window was wet, though it didn't seem to have been raining overnight: the park was dry, not a twinkle of rain.

The decks of the Liverpool ferry were crowded with shoppers. White stuffing bulged from splits in the blue sky. A pigeon on the mast of a yacht was modelling the metal bird on the tower of the Liver Building. A naked baby was crawling about behind the legs of the crowd. Of course it must have been a dog.

When he'd overseen the mounting of his exhibition in the Bluecoat Gallery, he sat on a bench on Church Street and watched people. A man with a bowler hat and umbrella danced by as though in search of the rest of his troupe. A scrawny man in a pinstripe suit sat opposite

Crosby, his limbs like sticks of mint rock. A whitish dog
that looked hairless vanished into the crowd.

By the time he reached home he knew what he was
going to draw. An hour later it was done: a chorus line of
businessmen, all shapes and sizes, trotting to the office.
He liked it enough to copy it for the exhibition before
sending it for syndication.

And yet he felt he'd overlooked a more important task.
He wandered through the house, feeling like a stranger
who had strayed into a gallery full of framed drawings
while it was closed to the public. "This is the Michelan-
gelo room," he muttered wryly. "This is the Cruikshank
room. And here is the Crosby room—the smallest room,
of course." Even if he was being unfair to himself, the
echoes agreed with him.

A stroll in the park might help clear his mind. Perhaps
his problem related to the smooth-faced sketch, but he felt
there was more to remember. When he went out the
twilight was deepening: the intricate lattices of grass blades
merged into a smouldering impressionistic glow; the pond
looked solid and dark as soil. He began to follow the path
around the water as the last fragments of light in the sky
went out.

Before long he felt uneasy. The path was caged by
railings, and hemmed in by trees and bushes on grassy
banks. It turned constantly back and forth in a series of
blind curves. Suppose he rounded a curve and bumped into
someone in the dark?

Why should that bother him? It was nothing that an
apology couldn't make right. Of course it would be unpleasant to touch an unseen face without warning—but
how could he do that when his hands were down by his
sides? There was no point in brooding, especially since he
knew that if he left the path now, even assuming he could,
he would be lost.

He hurried onward, stumbling. Tree roots forced open
the cracked lips of the concrete path. A white blotch on the

pond grew suddenly larger, flapping. The gray mass the size of his head which came at Crosby's face was a cloud of midges.

Though the park road was no lighter, he let out a guarded sigh of relief when he emerged from the path. He made his way along the road toward the shortcut beside the rugby ground, and had almost reached the dark gap when he faltered, his jaw lolling. A flat white face had peered over the next-door hedge at him.

He glared up at the seven-foot hedge. He'd had the impression of a face like a bulldog's, but it had only been a glimpse from the corner of his eye; perhaps it hadn't been a face at all, just a piece of paper fluttering in the grasp of the hedge. But weren't the chains of the swing squeaking faintly to a halt? Surely his neighbors wouldn't let their child play out so late; perhaps a strange child had squeezed through the hedge. Their garden was impenetrably dark. Crosby dodged through the shortcut and was blinded by the streetlamps until he reached them.

Next morning he had been dreaming of fire. He'd turned away in dismay, only to find himself surrounded by gloating eyes. More than that he couldn't recall, and had no time to try. He was already later than he'd meant to leave for the Manchester train.

When he arrived panting at the television studios, he had to wait while an old soldier misheard his name and announced him dolefully over the intercom. For a moment Crosby hoped the show had begun without him, but it wasn't that kind of a show. Eventually the producer appeared; his smile was more like a twitch. A makeup girl dabbed at Crosby's face as though cleaning a dusty waxwork before they rushed him into the studio.

The audience applauded, inspired by a placard, as the host strode onstage, a gleaming young man with a discjockey's brittle cheerfulness. Crosby was studying his opponents. The woman who drew feminist cartoons seemed all right, if rather lacking in detachment, but what of her partner on the team, "the wicked wit of Welwyn Garden City"? His hair resembled a shaving brush, his smile was as thin as his voice; his quips made Crosby think of a cruel child probing wounds.

Crosby's partner was a plump man who made jokes in the tone of a patient describing symptoms. What of Crosby himself? "He draws like an artist surveying today's world from a Victorian time machine," the host said, quoting. "Kindly but critical, amused but never spiteful." It must have been the only quote they could find, but it was true enough: Crosby did feel apart from the time in which he was living, a visiting observer—and never more so than today.

It wasn't only the game that alienated him, though that, now that he saw it, was repulsive enough: whichever team produced the first cartoon on a theme culled from the audience won a point, as did the team which provoked the loudest applause. The whole thing was as vulgar as its name, *Top Draw*—a debased circus with cartoonists instead of clowns.

But he was more disturbed by the blank gaze of the cameras—because they almost reminded him of something else. When had he suffered the judgment of expressionless gazes that pricked his skin with dread? Some childhood ordeal he'd forgotten, perhaps? He was still trying to remember when the show ended. The other team had won.

At least examples of his work had been displayed to the cameras, and the host had mentioned his exhibition, though Crosby doubted that the show's audience would be interested. When he arrived home that night, it was raining on a rugby match; bunches of floodlights glared on bony stalks, lines of rain looked like scratches on glass. Even the roar of the crowd seemed indefinably reminiscent—but why did he feel it wasn't savage enough? Shaking his head, to sort out his thoughts or dislodge them entirely, he let himself into his house.

He was drawing his bedroom curtains, and ready to enjoy the ineffectual assault of the rain on the house, when he saw the mark on the window. Momentarily the floodlights and his angle of vision made it resemble the impression which a flat drooping noseless face might have left on the glass. It must be a trick of the rain, which was pelting now; in a few minutes he couldn't even make out where the outline had seemed to be. Then why did he feel that he'd seen such a mark before?

A glimpse of movement in the park distracted him. The trees beyond the hedge were streaming with dim light. When he'd gazed at them so long that they swelled and shifted apart, he caught sight of the man who stood among them, gazing out of the park. It took him longer to distinguish the man's pale companion, for it was on all fours. How could anyone go out walking the dog in such a downpour? Crosby lay in bed and listened uneasily to the rain. Sometimes it sounded like a scratching at the windows; sometimes echoes made it sound to be inside the house.

He slept jerkily, and dreamed he was in bed with his wife, though in reality he had never even thought of marrying. Then he was betraying someone to the expressionless judges in order to save himself, and there was fire again. He spent the next day irritably pondering all this, which seemed just beyond his comprehension, and trying to draw a last piece for the Bluecoat Gallery. He had achieved nothing when it was time to leave for the private view.

It was hardly encouraging. The invited audience sipped sherry, smiled politely at his work or seemed afraid to laugh, talked of other things. He wouldn't have thought that dogs were allowed in here—but whenever he looked around, he couldn't be sure that anybody had brought one. When people met his eye, their faces turned hurriedly blank. Again he thought of expressionless judges.

At least Giulia was there, which was a pleasant surprise;

of course she would have been sent a ticket at the Lady Lever Gallery. "Don't take any notice of how they looked while you were watching," she said afterward. "They liked it, from what I overheard. They were inhibited, that was all." Perhaps sensing that he was unconvinced, she said, "Come to me tomorrow, and we'll read the reviews over dinner, if you like."

If only he could discuss his problems with her! How could he, when he had no idea what they were? That night in bed he tried to catch them in the dark. Though he wasn't aware of dreaming, he kept starting awake and wondering not only where he was, but who. Several times he restrained himself from getting up to look out of the window.

In the morning he was exhausted, but the notices revived him. They were more favourable than he would have permitted himself to hope: ". . . an impressively consistent exhibition . . ." ". . . real wit and style . . ." ". . . civilized humour of a kind one had ceased to hope for . . ." Perhaps his elation would help him discern the rest of his problems.

He spread out the sketch before him on the desk. There was a background that would make sense of the smooth face, if only he could draw it. He still had time to include it in his exhibition—but was that why it seemed so urgent to complete the picture?

The sketched eyes outstared him, challenged him to be sure they contained any secret at all. He had not the least idea what he was struggling to draw. Outside in the wind and the rain, trees tossed like the foot of a waterfall. Was it the wind or his awareness that kept fading? His pencil and his head were nodding, starting up. Perhaps he gazed at the smooth face for hours.

When eventually he fell asleep the pencil seemed about to mark the paper, yet he was too exhausted to intervene. Again he dreamed that he was in bed with his wife. He had woken beside her in the dark. She must be having a nightmare, for she was panting, though everything was all right now: he'd betrayed the smooth-faced man to save himself, betrayed the man who had corrupted him. All this was a dream, since he had never been married, and so he could wake up; please let him wake before he lit the candle! But the flint sparked, the wick flared, and he had to turn and look.

His wife lay face up beside him, her mouth gaping. She might have been panting in her sleep, except that her chest was utterly still. No, the sound was coming from the face that quivered above hers, the jowly face with its tongue gray as slime and its tiny pink eyes like pimples sunk in the white flesh. He thought of a bulldog's face, but it was more like a noseless old man's, and its paws on her chest looked like a child's hands.

Crosby woke, for the pencil had snapped in his fingers. The trees in the park were still now, and hardly distinguishable from the night. When he switched on his desk lamp, the reflection of his hand went crawling among the trees. He barely noticed, for he'd caught sight of the sketch. Before falling asleep, or while he had been dreaming, he had filled in the background at last.

Background wasn't precisely the word. The smooth-faced man had a body now, though not to his benefit; it was chained to a stake, and was burning. As Crosby stared at this, not at all sure that he wanted to understand, he remembered his spell under the anesthetic. As he'd drifted away he had begun to count backward, not random numbers but years—centuries of them.

All at once fear choked him, yet he wasn't sure what he feared. Once he was with Giulia he would be able to think. He switched off the desk lamp and hurried out, contorting himself into his coat. Why did it seem that a dim reflection of his hand stayed in the park?

He strode to the railway station, and kept close to the streetlamps. The downpour had moved on, but rain continued beneath trees. Dockers were yelling inside and outside

pubs. The platforms of the station were deserted, but
hardly quiet enough; he wished the noises would come out
and make themselves clear. The countryside, a glistening
blur, dashed past the train. Fireflies of houses and streetlamps
swarmed by.

He had just stepped onto the Port Sunlight platform, and
was glad to leave behind the foggy light and brownish
repetitive seats of the empty carriage, when something
darted out of the train and vanished up the passage to the
street.

At once his fear was no longer for himself. He ran along
the passage, which was deserted—not even a porter. So
were the half-timbered streets and avenues. The black and
white buildings looked dead as bone. Shadows or rain
bruised the pavements beneath trees. Far down a vista, the
beam of a headlight stretched between two rows of trees,
then broke up and was gone.

Giulia's cottage was rocking like an anchored boat, for
he was stumbling toward it at a run. Something pale was
waiting for him in the porch: a crumpled pamphlet, wet
with rain. Not even a pamphlet—just a ball of paper. But
perhaps it wasn't rain that had made it wet, for it was also
chewed. It was his sketch that had hung on the wall of
Giulia's parlour. It must have strayed out through the front
door, which was open.

Mightn't she have left it open for him? Yet when he
made himself enter, he couldn't bring himself to call out to
her. A tap ticked like a beetle in the bathroom to the right
of the narrow hall; at the end of the hall, light angled from
the kitchen and lay in wedges on the stairs. Amid the
smells of cooking was a stench reminiscent both of a zoo
and of decay.

He had almost reached the first door—the parlour's—when
something dodged out and past him, down the dark hall.
He thought of a slavering child on all fours. He kicked
out, but it eluded him. He knew instinctively that there was

no longer any reason to hurry into the parlour, and it was a long time before he could.

Giulia lay on her back on the floor, in an overturned chair. Her legs dangled from the seat. Her mouth and her eyes were gaping, her lips were wet. Stooping, he felt for her heartbeat. He was touching her at last, but only to confirm that she was dead. After a while he trudged to the kitchen and switched off the cooker.

Eventually he went back to the station. There was nobody to tell, nothing to do. In the empty carriage a lolling face peered out from beneath the seat opposite and drew back whenever he kicked at it. It was venturing closer, and so at last were his memories, but he was beyond caring.

His street was deserted. Light like glaring metal discs lay beneath the streetlamps. Something like a hairless dog vanished into the shortcut to the park. No doubt when Crosby looked out of his window, he would see it and its master waiting among the trees.

He was unlocking his empty house when he thought of Giulia. Both the shock and his sense of meaninglessness had faded, and he began to sob dryly. Suddenly he dragged the front door shut, sending echoes fleeing into the house, and strode toward the park.

His memories were flooding back. Perhaps they would help him. He was almost running now, toward the dark beneath the trees, where the smooth-faced man and his familiar were waiting. Once they were face to face, Crosby would remember both the man's name and his own. He'd got the better of the smooth-faced man once before, and this time, by God—even if it killed him—he would finish the job.

Missed Connection

OUTSIDE THE TRAIN the night rocked like a sea. Distant lights bobbed up and sailed away, waves of earth surged up violently and sank. The hurtling train swayed wildly. In the aisle crowds collided; people grabbed one another, clutching for support; their noise was deafening. But Ted had reached the door, and was wrenching it open.

"Oh no you don't," a voice said.

He woke. Was he home at last, and in bed? But already the jumble of sound had rushed into his ears: the harsh clicking repetitions of the tracks, the ebb and flow of tangled voices. He was still on the train.

He opened his eyes to glance at his watch. God, time seemed to have waited for him while he'd slept. Across the aisle the compulsive talker never faltered. "They're not what they used to be," he was saying. "Nothing is these days." Hadn't he said that before? No, Ted silenced himself: no déjà vu, thank you. He'd had enough philosophy of time this term to last him the rest of his life.

The train hadn't even left the city yet. Perhaps it had halted while Ted was asleep. He shifted so that he could look out of the window, trying to be stealthy: whenever he

moved, the fat woman next to him encroached further.
Specks of a new rain glittered on the windows. Beneath
streetlamps, gleams of orange light drifted across the mirrors of streets, drawn by the movement of the train. At the
end of a street, another train passed.

No, it couldn't have been. What, then? Momentarily
he'd seen windows passing beyond a street, a glimpse of
moving frames like a strip of film pulled through a gate.
An unlit bus, probably. It had seemed to pace the train,
but the far ends of streets were deserted now. Someone
trod on his toe.

Jesus, it was the whining child. He'd stood up to rum-
mage another toy out of the suitcase. "Watch the man's
feet," his mother shouted. "Just you sit down and shut up
or I'll belt you one." "Aw, I wanna get something else,"
the child whined. "I wanna play." God, Ted hoped they
weren't going to keep up their double act for the rest of the
journey. How much longer? He bared his watch. It had
stopped.

Well, that was great. Just fantastic. Now he couldn't tell
how long he had still to suffer; he hadn't been home by
this route before. All he needed now was for the train to
stall. Anything might happen on the railway; this train
wouldn't have been so crowded if there hadn't been some
foul-up elsewhere; the public address system had mumbled
an explanation. How long would he have to be stifled by
this crowd?

He glanced warily at them. The child toyed with a
gadget; his face grew petulant, preparing to whine. The
mother ignored him ostentatiously and pored over a love
story. The fat woman settled herself again; her lapful of
carriers crackled and rustled. The sounds were close, flattened; all sounds were—a perpetual coughing, the stream
of logorrhea across the aisle, the loud underlying tangle of
conversations, mixed blurrily with the rush of the train.
People spilled from the corridors into the aisle, swaying
expressionlessly as wax. Stale smoke drifted in, to hang in

the trapped June heat. Ted pressed himself closer to the window, trying to make even the tiniest gap between himself and the fat woman. He couldn't stand much more of this.

He must be overtired; he felt on edge, somehow vulnerable. The university term had been taxing. Still, he needn't be neurotic. The journey wouldn't last forever. He turned to the window, drawing into himself, itching with sweat.

The city was petering out. Jagged icicles of streetlamps hung beneath shades, houses gaped. A distant train crossed a vague street. Again? It had seemed to pass through a derelict alley. Perhaps a terrace walling off the end of a street had looked like a carriage. Or perhaps it had been the train on which he was trapped, reflected somehow. The night was seeping into the city; it swept away the last walls, and filled the windows of the train.

It made them into mirrors. The reflected carriage closed him in. The fat woman sat forward; her lap rustled loudly. Her reflection appeared, multiplied by the double glazing: her two noses overlapped, her four lips opened moistly. All the faces became explosions of flesh, far too much of it, surrounding him wherever he looked, hot and oily and luxuriantly featured. His own face had exploded too. He must distract himself. He dragged Robbe-Grillet from his pocket.

The child whined, the man talked, talked; the tracks chattered rapidly. Ted read the same words over and over, but they became increasingly meaningless; Ted read the same words over and over, but they became increasingly meaningless. He found himself hoping to find they had changed. He stared glumly through the window, which was thickly veined with rain. Then he peered closer. This time there certainly was a train out there.

It was perhaps two hundred yards away, and racing neck and neck with his own train. It squirmed a little, distorted by the watery veins. He strained to see more clearly. There was something odd about the train. The dimness of its windows could be an effect of the downpour. But why were the windows flickering, appearing and vanishing, like an incompetently projected film? Of course—the train was passing through a forest.

He gazed fascinated. The image seemed hypnotic; it drew him. He grew unaware of the stifling carriage, the rush of noise. The dim rectangular will-o'-the-wisps swayed jerkily between the glistening pillars of the trees. The forest was thinning. As a child might, he looked forward to the sight of the unobscured train. The trees fell back, giving way to a field. But nothing at all emerged.

He gasped, and craned back to peer at the swiftly dwindling forest, as though the train might be lurking in there like an animal. But there was only the long edge of the forest, fleeing backward. The bare fields spread around him, soaked and glittering.

He wished he could ask someone whether they had seen it too. But when he'd gasped, the mother and child had gaped only at him. Again he felt nervously vulnerable, as though his skin were drawn too tight, and thinning. Around him they coughed, whined, shouted, chattered incessantly; tracks clattered. Now he felt more than stifled by the crowd; he felt alienated. Hadn't he felt so earlier, before he'd had the dream? He couldn't talk to anyone; he was trapped in his own mind. The crowd was a huge muddled entity, hemming him in with flesh and noise.

He wanted a sandwich. He wanted to use the toilet. In fact he simply wanted to prove somehow that he wasn't helpless: even lean out of a window for a while. "Will you keep my seat?" he asked the fat woman, but she was asleep, jaw dangling. "Will you keep my seat?" he asked the mother, but she only murmured vaguely, shrugging. The child gaped at him. When Ted stood up anyway, the nearest of the standing passengers gazed speculatively at his place. He sat down again, muttering.

The fat woman snorted deep in her throat, as though choking rhythmically; she rolled against him. God! He shoved her away, but she rolled closer. He thrust his shoulder against hers and braced his feet. The mother and child stared at him. He gazed from the window, to ignore them.

The rain was thinning. Beside the train the ground soared abruptly; an embankment glistened with dim grass and flowers, skimming by. It pressed reflections closer to him; the faces overgrown with flesh became more solid. Surely he must be nearly home. Shouldn't the train reach a station soon? The embankment sank; wind cleared rain from the glass. The ground flattened and became fields, and a train matched the speed of his own.

It wasn't the same train, not the one from the trees. Its lights were dim, but why not? Of course, he thought gladly, it was being shunted into a siding. No doubt they shunted many trains at night, that was why the other train had vanished. But this train was closer, hardly a hundred yards away; and it was not empty. Dim faces rode in the dim carriages, bobbing slightly.

Perhaps the train was a reflection, on rain or mist. On bare fields? Sweat crept over him, making his skin uneasy; he felt a vague panic. It couldn't be a reflection, for the seat opposite him on the other train was empty. There was something wrong with the faces. Ahead the ground swooped up, carrying a road over a bridge. He heard his own train plunge into a short tunnel. But there wasn't a bridge for the other train, it was heading straight for—

The bridge swept over him, shouting; then fields sailed by. They were deserted. There was no second train.

Oh God, he was hallucinating. He hadn't taken many drugs in his time, surely too few to cause a flashback. Was he having a breakdown? For a moment he was unsure which train he was riding. Sweat stifled him; the noise of the carriage enclosed him, impalpable and roaring.

Oh come on, one needn't be mad to hallucinate. He'd decided earlier that he was overtired. Didn't tiredness sometimes force dreams into one's waking life? In any case, the train need not have been a hallucination. Its track must have curved beside the road; the bridge had prevented him from seeing where it had gone. The explanations soothed him, but still unease was planted deep in him. A thought lurked, something that had happened before, that he'd forgotten. It didn't matter. He must be near the end of the journey.

The crowd shifted restlessly, rocking; voices jumbled. Drifts of smoke sank through the ponderous heat; the cougher persisted harshly. The child banged his feet repetitively beneath his seat, the mother stared emptily away, the talker rattled on. Soon be home now, soon.

Outside the ground was rising. The luxuriant faces stared back from the window with their overlapping eyes. It's all right, nothing's wrong. But as the ground walled off the landscape, Ted felt panic growing. The embankment rushed by. He was waiting for it to sink, so that he could see what lay beyond. There was nothing, nothing lying in wait; why should there be? The embankment began to descend. Wind tugged the last lines of rain from the window. The embankment sped away behind, into the dark. At once its place was taken by a train.

It was much closer: less than fifty yards away. And it looked disturbingly similar to the last train. Though the dim carriages were crowded, their aisles clogged with people, the seat opposite Ted's was empty.

Panic threaded him like wire; his body felt unstable. There was something very odd about that train. Dim and vague though they were, the faces of its passengers looked even more abnormal than his own train's exploded reflections. Some were very pale, others looked vividly stained. The shapes of all of them were wrong.

His panic blazed up. He hardly knew where he was. He swayed, borne helplessly over clattering tracks; he was on one of the trains. He saw faces, flesh exploding beyond glass; they might be reflections, or—

The fat woman sagged against him, snatching him back

to himself for a moment. He was trapped in the hot suffocating carriage. A train, dim and flickering as though full of candlelight, was keeping pace with him. Within its windows, all the vague deformed faces were staring straight at him.

He struggled to rise. He had to get away. Where? If he found a guard, perhaps— He must get away from the window, from the staring vaguenesses. He fought to thrust back the fat woman; she was pinning him to the seat. Sweat clothed him. He was still struggling to free himself when he saw that the two trains were converging. They were going to collide.

"Ay, well," the talkative man said. "Not long now. We're nearly there."

He'd said that before: just before Ted had fallen asleep. Everything was wrong; there was no reality to hold the nightmare back. "Christ!" Ted screamed. One or two people stared at him, someone laughed; their eyes had gone dead.

He wrenched himself free. The fat woman toppled toward the window, snoring convulsively. He staggered down the aisle, hurled against seats and people by the swaying of the carriage. He glanced fearfully toward the window, and his mind grew numb. Perhaps it already was, for he thought that the ground had fallen away, leaving the other train still racing alongside, and closing.

He shouldered wildly through the crowd. People muttered resentfully. They moved aside sluggishly; some stood in his path, staring at him. The trains were almost touching now. A maze of hot moist flesh hindered him, choking the aisle, swaying repeatedly into his path. He clawed through. Behind him the muttering grew, resentful, furious; a hand grabbed at him. But he'd reached the end of the carriage.

Outside the door a dim distorted face lolled toward him, staring. He hurled himself toward the far door, against the swaying. He must throw himself clear. Any injury would be preferable to meeting his vague mounting dread. He wrenched at the handle.

''Oh no you don't,'' a voice said, and the trains collided.

There was no sound, and immediately no light. The trains seemed less to collide than to merge. In the absolute darkness, an image lit up in Ted's mind: a wrecked train lying beside a track, and himself crawling away from an open door. At once the image began to dwindle. He tried to hold on to it, but he was being borne away into the darkness. He wasn't the lone survivor, after all. They had come back to take him with them; they resented his escape. The image fled, was a point of light, went out.

He was lying back in his seat. He felt the carriage swaying, amid total silence. He kept his eyes closed as long as he could. When he opened them at last he tried to scream; but as he saw more, he tried to stay absolutely quiet, still, invisible. Perhaps that would make it all go away.

But the fat woman slumped against him. Without looking, he could make out that she had lost part of her face. The aisles were still crowded; objects swayed there. Outside the windows was nothing but darkness. Opposite him the mother's jaw hung far too wide. But despite their appearance his companions were moving, though slowly as clockwork on the point of running down, in the dim unsteady light. The child's body moved jerkily, and in the object dangling on its neck, a mouth began to whine.

Root Cause

I SAT BEHIND my second pint of beer and pretended to be unaware. Over by the billiard table a man in motorcycle leathers was selling a Japanese television; next to the fruit machine three sharp-faced youths in impeccable pastel suits seemed to be muttering about the supermarket across the road. Whenever I glanced at my book in case they thought I was watching, Vladimir said, "We're waiting for Godot." They must have suspected I could hear them, for suddenly all three were staring at me across the archipelago of tables, the frayed beermats and graying ashtrays. I headed for the door while gulping the last of the beer. In the doorway a girl of about sixteen was loitering. I hurried, anxious not to be late for work, and had reached the wasteland of the intersection when I saw the children beneath the overpass.

They were clambering up the concrete pillars as though the tangled graffiti were vines, toward the roadway overhead. Precisely because I was nervous, I had to intervene. I mustn't flinch away because their lives weren't like mine.

As I reached the concrete island in the middle of the crossroads, the children came scrambling down. They had almost dodged into the traffic before they saw I wasn't following. "He isn't anyone," said a ten-year-old, the daytime mother of the group. "He's only the library man."

"You mustn't play under there. You might hurt your-selves." I felt absurdly pompous, but I could only be true to myself. "If you come to the library, I'll find you some books to read."

"Come here till I tell you something," the ten-year-old hissed to the others. When she'd finished whispering, one boy peered beadily at me. "Are you a queer, mister?" he said.

"Certainly not." But I knew how my middle-class ac-cent, stiffened by years of elocution classes, must sound. The concrete gloom pressed down, the muffled hissing of cars overhead made the pillars sound like trees, and I was afraid that if I went toward the children they would run into the traffic without looking. "Don't come to the library if you don't want to," I said, turning away.

Of course I hoped that would lure them in. Certainly the library needed enlivening. Presumably the plate-glass walls had been intended to attract readers to the tens of thou-sands of new books, but when I arrived the place was almost deserted. The librarian gave me and the clock a sharp glance, and I hurried to deposit my coat in the staffroom, burping loudly enough to wake an old man who was dozing over the racing pages.

When I emerged, the children were swaggering toward the junior section. The uniformed attendant went after them at once, eager as a policeman on his first beat. Within a minute they were eluding him in four directions, punching the books as they ran, until the shelves looked gap-toothed. The librarian helped chase them while I served a pregnant woman who was returning an armful of overdue books. I didn't charge her a fine, for she already had three children, and I'd seen her husband a few minutes ago, drinking away his unemployment benefit in the Viscount of Knowsley. All at once my neck felt exposed and red-hot, for the librarian was frowning at me, but she hadn't seen me waive the rules. "Brian, did you tell those children to come in here?"

"Yes, I did, Mrs. Smullen. They didn't seem to have anywhere else to go."

"They most certainly have. They ought to be at school. If they choose to play truant, they mustn't think they have a refuge here. And apart from that, you saw how they behaved."

If the attendant had left them alone they might have found themselves books to read, but I refrained from saying so: I was on probation at the library for the first six months. As the afternoon wore on I stuck labels in books, dealt with a few readers, woke up a snoring drunk, read a landlord's letter to an old lady. The girl who had been loitering in the doorway of the Viscount sat waiting for her mother, a plump pink woman with the fixed thoughtless smile of an inflatable doll. At last the mother appeared in the lobby, beside a man who was averting his face, and beckoned her daughter out. I tried to watch where they went, but Mrs. Smullen was saying, "You weren't to know about those children, I suppose. You'll learn when you've been here a few weeks. I know it comes as a shock that anyone can live the way these people do."

But they had no choice, I thought as I waited for the bus that night outside the library. They were trapped here in the new town, miles out of the city from which they'd been rehoused. Half the firms which had promised jobs had set up factories elsewhere instead. That was why the overpass was empty now, robbed of the heavy traffic which had been supposed to feed the town.

The April twilight settled on the tower blocks—you couldn't tell it was spring out here, except by the green tips of the saplings beside the intersection—and I grew nervous about whether the bus had broken down, leaving me to wait another hour. Nothing moved on the narrow fenced-in pavements, the pale roads. Few people went out at night here, for there was nowhere to go. The overpass stood like a huge gray humped insect, a dozen legs supporting its midriff, and I found its utter stillness oppressive. It was enough to make me nervous all by itself.

Ten minutes later it was smudged by darkness. Now it looked like a petrified clump of trees. If I stared at it long enough I thought that the children were, back again, clambering. Once I was sure that they were, and made a fool of myself by hurrying to look. For a moment I thought they had dodged across to the trees and were peering out at me, as if anyone could hide there: the saplings were no thicker than the poles which were teaching them posture.

I didn't give them a second glance, for I had almost missed the bus. The driver grudgingly opened the doors, then sped up the overpass ramp. I could never understand why buses used the overpass, especially now when the roads were deserted. As the bus reached the top, he grimaced—perhaps at the sight of the miles of tower blocks with their racks of windows, or the way the bus juddered in a stray wind, or the only other passenger, who was complaining to nobody in particular that his nose was bleeding again. Neither of them worried me. Now that I was on the bus, I felt safe.

I felt safe until the next morning, when I saw the police cars outside the supermarket. The shattered hole beside the main lock made it clear what had happened, but I already knew. A policeman was talking to the manager, who wore a dark suit and five o'clock shadow. "Nine televisions, eight music centers," the manager was saying, like a belated carol of Christmas spending. I hurried into the library as if I were the culprit, averting my face.

I felt as if I were, but what could I have done? I had only suspicions to offer, and yesterday I would have had even less. Certainly I had no proof. Still, I felt on edge to speak to the police as I unlocked the front door to let in the old men. In they trooped, to squabble over first read of the newspapers.

I was stamping books at the counter when the police found the guard dog on the island beneath the overpass. As they carried it back to the supermarket I saw how its glassy-eyed head lolled, how the fur of its throat was darkly matted. I was angry, but I was more afraid, and very glad to be helping someone search for books when the police came to ask the librarian if she'd noticed anything suspicious yesterday. Until they left, I was afraid they would ask me.

And as soon as they left I was furious with myself, of course. The three youths would never have known that I was the one who had told the police. But then, I realized as lunchtime approached, they weren't the type that would need to be sure, and that made me nervous enough to stay away from the Viscount of Owsley in case they had seen the police in the library.

I was too tense to stay with Mrs. Smullen when we closed for lunch. Instead I went walking among the tower blocks. Draughty doorless entranceways gaped everywhere; broken glass glittered on stairs, graffiti dwarfed the walls. Here and there I passed terraces with ragged lawns and crippled fences; most of the houses were boarded up. On one of the few larger areas of green I saw children dragging a large plastic letter K and an N through the mud, which explained what had happened to the Viscount. Around the green, injured saplings tried to lean on splintered poles. It occurred to me that the only untouched saplings I'd seen were by the overpass.

I was on edge all day, and glad to leave. A teacher reserved all our junior books on ancient Britain for a school project, the teenage girl and her doll-faced mother strolled along opposite sides of the main road, slowing whenever they heard a car. That night as I waited for the bus I saw how the road stood over the place where the dog had been found, like a spider photographed in the act of seizing its prey. Had the thieves hidden the dog over there, or had it dragged itself? I found that until the bus was beyond the overpass, everything made me nervous—the way the driver grinned to himself, the smell of the raw meat which the woman at the far end of the bus must be carrying, even the distant chanting that drifted up from below, no doubt football songs in the Viscount. Once they'd begun singing football songs when I was in the pub, and I'd felt more out of place than ever.

At least next day was Thursday, my day off in the week. That afternoon I sat for a while on the pavilion and watched the bowlers, old soldiers and retired businessmen whose moustaches were neat as the green. I could almost believe there was nothing more important than the unhurried click of bowls. Later I strolled through the house of the family which owned the estate: elegant roped-off rooms, portraits safe in the past. Usually while I was there, I could pretend I had stepped back in time, but now the house reminded me how I was trying to forget about tomorrow.

When I arrived at the library, it was worse. Overnight half the windows had been smashed. Mrs. Smullen watched the workmen, her lips pursed, as they nailed boards over the gaps. She looked furious with everyone—no doubt the police had wakened her during the night—and I hardly dared say good morning. Besides, I was trying to ignore a secret fear that the windows had been smashed as a warning to me.

Now there was no daylight in the library. I was boxed in with relentless fluorescent light, like a laboratory animal. At lunchtime I sat on the far side of the staffroom from Mrs. Smullen and tried to hush the pages of the Vonnegut novel I was reading. I was afraid to show my face in the Viscount of Owly.

All at once, halfway through the afternoon, I was enough on edge to say "Shouldn't we do something about that girl?"

She was sitting at a bare table, waiting for her doll-faced

mother and whoever she might bring. "What do you suggest *we* do?" Mrs. Smullen said.

I ignored her sarcastic emphasis. "Well, I don't know, but surely there must be something," I pleaded, fighting to keep my voice low. "She can't be more than sixteen years old, and her mother seems to sell her to anyone who comes along."

"As a matter of fact I happen to know she's thirteen." Before I could react to that, she turned on me. "But what exactly are you implying? Are you alleging that I would allow my library to be used in that way?"

I might have been too shocked to pretend that I wasn't. In particular her words dismayed me: suggest, imply, allege—the language of a cautious newspaper. I hadn't replied when a woman came in with an armful of books. "See to the counter, please," Mrs. Smullen said.

The books were overdue, and I felt frustrated enough to take a sadistic delight in counting up the fines. When I announced the total, the woman stared unblinking at me. "My friend owed more than that the other day, and you didn't charge her," she said.

Mrs. Smullen intervened at once. "We aren't authorized to waive fines. If your friend wasn't charged, it must have been an oversight, and she should count herself lucky."

When the woman had gone, leaving her ticket with the unpaid fine and muttering that she'd rather watch television anyway, Mrs. Smullen demanded, "Is that true? Have you been waiving fines?"

"Well, there was one lady, that woman's friend." In fact there had been several. "She was pregnant for the umpteenth time, and her husband's unemployed."

"I pay quite enough tax to keep people like her without encouraging them. Because you're new I'll overlook this, but if it happens again I shall have to mention it in your probationary report," she said, turning away.

I might have retorted that it was also public money that paid her wages, but of course I didn't dare. Instead I tried to lose myself in work, though I was neurotically aware of every one of her movements, wherever she was in the library. The sky darkened, the fluorescent light seemed to intensify, the glossy spines of books glared discordantly. By the time Mrs. Smullen went for her afternoon break, it was pouring with rain.

As soon as the staffroom door closed behind her, I glanced about. Apart from the old men snoozing and mumbling at the tables, the library was deserted, and I didn't think that anyone else would come in until the rain eased off. I hurried to the phone at once, and called the police.

Immediately I heard a voice, I told it about the young girl and her mother. I'd hoped that would make me feel I had achieved something at last, but I only felt uncomfortably furtive, as guilty as if I were making a hoax call. Of course I didn't give my name, and wouldn't let the owner of the voice put me through to someone else. I replaced the receiver hastily, and spent five minutes worrying that Mrs. Smullen had heard the ring.

The girl at the table had found a picture book of Spain and was leafing through it rather wistfully, but I couldn't spare much time to watch her, for I was too busy watching for the police. Whenever the library doors opened, my stomach felt wrenched. I might have been the person they were looking for, not her at all.

I was glad when Mrs. Smullen reappeared. At least I could take refuge in the staffroom. But I couldn't read; I could only gaze out at the dark afternoon, the streaming road, a few cars ascending the overpass, their headlights swollen with rain. I was so nervous that I saw a figure being slashed with knives beneath the overpass. It must have been the shadow of a sapling, knives of rain and headlights. The rain made the graffiti on the pillars resemble huge blotchy faces.

When I emerged from the staffroom, the girl had gone. For a moment I felt guiltily relieved, then I realized that it didn't mean the police would stay away. Suppose they assumed the call had been a hoax? Suppose they recognized my voice? I was afraid to look up when the doors opened, and by the time the library closed I was near to panic. It was almost a relief to stand outside in the last of the rain and wait for the bus, even though I couldn't help peering across at the overpass. I saw nothing unusual, even when I hurried to the window of the bus and stared down from the overpass. There were only the saplings, glistening darkly.

I didn't sleep well that night. I dreamed I was in the staffroom, unable to look away from the overpass outside the window, while someone came into the room behind me. I jerked awake when I felt an icy touch on my throat. After that I couldn't sleep at all, and perhaps that was why, next morning on the bus, the noise of the engine seemed to turn into chanting as the bus reached the overpass.

At least there was no sign of the young girl. Perhaps Saturday was her day off. I managed to behave as if everything was normal: I asked people to keep their voices down, told readers I would put out the returned books in a few minutes, said, "Staff only behind the counter" when they tried to grab returned books from the trolley. Mrs. Smullen could have had no reason to suspect that anything was wrong, until I came out of the staffroom at the end of my morning break and saw her talking to the police.

My reaction gave me away. I hesitated long enough in the doorway for her to see that I wanted to hide. I snatched a handful of reservation cards and tried to look as if I were searching for the books on the shelves, but as soon as the police left she hunted me down. "Was it you who called the police?"

"Well, somebody had to do something . . ." I kept my voice low, and wished that she would do the same; readers were glancing at her. "You said she was only thirteen . . ."

"Let me make one thing perfectly clear to you." Her face was growing red, her voice was rising. "I am in charge of this library. From now on you will do exactly as I say, no more and no less. If that girl comes in here again you will tell her to leave at once.''

"But that won't achieve anything,'' I hissed. ''She'll only go elsewhere. What are the police going to do about her?''

"Will you go back to the counter and get on with your work.'' She turned her back on me at once and strode to her desk.

When I had to give a reader his tickets, I almost dropped them. My fingers felt swollen, my face was burning. Not only had all the readers heard Mrs. Smullen, some of them had given her approving smiles. When she went into the staffroom for her break I mouthed obscenities at her, but that didn't make me feel any less enraged. I was still standing at the counter, digging my fingers viciously among the book cards and readers' tickets, when the three sharp-faced youths came in.

They hardly glanced at me, but one of them murmured something. All of them sniggered as they sat down at the table farthest from the counter. They began to mutter, heads close together, a low blurred sound like the noise of a fly trapped in a room. Even if they had been three other people I would have found it nerve-racking. As soon as an old man turned to glare at them I strode over. ''Will you keep your voices down, please,'' I said, my lips trembling.

They took their time before they looked up at me, smirking. ''All right, squire,'' one said. ''You won't even know we're here.''

As soon as I turned away they burst out laughing and resumed talking. All at once I felt safe: they were on my territory here, I was in charge of the library while Mrs. Smullen was away, whatever she might think. ''That's enough,'' I said with all the violence I felt. ''I told you to keep quiet. Get out and make your plans somewhere else.''

"And what'll you do? Hit us with a book?'' one said. As they rose to their feet, the chair legs screeched over the linoleum. They were no longer smirking, because I'd revealed that I knew about them. One of them reached in his inside breast pocket, and my face and throat already felt raw.

Before he could withdraw his hand, the library attendant returned from a surreptitious visit to the Viscount of Owl. He saw what was happening, and intervened at once. "Go on, the lot of you," he snarled, exhaling beer over me and the youths alike. "Don't try it. I'll have the law on you." For a moment the youth stood there like Napoleon, then the three of them marched out, kicking all the chairs within reach.

I was relieved that the attendant had intervened—not only because he'd prevented whatever they might have done to me, but also because he had decoyed their hostility away from me. At least, I hoped he had. Certainly Mrs. Smullen assumed that I had been helping him throw out some troublemakers. It wasn't until the library closed for the night, and I was waiting for the bus, that I realized fully how blind my hope was. The youths had every reason to cut me up like the dog, and now was their chance.

I hid beneath the overpass and watched for the bus, but I felt by no means safe. Clouds were blackening the twilight; it was very dark among the pillars. I was surrounded by graffiti, incomprehensible as runes. They were confusing the edge of my vision, for there seemed to be far too many pillars, disfigured by huge looming faces. I wouldn't look up, even though I kept thinking that children were clambering overhead; I knew it must be an illusion of the graffiti—no children ever had such bright red mouths. I had enough trouble convincing myself that the spidery saplings weren't fat and darkly glistening.

When the bus came in sight I felt safe at last, but not for long. As soon as I sat down I caught sight of the driver's face in his mirror. The bus was racing up the overpass, and he was grinning mirthlessly, grinning like a wooden mask. He looked insane.

As the bus reached the top, it swerved. For a moment I was sure he was going to drive straight through the concrete railing. When I opened my eyes, we were a hundred yards beyond the overpass, and he looked perfectly normal, almost expressionless. Perhaps it was only my lingering nervousness that had made him look anything else.

My nervousness wouldn't go away. It loomed over me all Sunday while I tried to enjoy the spring among the large scrubbed houses near my home. I thought of calling Mrs. Smullen in the morning to say I was ill, but I knew she wouldn't believe me. My probationary report would no doubt be bad enough as it was.

I didn't get much sleep. On Monday I was tense long before I arrived at the library. Everything made me anxious, even a child who had fallen near the overpass and was crying about his bloody knees. But there was a surprise waiting for me. Someone had been sent on relief from another library, to make the staff up to three.

Mrs. Smullen must have known in advance, but it didn't matter that she hadn't mentioned it to me; I was too relieved not to be on my own with her. Jack, the new man, was an expansive sort who asked the readers what they thought of the books they were returning, something Mrs. Smullen never did. He joked with everyone, even with Mrs. Smullen, until her face made it clear that joking was against the rules. I felt at ease for the first time in days.

Perhaps Mrs. Smullen resented our rapport. Halfway through the morning she showed me an item in the local newspaper. The woman I hadn't charged fines had been arrested for shoplifting; her flat had proved to be full of stolen goods. "I hope that will make you think a little," Mrs. Smullen said, but I was less depressed by the report than by how triumphant she seemed. When Jack saw I was depressed, he winked at me, and I felt better.

"Coming for a drink, old son?" he said at lunchtime. I

didn't mind going to the Cunt of Owl now that there were
two of us. Jack challenged me to a game of billiards,
which I lost hilariously. He insisted on a third round of
beer, and we were gulping it down with barely a minute to
go before the library opened when the three youths appeared at the far end of the bar.

I choked on my beer, and stood coughing and spluttering while Jack thumped me between the shoulders. One
youth was dawdling ominously toward me along the bar,
but it didn't feel at all like a scene in a Western to me.
Then one of his companions caught his elbow and muttered something that turned him back, and at once I felt
impressive as John Wayne. I wasn't scared of them or of
Mrs. Smullen. I took my time finishing my drink; I wasn't
about to start coughing again.

When we returned to the library it was already open,
and the doll-faced woman was flouncing out with her
daughter. "You pack while I tell Reg we have to stay with
him," the mother was saying. So the police and Mrs.
Smullen had made them move elsewhere, but what had
that achieved? Still, I felt resigned to its inevitability,
thanks to the beer.

The beer helped me amble through the next hour or so,
chatting with readers and fumbling for their tickets in the
narrow metal trays, but by the time I went for my afternoon break I felt sleepy. I sat and blinked at the rain that
was striping the staffroom window. Before long I was
nodding. I thought there were too many pillars in the
gloom beneath the overpass, but then I saw that what I'd
taken for a mass of pillars was something else: a glistening
tangle of roots or branches or entrails, that were reaching
for me. They might have caught me if I hadn't been woken
by a crash of glass.

I sat and stared, and couldn't move. Just a couple of feet
in front of me, the staffroom window had been smashed. I
heard footsteps running away, and the clang of a metal bar
thrown on the pavement, but I could only stare at my

reflection in the fragment that remained of the window. I could feel glass in my throat, which was wet and growing wetter. Reflected against the streaming overpass, my chest was darkening with a stain.

Mrs. Smullen strode in almost at once. I managed to stand up, my feet crunching broken glass, so that she could see what had happened to me, but she hardly spared me a glance. She seemed almost to blame me for the damage. Perhaps she was right—no doubt the broken window was the revenge of the sharp-faced youths—but couldn't she see that my throat had been cut? At last I ventured to the mirror above the sink, and made myself look. There was a tiny splinter of glass under my chin, but no blood. My chest was soaked with rain.

Perhaps I should have been able to laugh at my panic, but the anticlimax only worried me: it seemed the worst was yet to happen. After all, I would have to wait by myself for the bus. The hammering of workmen at the staffroom window resounded through the library. Before long it felt as though they were hammering my ears.

But I didn't have to wait for the bus. Though he didn't live near me, Jack offered me a lift home. I felt limp with relief, even when he headed unnecessarily for the overpass. "Here goes the roller coaster," he cried.

As the car reached the top, it veered alarmingly. I thought there must be a crosswind, though I couldn't feel one. I glanced at Jack to make some such remark, and at once I was afraid to speak. He was grinning stiffly, showing his teeth. His eyes were fixed as glass.

I watched him, because I couldn't look away, until we were off the overpass. At once his expression began to fade, and a hundred yards farther on he looked at me. "What's up?" he said.

He seemed back to normal. "What were you thinking about when you made that face?" I said, trying to relax.

"What face?"

"You made a face just now on the overpass."

"Did I? I'll take your word for it, old son. I can't recall thinking of anything. This bloody place, I expect."

He obviously thought he hadn't told me anything, but I felt he had: it was just that I couldn't define it, especially while his hand kept touching my leg whenever he changed gear. Soon he let his hand rest on the gear lever and my thigh, until I drew away. Once I was alone I tried to pinpoint what I should have noticed, but my mind felt like a lump in my head. That night I kept waking, convinced that the prickling of my throat meant it had been slashed.

Next morning I almost fell asleep on the bus, but I alighted before it reached the overpass. Though I couldn't see the driver's face, I was almost sure that he lost control for a moment at the top. I didn't feel any more confident for having escaped the bus. As I hurried past the intersection the buds of the saplings looked too green, violent as neon.

Jack clapped me on the shoulder when he arrived. "How are you today, old son?" I tried to stay away from him and Mrs. Smullen; I didn't feel at ease with either of them. Old ladies jostled in front of the shelves of romances, the attendant threw out several children for giggling at picture books. I searched for adult books on ancient Britain for the class that was coming in later. Through one of the remaining windows I could see the overpass, rearing up as if to pounce.

When I went for my morning break I wasn't conscious of taking a handful of the history books with me. I sat in the boarded-up staffroom and tried to relax. Flats in the tower blocks must feel like this, like cells. More than the glaring light, it bothered me that I couldn't watch the overpass. I closed my eyes and tried to find a reason for all the tension and frustration I was suffering. If I could understand them, perhaps they would go away. If they lingered they would grow worse, and I couldn't imagine what I would do then.

My hands were clenching. They clenched on the books,

which I realized at last I was holding—and suddenly I realized what I'd overlooked.

For a while I stared at the unopened books. I had to know, and yet I was afraid to find out. Eventually I turned to the index of the first book. There wasn't much to find: most of England had been Celtic in the fourth century, the Druids had performed human sacrifices in sacred groves. Perhaps I was wrong, perhaps my impressions had no historical basis after all. In any case, how long could an area of land retain its character? Could any influence survive so long?

I opened the second book, and there it was: a Roman description of a sacred grove. Barbaric rites—*barbara ritu sacra deorum*—every tree sprinkled with human gore, altars heaped with entrails. Trees were carved to represent gods—*simulacra maesta deorum*—and I knew how the Romans must have felt to be hemmed in by the huge looming faces, for I had felt it myself. I was sure of myself now. Jack had said more than he knew when he'd called it a bloody place.

I was sure of myself, but not of what to do. Who could I tell? What could I say? I hurried out of the staffroom, trying to think whether there was anything at the intersection that might convince people, and saw the school bus full of children in the distance. It was heading for the library—for the overpass.

At once my sense of danger was so intense that I began to shake. There wasn't time to explain to anyone. I had to act, I mustn't fail again. My whole body was tingling with apprehension, and yet deep down I felt relieved, capable of dealing with the miles of concrete and everything within them at last. All at once everything seemed clear and simple. The bus came speeding down the long straight road as I ran panting toward the intersection. Before I reached it, my lungs felt raw.

By the time I stumbled to the far side of the intersection, the bus was only yards away. I stood in front of the overpass and gestured wildly for the driver to go round. When the grin formed slowly on his face I knew what I'd failed to anticipate, but it was too late. As he drove straight at me my vision blurred, and the saplings seemed to bend toward me like the tendrils of a carnivorous plant. As the bus knocked me down into darkness, I thought I heard the children chanting.

But perhaps I was wrong. Perhaps I was wrong about everything. When he came to visit me in hospital, the driver said that the steering had locked. He'd managed to brake, though not in time to prevent the impact from fracturing three of my ribs. Perhaps he had been grimacing as he fought the wheel, not grinning at all.

Yes, I think I was wrong. Now that I read over what I've written, I think that the unfamiliarity of everything distorted my view of it—of the intersection most of all. I can hear the birds in the trees outside the window, singing with their bright red beaks, and it seems to me that the saplings by the intersection may be the most important factor in the lives of all those people. When they grow into trees, surely their green must brighten those lives. Once I leave the hospital, I must do what I can to help the saplings grow as they should.

Looking Out

THE FIRST TIME Nairn saw the figures in his house, he thought the landlord had won.

Nairn hammered his stick triumphantly on the pavement as he neared home. Even his legs weren't hobbling him so much; he was almost striding. The girl at the supermarket had tried to cow him: "I can't let you have this sugar. You haven't bought enough goods. You can see the sign, a pound for a pound." I can read well enough, he'd thought; in my day we went to school to learn. When she continued to refuse he'd thumped the sugar down on her counter, and the bag had split. "You can't sell that to anyone else now," he'd pointed out. "It's damaged goods." She still hadn't sold it to him, bitch in the manger that she was, but they both knew she was the loser. He was smiling as he arrived home.

He was reaching in his pocket for the key, smiling more broadly as he remembered that for the first time in months he wouldn't be greeted by the scrabble of rats nagging at the house, when a movement in his bedroom caught his attention. He glanced up in time to see a group of dim-faced figures peering out at him.

At once he was hurrying toward the house, slashing his

stick through the net of grass which overgrew the path. He locked the front door behind him and hobbled toward the back, kicking a letter along the hall. When he'd locked the back door he leaned on his stick, smiling grimly. Let them try to get out now without his seeing who they were. Both doors had mortice locks. The intruders would get the keys over his dead body. No doubt they were capable of that, if they were like most people today. But let them try to explain away his corpse. Eventually, when they'd still made no sound, he crept upstairs in search of them.

The house was empty. It took Nairn some time, his heart labouring despite his resolve, to be convinced of that. They weren't hiding behind his dressing table, and they couldn't be under the bed: the bedclothes didn't hang so as to conceal anyone, they were folded over in the centre of the double bed for warmth. But nor could anyone hide in the other two bedrooms; the door of one was missing, the other room was crowded with furniture and trunks unbrokenly coated with dust.

Nairn crept back through the house. Even he, knowing where to tread, couldn't avoid making the loose boards spring and creak beneath the mangy carpets. Nobody could have left the house before he locked the back door without his hearing them.

He was stooping to pick up the letter from the hall floor when he realized what he must have seen. Through the fanlight above the front door he could see people bunched in the window of the first-floor flat opposite. He'd glimpsed their reflections in his bedroom, staring out, possessive and darkly faceless. Let them watch, he thought. They won't see much. They'd love to come in and look round, I know. Over my dead body. He took the letter into the living room, his feet gritting on coal dust.

It was from the landlord. Nairn could tell by the envelope, by the misspellings and the handwriting, which was that of an ignorant man. The sort who thinks everyone as ignorant as himself, Nairn thought. On his last visit the

landlord had scurried through the house, not even waiting
for Nairn to catch up; he'd stared at the bedroom door
leaning next to the frame from which its hinges had rusted
free, he'd peered at the damp peeling away the sitting-
room wallpaper, he'd gazed into Nairn's bedroom, sniffing. "I'm sorry to hear you've a cold," Nairn had said
satirically. The man had offered to ask friends to do the
repairs, but Nairn knew what that meant: sending his
friends to sneer at the way the old fool couldn't cope, to
snoop and report back. "I'll see to it myself," Nairn had
said, "when I have the money and time."

The following day he'd had the mortice locks fitted.
Since then he'd had three letters from the landlord, and
here was the fourth. He tore it up unopened and built a
small pile of coal over it, in the grate. Soon the brownish
walls and ragged floor were fluttering about him, amid the
darkness; a cold fire flickered in the mirror on the wall. He
sat gazing at the sputtering coal. If the landlord and his
friends thought they'd picked a helpless victim, they'd find
out how mistaken they were.

On the day the next letter arrived, he saw the face.

The postman was crossing the road to the flats opposite
when Nairn returned from collecting his pension. "Good
day," Nairn said, but the man didn't touch his cap, though
he couldn't have been more than twenty. Watching him
pass, Nairn saw that the first-floor flat was still curtained.
You'll have to get up earlier than that to catch me, he
thought. He turned toward his house, and saw it staring
down at him from his bedroom window.

The face seemed to be perched on top of a shapeless
heap of gray material. The body must be hidden within the
mass, Nairn thought, even though he found it impossible
to distinguish the material: they couldn't trick him into
believing anything else, his eyes might be growing weak
but not his mind. The face, however, he could make out
clearly enough: a thing of bone and discoloured sucked-in
skin, patched with colourless hair that was sodden with

sweat, grinning out at him. The dark October sky drifted across it and peeled away, leaving the wide mirthless grin untouched.

Nairn limped toward the house, stamping his stick. He locked the doors and searched. When he'd searched twice and found the building empty, he knew the landlord and his friends were responsible. Nobody else would have had keys to the house. The man was trying to frighten Nairn out. He'd soon see who he was dealing with. Nairn strode unsteadily back to the hall, drubbing dust from the carpet with his stick.

Though Nairn's name was still misspelled on the envelope, the letter wasn't from the landlord. It was officially franked, from the courts: a summons. Another attempt to frighten him. He halved the unopened envelope slowly and deliberately, until the pile was too thick to tear. He couldn't bear a man who was underhanded. If the landlord had anything to say to him, let him come and say it to his face.

It took him most of the day to drag the bed into a position from which, lying down, he could watch his bedroom door. He'd managed to manhandle chairs to block the front and back doors, skinning the walls as he did so. He lay on the bed in the dark, resting sleeplessly. The bedroom door, which he'd closed fast, merged with dimness; closed fast, it hung in the darkness, distant and invisible. He lay waiting for the dark and the silence to burst open. He must hear a chair fall first. He saw the gray shapeless mass advancing toward his room, bearing the yellowed grinning face toward him. "Come on!" he shouted furiously, but only his voice clattered flatly about the house.

Nothing came that night, nor the nights following. But each time he made to pull the chair away from the front door, he halted. Maybe they thought he was a fool, who'd go out and give them the chance to get in. He knew they were watching. He was sure they were in the first-floor flat opposite. If the people there felt about him as he felt about them, they would be delighted to see him beaten. Besides, the landlord owned them. No doubt he thought Nairn hadn't noticed him collecting rent from the flats.

When at last he had to go out, he gathered dust in a dustpan beforehand and spread it over the sashes of the windows and on the floor in front of the exterior doors. Perhaps their footprints would betray them; the landlord's shoe soles were imprinted in the mud of the lawn. Let them explain that away.

Nairn collected his pension and shopped on the same journey. Long before he reached home he was exhausted; the November wind tugged viciously at his wheeled basket, like a dog. His legs ached dully, and the pain left him no room to be surprised to see his bedroom crowded with figures.

The face was there, protruding from its gray mass and grinning. The other figures, four or five of them, clustered dimly behind it, staring out. Nairn was sure that they were all sneering down at him. He stared up at the window, clenching his fist on his stick, to see how long they dared taunt him.

At last he hurled himself forward, nearly falling, and wrenched open the front door. They hadn't time to descend the stairs, and nobody was halted in flight on the staircase; but his bedroom was empty. He hardly bothered to search the house and confirm that the dust on the sashes was undisturbed. He already knew that the dust before the doors was untouched.

They were very clever. Too clever for their own good. They'd shown they could enter his house whenever he was out, without leaving a trace. But they had overlooked one possibility: that he would never go out. Then let them try to take over his house. "Over my dead body," he shouted, sending his voice to stake his claim on every recess of the building.

They didn't believe him, didn't they? He stumped into the kitchen and grabbing the rat poison, thumped his way upstairs and dropped the packet triumphantly by the bed. Let them try to bully him out now, let them lay a finger on him, they'd see what would happen.

He spread his food more thinly on his plate. He sat nearer to a smaller fire. He tore up a letter. He lay in his cocoon and heard the restless sounds of the house tiptoeing toward him through the dark. He saw the sunken patched face grinning at him, perched atop the gray mass. He started awake and saw it at the end of his bed, hulking. But it was only the dawn, creeping into his room like a cloud of dust.

Soon he'd used up all his coal. He sprinkled a last crackle of dust from the coal scuttle and watched the fire dimming again to somnolent pink. About to brew a cup of tea, he controlled himself. He'd only start nibbling at food if he went into the kitchen. He wasn't a rat. And he didn't need tea just to cheer himself up. He could keep warm in bed.

The first thing he saw when he entered his room was the packet of poison. He stared at it, confused. Had he intended to use that on himself? Oh no, they wouldn't drive him to that. They thought they could win that way, did they? He'd bent stiffly to pick up the poison when, reflected in the muddy sky in the window, he saw the figures behind him.

There were five of them, converging swiftly on him, a fluttering heartbeat away. He twisted about; his stick slipped on a board, and he fell. By the time he'd levered his throbbing body to its feet it was useless to pursue them; he hadn't even glimpsed which way they'd fled.

They were showing him how bold they could be, were they? His fury mounted in time with the pulsing of his bruises. Their spies had told them he had to go out now to get coal, had they? Then he wouldn't move from this room except for the calls of nature.

Nor did he. He lay thinking: if they want to get me out now they'll have to carry me, bed and all. Such big brave fellows, it should be easy for them to carry an old man downstairs. They'll see what sort of old man they're dealing with if they try.

The house creaked like a boat, the light swelled and drained away; Nairn drifted. Once he heard a sound at the front door, a metallic snap. He reached the window in time to see that it had been the postman, but after that he sat in a chair at the bedroom window, wrapped in his blankets. They would have to come through the front garden to reach the house. Even they wouldn't dare to be seen climbing over the backyard wall.

His mouth, his throat, his stomach felt like parchment. His body seemed light as paper. They won't blow me away, he thought. The postman stared back at Nairn's window, frowning. No, they haven't got rid of me, Nairn told him. Frown all you like.

The walls of the room looked, and moved, like a stormy sky. As the December clouds sailed by Nairn felt them pulling gently at him, coaxing him out of his room. You won't get me out, he thought. Not you or anybody else. He kept his eyes on the garden gate, through which any intruders had to pass; he ignored the stealthily pacing creak of the floorboards, ignored his bedroom door as it fumbled in its frame.

Once, downstairs, something fell, its hollow clatter cackling through the house. Nairn turned sharply and saw his wife lying on the bed, a gray stick figure gasping openmouthed but voicelessly. Only in his dreams had the doctor let him see her like that. He turned his back on the room, on the walls that rose slowly like smoke, and felt the room turn with him like a staggering roundabout. His unkempt beard crawled moistly on his cheeks. As he gripped the arms of the chair and fought dry nausea, he caught sight of figures in the flat opposite, watching him. Keep watching, he told them. You won't see me blow away.

When he saw the policeman ring the bell of the flat,

when someone came to the street door and pointed to Nairn's room, he knew they thought they'd won. He was hardly surprised, as the dark sky began to hang lower like damp paper, to see the landlord drive up and join the watchers.

Nairn tried to hook the poison toward him, but his stick flew from his hand and slid under the bed, and he had to crawl to the poison. Never mind the stick. He didn't need that to beat them. He grasped the chair, fell back on the floor and the second time managed to clamber in, wrapping the blankets about himself.

The watchers were standing outside the flats, no doubt to taunt him. No, because now he could see what they'd been waiting for: an ambulance. They were striding toward the house, two ambulancemen, the policeman, a man from the flat, the landlord. Even now the landlord didn't dare tackle Nairn alone. This time he'd tricked himself, for there would be witnesses to what he'd made Nairn do. Nairn gripped the poison beneath the blanket, like a concealed weapon.

They were knocking on the front door, knocking louder, battering. That's right, Nairn thought, break it down. Eventually they did so, by the sound of it. He heard their footsteps beating the boards of the hall, knocking on the house to show how hollow it was. As their tread came thudding upstairs, he remembered the day the landlord had given him the key, remembered his wife running up the stairs, agog at the size of the house.

As they strode across the landing, he tried to rise and face them, but his legs trembled and threw him back into the chair. To face them would give them the satisfaction of being acknowledged, anyway. Better to ignore them. He turned to the window as his bedroom door slammed back and saw the five of them hurry into the room, spreading out to converge on him. He cupped his hand to his mouth and swallowed the poison.

There's your house, he told the landlord. You didn't

believe it would be over my dead body, did you? Try and make your tenants forget this was my house now, if you can. He grinned at himself in the glass of the window, as the blackening sky reached out for him. He saw the five of them at his back, staring. He saw his own starved, hair-patched face grinning through the window, above the gray shapeless swathe of the blankets.

Then the poison clamped the grin to his face.

Bedtime Story

SOON JIMMY GREW bored with watching his parents holding tiny saucers and sipping coffee from tinier cups. They looked awkward as grown-ups playing tea parties. He could tell that they wanted him out of the way while they talked, and so he ventured upstairs, though he wasn't sure his grandmother would want him to. All at once he was breathless, because there was so much he hadn't seen before: an attic full of objects made mysterious by dust, polished banisters that begged to be slid down, a small room halfway up the house, that faced the park. Down in the rose garden paths split the lawns into pieces of a giant green jigsaw, over by the lake trees waited in line to be climbed, and suddenly he wished this was his room—but when he turned, there was already someone in the room behind him.

It was only himself in the wardrobe mirror. The dusty sheen of the glass made it stand out from the backing, made it look like a mirror into another room. He stared until his face grew flat and glary, until he felt as papery as his reflection looked, and very aware of being only seven years old. As he crept downstairs his father was saying that once he found another teaching job he was sure they'd get a mortgage, Jimmy's grandmother was saying she had friends who would bring his mother work if she learned how to sew, and Jimmy thought they'd finished wanting him out of the way.

From her look he thought his grandmother was about to tell him off for going upstairs. "Well, James, you're going to live with me for a while. Will you like that?" she said.

He could feel his parents willing him to be polite. "Yes," he said, for it was the first week of the summer holidays and everything felt like an adventure. Even living here did, especially when he found he was having the room with the mirror. It was as though finding himself already in the mirror had made his wish come true. He didn't even mind when that night his mother stayed downstairs while his grandmother tucked him into bed and gave him a wrinkled kiss. He made a face at the mirror, where he could just see himself in the light from the park road. Then she turned in the doorway to look at him, that look which made him feel she knew something about him she wished were not so, and he hid under the sheets.

Next morning he ran into the park as soon as he was dressed. It was like having the biggest front garden in the world. Soon he'd made friends with the children from the flats next door, Emma and Indira, who had to wear trousers under her skirt, and Bruce, who was fat and always sniffing and would blubber gratifyingly if they pinched him when they were bored. The children made up for being put to bed too early by Jimmy's grandmother, who had somehow taken over that job, for having to be exactly on time for meals, which were as formal as going to church. Then his mother started her job at the nursery, and his father kept having to go for interviews, and Jimmy realized his life had scarcely begun to change.

At first she only fussed over him and told him not to do things, until he felt he couldn't breathe. Once, when he lifted down his father's first examination certificate—the glass gleamed from her polishing it every day—she cried,

"Don't touch that" so shrilly that he almost dropped it.
Worse, now he was forever catching her watching him as
if she was trying not to believe what he was.

One day, when a downpour crawling on the windows
made even the trees look gray, he went up to the attic.
Behind a rusty trunk he found several paintings, one a
portrait of his father as a child. Before he knew it she was
at the door. "Must you always be into mischief, James?"
Yet all he was doing was feeling sad, that she must have
taken weeks over each painting only to leave them up
here in the dust.

That night he lay wondering what she'd thought he
would do to her paintings, wondering what she knew. The
dusty reflection reminded him of a painting, the dim figure
still as paint. It was a painting, and that meant he couldn't
move. By the time he managed to struggle out of bed he
didn't like the mirror very much.

Downstairs his grandmother was saying "You must say
if you think I'm interfering, but I do feel you might choose
his friends more carefully."

Jimmy could tell from his father's voice that he'd had
another unsuccessful interview. "Who do you mean?"

"Why, the children from the flats. The darkey and the
others."

"They seem reasonable enough kids to me," his mother
said.

"I suppose it depends what you're used to. I'm afraid the
class of people round here isn't what it was when I was
young. I know we aren't supposed to say that kind of thing
these days." She sighed and said, "That sort of child
could make life difficult for James if they found out what
he is."

Jimmy realized he'd been clinging to his bedroom door,
for as he crept forward to hear better it slammed behind
him. "I'll see what's wrong," his mother said sharply.
"You've done enough for one day."

Jimmy hurried back to bed and tried to look as if he

hadn't left it. In the dimmer bed, someone else was hiding beneath the sheets. His mother tiptoed into the room. "Are you awake, Jimmy?"

"I heard Granny. What did she mean? What am I?"

"Bloody old woman," his mother whispered fiercely. "I was going to have you when we got married, Jimmy, that's all. It doesn't mean a thing except to people like your grandmother."

As she kissed him goodnight, he saw her stooping to the dim face in the mirror, and suddenly it seemed more real than he was. Whatever was wrong must be worse than she'd said, for how could that make his grandmother watch him that way? After that night he could never be quite sure of Emma and her friends. He was afraid they might find out what he was before he knew himself.

One day they came into the house. His grandmother was in the park, calling "Mrs. Tortoiseshell" after a lady who appeared to be very deaf. Jimmy had grown bored with watching the chase when the others came to find him. "I've got to stay in until she comes back," he said. "You can read my comics if you like."

He led them up to his room. Bruce had to read everything out loud, though he was two years older than Jimmy, and the best he could make of Kryptonite was "k, k, kip tonight." Jimmy laughed as loudly as the others, but he didn't like the way they were crumpling his comics. "I know where we can go," he said. "There's a great cellar downstairs."

There were mountains of coal, and a few graying mops and pails that looked stuck to the walls by shadow, and the furnace. That was a hulk like a safe taller than his father, overgrown with pipes. Jimmy wished it were winter, because then he could open the door and watch the blaze; now there was nothing inside but a coating of soot and ash. The three of them were hiding from Bruce to make him blubber when Jimmy's grandmother found them.

"Don't you dare come in here again. Just you remember

the police are only up the road." She warned Jimmy that she'd tell his parents when they came home, but they didn't seem very concerned. "I can't see what you have against his friends," his mother said.

His father clenched his forehead against a headache. "Neither can I."

"Oh, can't you? Once you could have. Anyway," she said, gazing at Jimmy's mother, "I'm afraid I insist on choosing who comes into my house."

After a painful silence his father said, "That's it, then, Jimmy. You'll have to do as your granny says."

Jimmy sensed his mother was more disappointed than he was. "Do I have to?"

"There, you see, he won't be told. What he needs is a good thrashing."

"He won't get one from us," his mother said. "And anyone else who touches him will be very sorry."

His grandmother ignored her. "Thrashing never did you any harm."

Jimmy found the idea of her beating his father so disturbing that he ran blindly upstairs. His body seemed to have made the decision to run while he tried not to think. What was he that his grandmother hated so much? He reached the landing and was suddenly afraid to open his door in case there was already someone in his bed. Yes, someone was beyond the door, creeping toward it as Jimmy went helplessly forward. Once the door was open, they would be face to face, and what would happen to Jimmy then? He was fighting not to turn the doorknob, and unable to be sure that it hadn't already begun to turn, when his mother came upstairs. "That's right, Jimmy," she said, suppressing her anger. "Time for bed."

Nobody was in his room except the face that peered around the edge of the mirror. He could tell it was his own face until he got into bed. His mother seemed anxious to go downstairs—because she wanted to hear what the others were saying, he told himself, not because of anything in his room. "Don't worry, we won't let anyone harm you," she said, but he wasn't sure she knew the nature of the threat.

The night was hot as a heap of quilts. He was nowhere near sleep when his grandmother came up. She tucked in the sheets which he'd kicked off, and shook her head as if someone hadn't done her job. "You must promise me never to go near the furnace again. Do you know what happens to little boys who go near ovens?" She told him the story about the children whom the old witch lured into the gingerbread house, except that when his mother used to read him the story the children had escaped. He tried to make faces at the mirror so that he wouldn't be frightened, but couldn't be sure of the face in the other bed; it seemed to be grinning, which wasn't at all how he felt. He squeezed his eyes shut, and when she left, having given him a withered kiss, he was afraid to open them; he felt he was being watched.

His father was growing short-tempered as one interview after another proved to be fixed in someone else's favour. In the mornings he loitered near the front door until the mail arrived, and Jimmy heard him saying "Shit" when he opened his letters or when there weren't any. The house felt as if it was waiting for a storm, and it was on the day of the tea party that the nightmare began.

Usually Jimmy managed to avoid these gatherings, but this time his grandmother insisted on showing him to her friends. He stood awkwardly, surrounded by faded tasselled lamps and the smells of age and lavender water, while the old ladies dramatized appreciation of their microscopic sandwiches and grumbled about strikes, crime, Russians, television, prices, bus timetables, teachers, children. "He isn't such a bad boy," his grandmother said, holding his hand while they gazed at him. He was seeing a hairy wart, a hat like a green and purple sea urchin, mouths the colour and texture of healing wounds. "He got off to a bad start, but that isn't everything. He just needs proper handling.''

Jimmy felt more confused than ever, and escaped as soon as he could. As he stepped onto the sticky road, Emma waved at him from her window. ''Everyone's gone out. We can play being mummy and daddy.''

He and his parents had often used to wear no clothes in their flat, but now they wouldn't even let him go undressed. Sure enough, Emma suggested they take off their clothes before dressing up, and he was almost naked when Mrs. Tortoiseshell saw him. She was holding a plastic bag of ice cubes on top of her head. She stood there aghast, one hand on the bag and the other on her hip, like a caricature of a ballerina. Then she vanished, crying so loudly for his grandmother he could hear her through the two windows.

He felt infested by guilt. Mrs. Tortoiseshell must know what he was. He fled into the park, because he couldn't look at Emma, and hid behind a bush. Soon the old ladies emerged, calling ''Bye-ee'' like a flock of large pale birds, and his grandmother saw him. ''James, come here.''

She only wanted to show him an old book. That made him think of a witch in one of his comics, except his grandmother's book was for doctors. ''Just you leave girls alone,'' she said, ''unless you want this to happen to you.'' She seemed to be showing him a picture of a decaying log: did she mean his arms and legs would drop off? He was still trying to make it out when his mother came home and saw the picture. ''What the Christ do you think you're doing? What are you trying to turn him into?''

''Someone has to take him in hand while you play nursemaid to other people's children. I never thought my son would end up married to a nanny.''

Jimmy thought his mother would explode, her face had turned so mottled. Then his father came in. One look at the tableau of them, and he groaned. "What's wrong now?"

"You tell me. Tell me why she's showing him this crap if you can."

"Because he was up to no good with the little strumpet next door." When his parents demanded what she meant she said "I should think you would know only too well."

"Don't be ridiculous. He's seven years old," his father said, and Jimmy felt as if he wasn't there at all.

"That means nothing with all this sex you're teaching them in school."

"I can't teach anybody anything with all the education cuts your bloody government is making."

"Oh, is it my fault now that you can't get a job? Well, I shouldn't say this but I will: if it were up to me I wouldn't send you to your interviews looking like a tramp."

It seemed the storm was about to break, when Mrs. Tortoiseshell appeared from upstairs in search of her hat. She was still clutching the bag of melted ice to her head, as if it were a hat someone had left in exchange for hers. "I shouldn't have taken it off," she wailed, and Jimmy imagined her wearing her hat on top of the bag. Eventually he found it, a helmet like a pink cake curly with icing. "That's a good boy," his grandmother said, enraging his parents.

The interruption had turned the row into a hostile silence. Jimmy was almost glad when bedtime came. As his mother tucked him in she said, "I don't know what you were doing with Emma, but don't do it again, all right? We've enough problems as it is." He wanted to call her back to tell her what had really happened, but instead he huddled beneath the sheets: he'd glimpsed the face in the other bed, the face that looked swollen and patchy, just like the picture his grandmother had shown him. He was afraid to touch his own face in case it felt like that. He could hardly convince himself he was there in his own bed at all.

The morning was cold and wet, and so was the week that followed. He avoided his room as much as he could. It wasn't only that it seemed the darkest place in the house, its walls swarming with ghosts of rain; it was the face that peered around the edge of the mirror whenever he entered the room. He had to step in before he could switch on the light, and in that moment the puffy blackened face grinned out. When he switched on the light his face looked just as it did in any other mirror, but he'd seen in comics how villains could disguise themselves.

The day it stopped raining was the day his grandmother let him know he was a villain. The wet weather must have made her rusty, for whenever she stood up she winced. She gave him a five-pound note to buy liniment at the chemist's. He was feeling grown-up to have charge of so much money when she fixed him with her gaze. "Just remember, James, I'm trusting you."

He had never felt guiltier. She expected him to steal. Since she did, he hardly paused when he saw the new red ball in the toy shop by the chemist's. It cost nearly a pound, and the wind was trying to snatch the four pound notes out of his fist; he'd only to tell her that one had blown away. Buying the ball made him feel vindicated, and he was almost at the house before he wondered how he could explain the ball.

He must hide it before she could see it. He ran in— she'd left the porch door open for him—and was halfway to the stairs when she came out of the living room. He threw the ball desperately onto the landing above him. "Who is it?" she cried as it went thud, thud. "Who's up there?"

"I'll go and see," he said at once, and was running upstairs to hide the ball when she said "My liniment and four pounds ten pence, please."

"I put it there." He pointed at the jar of liniment on the hall table, but she gazed at his clenched fist until he went reluctantly down and opened his hand above hers. "And the other pound, please," she said as the notes unfurled.

"I haven't got it." He realized too late that he should have said so at once. "It blew in the lake."

She made him turn out his pockets. When they proved to be empty except for a clump of sweets, her face grew even stiffer. "Please stay where I can see you," she said as he followed her upstairs.

The ball wasn't on the landing. It must be in one of the rooms, all of which were open except his. As she looked into each and pushed him ahead of her, the sky grew dark, the trees began to hiss and glisten. She pushed him into his room. The figure with the crawling blotchy face stepped forward to meet him, and the ball was at its feet, beneath the wardrobe. Yet Jimmy's grandmother hardly glanced at the ball, and it took him a while to understand she didn't realize it was new.

She said nothing when his mother came home. She was waiting for his father, to tell him Jimmy had stolen from her. "Is that what happened, Jimmy?" his father said.

"No." Jimmy felt as if he were talking to strangers—as if he were a stranger too. "It blew in the lake."

"That sounds more like it to me." When the old lady's pursed lips opened, his father said, "Look, here's a pound, and now let's forget it. I don't want to hear you saying things like that about Jimmy."

Jimmy felt strange. He could no longer recall taking the money. Someone else had stolen it: whoever had the ball. The idea didn't frighten him until he went to bed and lay there dreading the moment when his mother would leave him in the dark. He wasn't frightened of being alone, quite the opposite. "Don't switch off the light," he cried. "I don't want to live here anymore."

"We have to for a little while. Be brave. Your father had an interview that looked promising. We're waiting to hear."

He felt a hint of their old relationship. "Don't go out and leave me all day. I have to stay in with her."

"No you haven't. If it's too wet to play you can go to Emma's. I say you can. Now be a big boy and do without the light or you'll be getting us told off for wasting electricity."

Eventually he slept, praying that the noises at the end of the bed were only the stirrings of the radiator. Rain like maracas woke him in the morning, and so did a surge of delight that he wouldn't have to stay in. Emma was glad to see him, for she had a cold. They played all day, and he didn't go home until he heard his parents.

His grandmother wasn't speaking to them. Whenever she spoke to him, it was a challenge meant for them. He felt as if the burning silence were focused on him, especially when, nearly at the end of the endless dinner, they heard Emma sneezing. His mother felt his prickling forehead. "You'd better go to bed," she said at once.

He couldn't protest: something had drained that strength from him. As his mother helped him to his room, no doubt thinking it was illness rather than fear that was slowing him down on the stairs, he heard his grandmother. "I hope you're satisfied now. That's how she cares for your child."

His mother put him to bed and gave him a glass of medicine. All too soon she was at the door. "Leave the light on," he pleaded in a voice he could scarcely hear.

"You certainly can have the light on," she said, loudly enough to be heard downstairs. "Call me if you need anything."

For a while he felt safe, listening to the downpour whipping the window. When his parents came upstairs he thought he would be safer, but then he heard his mother. "You won't stand up to her at all. You as good as admitted he was a thief by giving her that money. I really think you're still afraid of her. Being near her makes you weak." That made Jimmy feel weak himself, made him think of his father being beaten. He buried his head in the

pillow, and was trying to decide whether he felt hot or
cold when he fell asleep.

When he awoke, the rain had stopped. There was silence except for a faint dull repetitive splashing. Everyone
must be in bed. He clawed the sheet away from his face
and opened his eyes. He was still in the dark. Someone
had switched off the light.

Above his head the window must be streaming, for the
wall and the door beyond the foot of the bed were breaking
out in glistening patches. The outline of the switch beside
the door was crumbling with darkness, it looked ready to
fall and leave him with no hope of light, but if he could
struggle out of bed it was only a few paces away. Surely
he could do that if he closed his eyes, surely he could
reach the switch before he saw anything else. But he was
already seeing what was in the corner by the window,
nearest his face: a small round shape just about the size of
his head.

When he saw the blotches breaking out on it he knew it
was about to grin—until he saw it was the ball. It had been
sent out of the dark to him. He lay staring fearfully, alone
but for the muffled regular splashing, and tried to believe
he could move, could dart out of bed and out of the room.
The mirror was farther from the door than he was. When
he tried to take deep breaths, they and his heart deafened
him. He was afraid not to be able to hear.

Or perhaps he was afraid of what he might hear, for the
soft dull sound wasn't quite like splashing. To begin with,
it was in the room with him. It must be growing louder: he
no longer had to strain to hear that it was a thumping, a
patting, the sound of squashy objects striking glass. No, it
wasn't at the window. It came from beyond the foot of the
bed.

At last he managed to raise his head. He would be able
to see without being able to escape. His neck was at an
angle—a blazing pain was trying to twitch his head back
onto the pillow—but now he could see over the footboard.

It was terror, not pain, that made his head fall back. The
dim bed in the mirror was empty. A figure covered from
head to foot with blotches was standing beyond the bed,
pressing its face and hands against the glass, gazing out at
him.

As soon as his head touched the pillow he screamed and
threw himself out of bed. A moment later he wouldn't
have been able to move. He fled toward the door, but the
sheets tripped him. As he fell he twisted his ankle. The
soft thumping recommenced at once, more strongly. It
sounded determined to break through the glass.

He clawed at the floor above his head and hurled the
ball without thinking. It was out of his hands when he
realized that it was too light to break a mirror. Yet he
heard the smash of glass, fragments splintering on the
floorboards. The mirror must have been thin as eggshell,
and now he had made it hatch. When he heard the footsteps, which sounded like pats of mud dropped on the
floor, he could only shrink into a corner with his hands
over his face, and scream.

Though he heard the door opening almost at once, it
was some time before the light went on. He dared to look
then, and saw his grandmother staring at the broken mirror. "That's the end," she said as his parents pushed past
her. "I won't have him in my house."

Jimmy took that as a promise, and wished it could be
kept at once, for someone else was at large in the building.
It hadn't been his grandmother who had opened his bedroom door. When he heard the crash of glass downstairs,
he began to shiver. His grandmother hurried down, and
they heard her cry out. Soon she returned, carrying his
father's framed certificate, her treasure, smashed and torn.
She looked as if she blamed Jimmy, but he couldn't be
sure if it was his fault. Perhaps it was.

When his grandmother went away to cry, his mother
persuaded him back into bed, but he wouldn't let her leave
him or switch off the light. Eventually he dozed. Once he

woke, afraid that someone was lying in bed with him, but the impression faded almost at once. His mother was still in her chair by the bed. Surely she wouldn't have let anyone creep into the room.

The morning was cloudless, and everything seemed to have changed. His father had been accepted for a teaching post. Perhaps that was why Jimmy felt as if he hadn't caught Emma's cold after all. Perhaps something else had been draining him.

His grandmother said nothing. Jimmy thought she wished that she hadn't sounded so final last night, hoped they would say something that would let her take it back. But his father had already arranged for them to use a friend's flat while she was in London. Jimmy was so elated that when the moving van arrived, he hadn't even parcelled up his comics.

In any case, he hadn't said good-bye to Emma. He said he would stay until their friend came back with the van. "I'll stay too if you like," his mother said, but he found her concern irritating. He could look after himself.

As soon as they left, his grandmother went upstairs. He rang Emma's bell, but there was no reply. His grandmother's house was hotter than outside. She'd forgotten to turn off the furnace. He could hear her in her room, weeping as if nothing mattered anymore. He felt rather sorry for her, wanted to tell her he would come and see her sometimes. He didn't mind now, since he was leaving. He ran upstairs.

She must have heard him coming. She was dabbing at her eyes and making up at the dressing table. He opened his mouth to promise and heard himself saying "Granny, there's something wrong with the furnace. I didn't go down, you said not to."

"That's a good boy." She turned to give him a brave moist-eyed smile, and so she couldn't see what he was seeing in the mirror: his face just managing to conceal its grin. For an instant, during which he might have been able to cry out, he saw how another face was hiding beneath his. He remembered the impression he'd had, fading into himself, that someone had crept into bed with him.

"You can come down with me if you like," his grandmother said forgivingly, and he could only follow. He wanted to cry out, so that she or someone else would stop him, but his face was beyond his control. He hurried down the cellar steps behind her, hearing the muffled roar of flames in the furnace, grinning.

Beyond Words

LIVERPOOL'S DYING OF slogans, Ward thinks. Several thousand city council workers are marching through the littered streets under placards and banners and neon signs, Top Man, Burger King, Wimpy Hamburgers, Cascade Amusements. Songs that sound like a primer of bad English blare from shops under failing neon that turns words into gibberish. The chants of the marchers and the chattering of signs lodge in Ward's skull, crushing fragments of the story he's trying to complete. He dodges between stalls that have sprung up in Church Street, hawking cheap clothes and toys and towels imprinted like miraculous shrouds with a pop star's face, and into the optician's.

"So you're a writer, Mr. Smith. I don't get many of those in my chair." The optician's round smooth face is a little too large for the rest of him; Ward is reminded of a lifesize seaside photograph with a hole to stick your face through. "You must need eyes in your job. We'll just have these off," the optician says, and deftly removes Ward's spectacles.

Just a few words may be all that he needs, a solution hidden deep in his mind, but the slippery idea seems more distant than ever. Ward imagines the unwritten words turning red, the bank manager frowning and shaking his head, and is terrified that the resolution of the story may be gone forever—terrified of losing the ability to write now that Tina is soon to quit her job to bear their child. He's straining his mind desperately when the optician fits a pair of medievally-heavy glassless spectacles on his nose and slides an eye patch in front of his left eye, a lens before the other.

As the eye chart lurches into focus, its letters glaring blackly out of the backlit rectangle, Ward reads it all at once, instantly. The words seem a solution to everything, to problems which have yet to arise as well as those he's grappling with. Then he sees that they aren't words at all; what's sounding in his inner ear is the rhythm of the letters, the way he thought their groups should sound. He sets about pronouncing the letters, down to the bottom line that's almost as small as his handwriting.

"Well, Mr. Smith, you'll be glad to hear you don't need new glasses." Seeing that Ward isn't entirely, the optician continues "I should see your doctor about your headaches or give yourself a holiday from writing."

If I go away the writing comes too, Ward thinks, shivering in the April sunlight at the bus stop. A windblown polystyrene tray squeals along the stained pavement like a nail on slate. The ghost of a giant spinal column fades from the rumbling sky, a fat woman trots delicately past him—a ball trying to grow into a ballerina, Ward thinks, fighting off the crowd of images that clamour to be caught in words. A bus carries him through Toxteth, where youths with bricks are besieging a police station, and into Allerton, shops growing smaller under signs like samples of typefaces. In Penny Lane, where Ward lives, a coachload of Beatles fans is chattering in Japanese as he lets himself into the house. He runs up the stairs, whose well is smaller than its echoes pretend, and into the flat overlooking the school.

Tina's lying on the sheepskin rug. Her hands are splayed

on the bare floor, her red hair seems to stream across the
boards from her pale delicate face. Her four months' preg-
nancy bulks above her in the flowered mound of her
maternity smock. "How are you?" Ward says.

"We're both fine. Listen." She clasps his head gently
while he rests one ear against her belly. He thinks the
heartbeat he's hearing is his own, racing in an elusively
familiar rhythm. "How about you?" Tina murmurs.

"Just eyestrain, he said."

"You shouldn't write so small. No good saving paper if
you end up losing your vision. Even I couldn't read that
last story."

"Guards against plagiarism," Ward says, then smiles.
"You know I don't mean you. We're collaborators. That's
our first collaboration swimming round in there."

"I'm glad we'll be together."

She means at the birth, and perhaps she's referring to
the way she feels excluded from his work. He can't see
how to share a process that takes place in his head and on
the blank page. "Publisher called, by the way," she says
as if reminded. "It's all written down."

It isn't Ward's publisher. He doesn't recognize the name,
not that many people seem to know his or that of his
publisher. He calls and finds he's reached a new house.
"When can we meet for lunch?" Kendle Holmes demands
heartily. "I've a proposition to put to you."

"I could come down to London tomorrow?" Ward asks
Tina, who nods.

"I'll see you here at one," Holmes says, and tells him
where.

Anxious to round off his story so as to be ready for
whatever Holmes may propose, Ward heads for the library. In the story a writer haunts libraries in search of
comments readers scribble in his books. He begins to find
the same handwriting in the margins of every copy wherever he goes, comments addressed more and more directly
to him. He becomes obsessed with catching the culprit, but

what happens when he does? Nothing Ward can think of
that he finds worth writing. When schoolchildren crowd
into the library, disarraying his thoughts and the already
jumbled shelves of books, he gives up wandering the aisles
in a vague vain quest for his own work and walks home as
the shops light up the streets.

Tina's lying on the bed in the main room, a computer
manual propped against her belly. Ward makes omelettes
in the small not quite upright kitchen before she goes to
work. Later he listens to the radio, wincing at abuses of
language; he can never shrug off the proliferation of sole-
cisms until he's composed a letter of protest in an attic of
his mind, even though he never commits it to paper. He's
still listening in the dark when Tina comes home, too tired
to make love.

In the morning he goes to London, so early that he's a
hundred miles from Liverpool before he feels awake. Trees,
irrepressibly green, pirouette intricately in the fields while
he listens to the rhythm of the wheels, muffled by the
vacuum within the panes. Fitting words to the rhythm
might lessen his awareness of the sound and let him think
what the writer has to confront in the library, but all he can
make of the rhythm is *WHAT THE WORDS ARE WHAT
THE WORDS ARE WHAT THE WORDS ARE* . . . The
rhythm seems almost familiar, but he can't tell what's
missing, any more than he can put an ending to his story.

Dozens of black cabs pile down the ramp below Euston;
Ward thinks of a coal chute. One carries him up into the
sunlit maze of traffic, past pavements laden with pedestrians and words. It's his first experience of London, and the
rifeness of streets overwhelms him; so does the cost of the
ride. By the time he reaches Greek Court, where Hercules
Books have their office, his ears are throbbing rhythmically.

As soon as Ward announces himself to the brisk young
woman behind the glossy white horseshoe desk, Holmes
strides out of his office like someone who's been waiting
impatiently for the doors of a lift to open. He's thinner

than he sounded on the phone, and dressed in a green suit. When he sways forward to give Ward a darting handshake Ward thinks of a sapling, bowing.

He sweeps Ward round the corner, into an Italian restaurant, where he orders drinks and conveys Ward's order for lunch to the waiter. "Now, are you going to be the next Tolkein?"

Ward's at a loss for words. "Well . . ."

"Of course you aren't. You're the first Ward Smith, the voice of modern British fantasy. That's what the public will say when they've heard of you, and I'm saying it now."

"That's very kind."

"Not kind at all. It's true." Holmes blinks his bright blue eyes twice and rubs his long smooth chin. "I really like your one about the scriptwriter who's haunted by the character he created, can't get rid of him because he's forgotten where he got the name from."

"Gnikomson."

"Right, the Swedish detective. I love the ending when the writer's going to light his first cigarette in years until he sees the No Smoking sign reflected in the train window. 'And then, of course, Gnikomson stood on his head and vanished.' How did that collection of yours do?"

"Pretty well for a book of short stories, they tell me," Ward tells him, shaking his head.

"I take it your wife works too."

"Until she has our baby."

"Good, good, but dear, dear. And will Clarion Press have something else by you out by then?"

"I'm just trying to finish a story to round off another book," Ward says, shaking his head again as if that may dislodge the throbbing.

Holmes rubs his chin as if it's a magic lamp. "Sounds to me as if they aren't looking after you as you deserve to be looked after. If they haven't commissioned you to write a novel yet, I'd like to."

The rhythm in Ward's ears is becoming entangled in his thoughts. "Tell me what to write, you mean?"

"Have you a novel in mind yourself?"

"I've been thinking about one off and on." Ward doesn't mean to shout, but he has to speak up to be sure of what he's saying. "I had the notion of a story from two viewpoints, only really you're always reading the opposite viewpoint from the one you think you are. You'd realize that when you notice wrong words cropping up in each one, and then the whole meaning of the story would change completely."

Holmes gazes at him to make sure he's finished. "Sounds fascinating. A bit obscure for a first novel, don't you think? We want to put your name in as many heads as possible. I think a writer who's as much in love with words as you are has a trilogy in him. Say a trilogy about magic, the power of words. Say a professor of languages who finds he's a magician and he's needed to save humanity. Does that get you thinking?"

Ward's backing into himself, he finds the attempt to shape his ideas so threatening. "I don't know if the people at Clarion Press would want me to write for someone else."

"If you feel they've earned your loyalty that much you mustn't let me come between you. Take a look at how they're doing in the shops before you go home." Holmes changes the subject, so abruptly that Ward feels as if it has been snatched from beneath him. As they part after lunch, Holmes says "Think about what I said, if you like, and let me know if you change your mind."

Ward feels vulnerable again at once. The prospect of writing someone else's idea seems threateningly meaningless, as meaningless as the cadence that's repeating itself over and over in his ear, like a distant muffled voice he's never heard yet feels he ought to recognize. It's between him and the world. He goes looking for his book in Charing Cross Road, to bring the world closer.

The first two shops sell secondhand books only. The dusty ranks of forgotten names, books like so many decaying untended gravestones, dismay him. He heads for Foyle's, the bright spines, the outstanding embossed titles. But the subdued cover of his book isn't there, nor in any other bookshop. "*Whispers and Titters*," he mutters fiercely over the murmur in his ears, as if pronouncing the title will make it appear on the shelves.

He hasn't time to visit Clarion Press. He jogs to Euston so as to save money, then tries to phone Clarion before he's stopped panting, but there's no reply beyond the sound that has lodged in his ear. On the train he tries to doze, and eventually the song of the wheels lulls him: whispers and titterings, whispering titterings, waspishly tittering, waspishly whispering . . . But when he lurches awake as the Liverpool suburbs speed by, the cadence he's been carrying with him fills his ears like water, and he feels as if he's drowning.

Tina's waiting for him, beaming expectantly over the spread of her computer manuals on the dining table. "How did it go? Was it worthwhile?"

"I can't tell you yet. I mean, I don't know." He feels as if he won't know anything until his ears are clear. He can't even taste the chili con carne she has waiting for him. Nor can he make love; his sensations are on the other side of the noise in his ears, and feel as if they belong to someone else. Floppy's a disc, not an impotent dick, his mind chants in time with the noise.

He can't sleep for more than a few minutes. Whenever he jerks awake he thinks an intruder is in the room, stooping at him in the dark and muttering. He holds himself still; it takes very little to wake Tina just now. For hours he feels as if the day will never come, as if he'll never see the doctor.

"Tinnitus," the doctor says.

Ward has waited over an hour to see him, but at once he's glad he has: there's a word for what he's suffering, and that must mean an answer, a cure. "What causes it?" Ward says eagerly.

"Deafness, possibly. You don't suffer from deafness? Catarrh, then, or wax in the ears." When he fails to find either he measures Ward's blood pressure, and frowns. "Of course there are cases where it doesn't seem to be a symptom of anything else."

"I'm one of those, am I? What can we do?"

"To be blunt, nothing except hope it goes away eventually."

"But I make my living as a writer," Ward pleads. "How can I work like this?"

"Many tinnitus sufferers have to cope with more difficult jobs." The doctor lets his face soften. "If you find you aren't able to sleep, sufferers often leave a radio playing."

Ward buys a pair of headphones, whose price dismays him. As he lets himself into the flat he's dreading Tina's sympathy, her sense of being unable to help him. He avoided telling her that he was seeing the doctor, in the hope that he'd come home cured. When he tells her why he bought the headphones she takes his hands, but even this contact seems to be taking place in the distance beyond the incessant noise. "Is there anything I can do?" she murmurs.

"Not unless you can get inside my head."

"I wish I could, believe me."

He dons the headphones and lies on the bed while she works at the table. He can tell by the way her hands creep up the sides of her face that she hears the headphones squeaking. His only chance of ignoring the tinnitus, however momentarily, is to turn the radio up loud enough to blot it out.

He has to grow used to it, he tells himself as he lies sleeplessly beside Tina. People adjust to living next to motorways or near airports. People cope with tinnitus, the doctor said so. Yet being one of many doesn't make it any easier for Ward. In fact, he thinks he might have coped better if it were unique to him, instead of something that can afflict anyone, randomly and meaninglessly. Whenever he turns up the volume minutely on the radio, seeking to fill his head with late-night chatter, Tina stirs beside him.

When the night's darkest, exhaustion overtakes him. A silence between radio programs wakens him. For a few seconds he's alone with the noise in his ears, and as he hangs between sleeping and waking, he hears precisely what it has been trying to say, sees the glowing letters whose message has grown blurred with so much repetition. The simplicity and profundity of the message, such a secret contained in so few words, makes him feel large as the night, immensely meaningful, utterly peaceful. Before he knows it, his peace turns back into sleep. He doesn't waken until daylight probes the room. He can't remember a word of the secret he heard in the dark.

His ears continue mumbling when he pulls off the headphones. The message is still there if only he can clarify it to himself. As soon as Tina leaves for the office, glancing anxiously at him as if she feels her sympathy hasn't reached him, he begins to write. He writes every phrase he can think of that fits the rhythm of the mumbling. At first he writes only phrases that mean something to him, then he makes himself relax and scribbles anything that comes to mind, scribbling larger so as not to strain his eyes. Before lunchtime he has to go out for more exercise books.

When he hears Tina's key in the lock, he slaps the latest book shut and stows the pile under the bed, his head aching with the notion that he was about to stumble on the message. She wouldn't have noticed; she rushes straight to the bathroom. He strokes her head and murmurs consolingly and tries to feel the emotions he's enacting. "Don't worry about me," he mutters when she's able to ask how he is. All he wants to hear now is the mumbling.

But he has to sleep. In the darkest hours he gives up

trying to hear words, only to find as he reaches to turn on the radio that Tina's still awake. "Sorry," he whispers. "Go to sleep."

"I'm trying."

"I'm not much use to you, am I?"

"I love you all the same."

"I'm serious." He pulls off the headphones and props himself against the pillow, which feels no softer than the rest of reality. "You're going to need more support than I can give you while I'm like this. Do you think you ought to move in with your folks for a while? Then you'd be able to sleep as you should."

"Would that make life easier for you?"

"It might."

"I'll call them in the morning."

He can't interpret her tone, out there beyond the tinnitus. He'll leave the radio alone and put up with a sleepless night on her behalf. Whenever he drifts toward sleep he feels close to distinguishing the words. Every time he jerks awake before he can grasp them, and realizes that Tina's still awake beside him.

In the morning, when she calls her parents, her eyes are red and moist: from sleeplessness, he assumes. He collects the mail from the downstairs hall, two bills and a letter from Clarion Press. Tina's arranging to go to her parents after work as he tears open the letter. The tinnitus seems to lurch closer as he reads the photocopied paragraphs. Clarion Press has been declared bankrupt. Not only have they ceased publishing, but even the unsold copies of his book are in the hands of the receiver.

Tina blinks at the letter as if she's not sure how she feels about it. "What do you want me to do now?" she murmurs.

"What you were going to do. What else?"

"I thought you might be glad of my support, that's all. I thought you were."

"Yes," Ward says with all the conviction he can muster. He hugs her tight, willing her to leave so that he may be able to think. Everything she says now distracts him—everything she says is pulled into the shape of the tinnitus. "I'll call you," he says as he walks her to the bus, "I'll come and see you," but he thinks she can sense his imminent overwhelming relief.

He sits at the table and tries to think. Hercules Books are the answer for you, his mind throbs; children chanting tables in the school seem to be chanting that too. He has no chance of finding another job to support himself and Tina, not with the clamour in his ears; he can't imagine even coping with interviews. But there's still Hercules Books, still Holmes' proposal of a trilogy, and if Ward can finish the library story there will be a collection for Holmes to publish while Ward tries to work on the novels. He carries the phone as far from the chanting as the cord will stretch.

"Hercules Books? Kendle Holmes, if he's there. Sorry, speak up, I can't make out a word. Ward Smith is speaking. He asked me to call."

The rhythm's deafening. It has invaded his speech. Even if he gets through to Holmes, he won't be able to hear him. They have to meet face to face. "Coming to town now. I won't expect lunch," he shouts, and replaces the receiver gently as if that may make up for his hysteria. But when he carries the phone back to its dark square beside the bed, he finds that at some point he has pulled the plug out of the wall.

It mustn't matter. He can only go. He gathers the typescripts of all the stories he's completed for the book and stuffs them into a Safeway bag. A bus carries him through charred streets to a train that's leaving for London in five minutes. He should be there just after lunch.

He tries to doze, rocked by the train. A slowing wakens him. The chattering arable landscape is winding down; it stops outside his window. Apart from the odd timid lurch of a few feet, the train makes no further move for almost two hours.

He avoids looking at the stoical pensioners opposite

him, who appear to be chanting even though their lips are pinched shut, and leafs through his typescripts. "Phosphorescent Montmorency," "Cave Maria"—the titles he worked so hard to frame no longer convey anything to him, and he can't read more than a few words of the stories. A few pages of computer printout have strayed into the pile, and the stories mean as little to him. He shoves the pile into the bag and shrinks into himself, away from the wordless clamour, the senseless framing of landscape.

At last the train jerks forward, speeds to Euston. A huge voice explains the delay as Ward runs along the platform, but even that voice can't reach him. He mustn't take a taxi, he still has time to run. Euston Road, Tottenham Court Road, Charing Cross Road—he dashes past miles of signs, hugging himself to squeeze the spikiness out of his armpits. Hordes of books and commuters and vehicles jumble by, and give way to Greek Court. Ward dodges out of the crowd, taking the uproar with him, and shoulders his way into Hercules Books.

The receptionist in the melamine horseshoe mouths at him, but he hears a different rhythm. "Sorry I'm late, but my train was held up," Ward shouts. "Ward Smith, the writer. I'm here to see Holmes."

He stands his ground when she steps round the horseshoe, shaking her head and pointing at her watch. Suddenly he darts past her and flings open the door of the inner office. Holmes is alone, leaning back in his chair, reading a manuscript piled on his desk. He looks more surprised than pleased to see Ward. "Kendle, it's me," Ward says, trying not to bellow. "I've got something for you."

He hands Holmes the Safeway bag, waits while he frowns over the contents. "You'll publish these, won't you, while I compose. A fantasy trilogy, that's what you said. About time I extended myself."

When Holmes looks up, Ward hardly needs him to

speak, his eyes say so much. "I *can* write your novels. Give me a chance," Ward pleads.

Holmes speaks then, though inaudibly to Ward. He points at the manuscript he's been reading. Surely nobody could have written a trilogy so swiftly, but perhaps he's claiming that the manuscript or the writer can be developed. A sense of meaninglessness more profound than any he's experienced hitherto spreads through Ward, so profound that it feels like relief. He can do nothing for anyone, and nobody can need him as he is now. He swings round dizzily and heads for the street, feeling as if he may fly.

The thought of Tina slows him. He should call her, not least to explain that Kendle Holmes will presumably be returning the typescripts, which she's welcome to sell on her own behalf if she can. He huddles in the nearest phone booth as the hordes of books surrounding him decay imperceptibly, as the commuters and the traffic do, dust of the future. All the sounds around him are decaying too, merging into a single rhythm. If anyone answers the phone he won't even know whose voice it is, let alone what she's saying.

He makes for Euston through the evening streets, the dwindling crowds. He's glad he knows his way there, doesn't have to try and read the street names. But going to Tina will only make the situation harder for them both. On the way to Euston he repeats her parents' number over and over to himself. Thank heaven it fits the rhythm. At Euston he dials it, then counts to ten. "I'm not coming back," he says. "Blame me, not yourself. All my money is yours, all my manuscripts too. Look after the baby. I love . . ." He can't say he loves her, it doesn't fit the rhythm. Perhaps emotions don't. He repeats everything he's just said, then he makes for the ticket windows.

Scotland is farthest and sparsest, he thinks. Tinnitus booms in his ears and his brain. Signs all around him are chanting the chant. He must get beyond signs, the unbearable clamour, unstable changing of signs. Ten hours to Inverness, farthest of all—details he learned for an unwritten tale. Night wipes out England, the train races in. The fluorescent cradle rocks him to sleep.

Dawn is in Inverness, lighting the signs. Ward leaves the town just as fast as he can. Opticians' shops make him falter, then run. He heads for the mountains beyond the firth, for the unpeopled roads and peaks, for the comfort of names in no language he knows.

Winds and rain slash him, mists isolate him. Food he finds growing, and sometimes in bins. He no longer remembers his life or his name, he no longer washes or cares how he smells. His body is something that carries him on; he is only the chant. What remains of his voice chants it constantly now. Perhaps he is chanting words that he can't hear. Perhaps he must walk until he's understood. Should he welcome that prospect or shrink from it fearfully? The rhythm must go on, must go
on,

LISA
TUTTLE

for Garry

*There are two lives, the natural and the spiritual,
and we must lose the one before we can participate
in the other.*

William James,
The Varieties of Religious Experience

Every fear is a desire. Every desire is fear.
James Fenton, ''A Staffordshire Murderer''

Riding the Nightmare

TWILIGHT, *l'heure bleu*: Tess O'Neal sat on the balcony of her sixth floor apartment and looked out at the soft, suburban sprawl of New Orleans, a blur of green trees and multicolored houses, with the jewels of lights just winking on. It was a time of day that made her nostalgic and gently melancholy, feelings she usually enjoyed. But not now. For once she wished she were not alone with the evening.

Gordon had cancelled their date. No great disaster—he'd said they could have all day Sunday together—but the change of plans struck Tess as ominous, and she questioned him.

"Is something wrong?"

He hesitated. Maybe he was only reacting to the sharp note in her voice. "Of course not. Jude . . . made some plans, and it would spoil things if I went out. She sends her apologies."

There was nothing odd in that. Jude was Gordon's wife and also Tess's friend, a situation they were all comfortable with. But Jude was slightly scatterbrained, and when she confused dates, it was Tess who had to take second place. Usually Tess did not mind. Now she did.

"We'll talk on Sunday," Gordon said.

Tess didn't want to talk. She didn't want explanations. She wanted Gordon's body on hers, making her believe that nothing had changed, nothing would ever change between them.

They're in it together, she thought. Him and his wife. And I'm left out in the cold.

She looked up at the darkening sky. As blue as the nightmare's eye, she thought, and shivered. She got up and went inside, suddenly feeling too vulnerable in the open air.

She had never told Gordon about the nightmare. He admired her as a competent, sophisticated, independent woman. How could she talk to him about childhood fears? Worse, how could she tell him that this was one childhood fear that hadn't stayed in childhood but had come after her?

As she turned to lock the sliding glass door behind her, Tess froze.

The mare's long head was there, resting on the balcony rail as if on a stable door, the long mane waving slightly in the breeze, the bluish eye fixed commandingly on her.

Tess stumbled backward, and the vision, broken, vanished.

There was nothing outside that should not be, nothing but sky and city and her own dark reflection in the glass.

"Snap out of it, O'Neal," she said aloud. Bad enough to dream the nightmare, but if she was going to start seeing it with her eyes open, she really needed help.

For a moment she thought of phoning Gordon. But what could she say? Not only would it go against the rules to phone him after he'd said they could not meet, but it would go against everything he knew and expected of her if she began babbling about a nightmare. She simply wanted his presence, the way, as a child, she had wanted her father to put his arms around her and tell her not to cry. But she was a grown woman now. She didn't need anyone else to tell her what was real and what was not; she knew that the best way to banish fears and depression was by working, not brooding.

She poured herself a Coke and settled at her desk with a stack of transcripts. She was a doctoral candidate in linguistics, working on a thesis examining the differences in language use between men and women. It was a subject of which, by now, she was thoroughly sick. She wondered sometimes if she would ever be able to speak unselfconsciously again, without monitoring her own speech patterns to edit out the stray, feminine modifiers and apologies.

The window was open. Through it, she could see the black and windy sky and there, running on the wind, was the creamy white mare with tumbling mane and rolling blue eye. Around her neck hung a shining crescent moon, the golden *lunula* strung on a white and scarlet cord. And Tess was on her feet, walking toward the window as if hypnotized. It was then that she became aware of herself, and knew she was dreaming, and that she must break the dream. With a great effort of will, she flung herself backward, toward the place where she knew her bed would be, tossing her head as she strained to open her eyes.

And woke with a start to find herself still at her desk. She must have put her head down for a moment. Her watch showed it was past midnight. Tess got up, her heart beating unpleasantly fast, and glanced toward the sliding glass door. That it was not the window of her dream made no difference. The window in her dream was always the bedroom window of her childhood, the scene always the same as the first time the nightmare had come for her. There was no horse outside on the balcony, or in the sky beyond. There was no horse except in her mind.

Tess went to bed, knowing the nightmare would not come again. Never twice in one night, and she had succeeded in refusing the first visit. Nevertheless, she slept badly, with confused dreams of quarrelling with Gordon as she never quarrelled with him in life, dreams in which

Gordon became her father and announced his intended marriage to Jude, and Tess wept and argued and wept and woke in the morning feeling exhausted.

Gordon arrived on Sunday with champagne, flowers and a shopping bag full of gourmet treats for an indoor picnic. He gave off a glow of happiness and well-being that at once put Tess on the defensive, for his happiness had nothing to do with her.

He kissed her and looked at her tenderly—so tenderly that her stomach turned over with dread. He was looking at her with affection and pity, she thought—not with desire.

"What is it?" she asked sharply, pulling away from him. "What's happened?"

He was surprised. "Nothing," he said. Then: "Nothing bad, I promise. But I'll tell you all about it. Why don't we have something to eat, first? I've brought—"

"I couldn't eat with something hanging over me, wondering . . ."

"I told you, it's nothing bad, nothing to worry about." He frowned. "Are you getting your period?"

"I'm *not* getting my period; I'm *not* being irrational—" She stopped and swallowed and sighed, forcing herself to relax. "All right, I am being irrational. I've been sleeping badly. And there's this nightmare—the same nightmare I had as a kid, just before my mother died."

"Poor baby," he said, holding her close. He sounded protective but also amused. "Nightmares. That doesn't sound like my Tess."

"It's not that I'm superstitious—"

"Of course not."

"But I've been feeling all week that something bad was about to happen, something to change my whole life. And with the nightmare—I hadn't seen it since just before my mother died. To have it come now, and then when you said we'd talk—"

"It isn't bad, I promise you. But I won't keep you in suspense. Let's just have a drink first, all right?"

"Sure."

He turned away from her to open the champagne, and she stared at him, drinking in the details as if she might not see him again for a very long time: the curls at the back of his neck, the crisp, black beard, his gentle, rather small hands, skilled at so many things. She felt what it would be to lose him, to lose the right to touch him, never again to have him turn and smile at her.

But why think that? Why should she lose him? How could she, when he had never been "hers" in any traditional sense, nor did she want him to be. She liked her freedom, both physical and emotional. She liked living alone, yet she wanted a lover, someone she could count on who would not make too many demands of her. In Gordon she had found precisely the mixture of distance and intimacy that she needed. It had worked well for nearly three years, so why did she imagine losing him? She trusted Gordon, believed in his honesty and his love for her. She didn't think there was another woman, and she knew he hadn't grown tired of her. She didn't believe he had changed. But Jude might.

Gordon handed her a long-stemmed glass full of champagne, and after they had toasted one another, and sipped, he said, "Jude's pregnant. She found out for sure last week."

Tess stared at him, feeling nothing at all.

He said quickly, "It wasn't planned. I wasn't keeping anything from you. Jude and I, we haven't even—hadn't even—discussed having children. It just never came up. But now that it's happened . . . Jude really likes the idea of having a baby, she's found, and . . ."

"Who's the father?"

She felt him withdraw. "That's not worthy of you, Tess."

"Why? It seems like a reasonable question, considering—"

"Considering that Jude hasn't been involved with anyone since Morty went back to New York? I thought you and Jude were friends. What do you two talk about over your lunches?"

The brief, mean triumph she had felt was gone, replaced by anguish. "Not our sex lives," she said. "Look, you've got an open marriage—you tell me it was an accident—I'm sorry, I didn't know you'd take it that way. I was just trying to find out what—forget I asked."

"I will." He turned away and began to set out the food he had brought onto plates. The champagne was harsh in her mouth as Tess watched his so-familiar, economical movements, and she wanted to touch his back where the blue cloth of his shirt stretched a little too tightly.

She drew a deep breath and said, "Congratulations. I should have said that first of all. How does it feel, knowing you're going to be a father?"

He looked around, still cautious, and then smiled. "I'm not sure. It doesn't seem real yet. I guess I'll get used to it."

"I guess it'll change things," she said. "For you and me."

He went to her and took her in his arms. "I don't want it to."

"But it's bound to."

"In practical ways, maybe. We might have less time together, but—we'll manage somehow. Jude and I were never a traditional couple, and we aren't going to be traditional parents, either. I'll still need you—I'm not going to stop loving you." He said it so fiercely that she smiled, and pressed her face against his chest to hide it. "Do you believe me? Nothing can change the way I feel about you. I love you. That's not going to change. Do you believe me?"

She didn't say anything. He forced her head up off his chest and made her look at him. "Do you believe me?" He kissed her when she wouldn't reply, then kissed her again, more deeply, and then they were kissing passionately, and she was pulling him onto the floor, and they made love, their bodies making the promises they both wanted.

After Gordon had left that night, the nightmare came again.

Tess found herself standing beside the high, narrow bed she'd slept in as a child, facing the open window. The pale curtains billowed like sails. Outside, galloping in place like a rocking horse, moving and yet stationary, was the blue-eyed, cream-colored mare.

With part of her mind Tess knew that she could refuse this visit. She could turn her head, and wrench her eyes open, and find herself, heart pounding, safe in her bed.

Instead, she let herself go into the dream. She took a step forward. She felt alert and hypersensitive, as if this were the true state of waking. She was aware of her own body as she usually never was in life or in a dream, conscious of her nakedness as the breeze from the open window caressed it, and feeling the slight bounce of her breasts and the rough weave of the carpet beneath her feet as she walked towards the window.

She clambered onto the windowsill and with total confidence leaped out, knowing that the horse would catch her.

She landed easily and securely on the mare's back, feeling the scratch and prickle of the horsehair on her inner thighs. Her arms went around the high, arched neck and she pressed her face against it, breathing in the rough, salty, smoky scent of horseflesh. She felt the pull and play of muscle and bone beneath her and in her legs as the mare began to gallop. Tess looked down at the horse's legs, seeing how they braced and pounded against the air. She felt a slight shock, then, for where there should have been a hoof, she saw instead five toes. Tess frowned, and leaned further as she stared through the darkness, trying to see.

But they were her own hooves divided into five toes— they had always been so since the night of her creation.

The thinly beaten gold of the *lunula* on its silken chain
bounced against the solid muscle of her chest as she loped
through the sky.

Some unquestioned instinct took her to the right house.
Above it, she caught a crosswind and, tucking her forelegs
in close to her chest, glided spirally down until all four
feet could be firmly planted on the earth. This was a
single-story house she visited tonight. She turned her head
and, at a glance, the window swung open, the screen that
had covered it a moment earlier now vanished. The mare
took one delicate step closer and put her head through the
window into the bedroom.

The bed, with a man and woman sleeping in it, was
directly beneath the window. She breathed gently upon the
woman's sleeping face and then drew back her head and
waited.

The woman opened her eyes and looked into the mare's
blue gaze. She seemed confused but not frightened, and
after a moment she sat up slowly, moving cautiously as if
for fear of alarming the horse. The horse was not alarmed.
She suffered the woman to stroke her nose and pat her
face before she backed away, pulling her head out of the
house. She had timed it perfectly. The woman came after
her as if drawn on a rope, leaning out the window and
making soft, affectionate noises. The mare moved as if
uneasy, still backing, and then, abruptly flirtatious, offered
her back, an invitation to the woman to mount.

The woman understood at once and did not hesitate.
From the window ledge she slipped onto the mare's back
in a smooth, fluid movement, as if she had done this every
night of her life.

Feeling her rider in place, legs clasped firmly on her
sides, the mare leaped skyward with more speed than
grace. She felt the woman gasp as she was flung forward,
and felt the woman's hands knot in her mane. She was
obviously an experienced rider, not one it would be easy to

throw. But the mare did not wish to throw her, merely to give her a very rough ride.

High over the sleeping city galloped the nightmare, rising at impossibly steep angles, shying at invisible barriers, and now and then tucking her legs beneath her to drop like a stone. The gasps and cries from her rider soon ceased. The woman, concentrating on clinging for her life, could have had no energy to spare for fear.

Not until dawn did the nightmare return the woman, leaping through the bedroom window in defiance of logic and throwing her onto the motionless safety of her bed, beside her still-sleeping husband.

When Tess woke a few hours later she was stiff and sore, as if she had been dancing, or running, all night. She got up slowly, wincing, and aware of a much worse emotional pain waiting for her, like the anticipation of bad news. The nightmare had come for her, and this time she had gone with it—she was certain of that much. But where had it taken her? What had she done?

In the bathroom, as she waited for the shower to heat up and wracked her sleepy brain for some memory of the night before, Tess caught a glimpse in the mirror of something on her back, at waist level. She turned, presenting her back to the glass, and then craned her neck around, slowly against the stiffness, to look at her reflection.

She stared at the bloodstains. Stared and stared at the saddle of blood across her back.

She washed it off, of course, with plenty of hot water and soap, and tried not to think about it too hard. That was exactly what she had done the last time this had happened: when she was nine years old, on the morning after the night her mother had miscarried, on the morning of the day her mother had died.

All day Tess fought against the urge to phone Gordon. All day she was like a sleepwalker as she taught a class, supervised studies, stared at meaningless words in the library, and avoided telephones.

She thought, as she had thought before, that she should see a psychiatrist. But how could a psychiatrist help her? She *knew* she could not, by all the rules of reason and logic, have caused her mother's death. She knew she felt guilty because she had not wanted the little sister or brother her parents had planned, and on some level she believed that her desire, expressed in the nightmare, had been responsible for the miscarriage and thus—although indirectly and unintentionally—for her mother's death. She didn't need a psychiatrist to tell her all that. She had figured it out for herself, some time in her teens. And yet, figuring it out hadn't ended the feeling of guilt. That was why the very thought of the nightmare was so frightening to her.

If Jude is all right, she thought, if nothing has happened to her, then I'll know it was just a crazy dream—and I'll see a psychiatrist.

Gordon telephoned the next day, finally. Jude was all right, he said, although Tess had not asked. Jude was just fine. Only—she'd lost the child. But miscarriage at this early stage was apparently relatively common. The doctors said she was physically healthy and strong and would have no problem carrying another child to term. Only—although she was physically all right, Jude was pretty upset. She had taken the whole thing badly, and in a way he'd never expected. She was saying some pretty strange things—

"What sort of things?" She clutched the phone as if it were his arm, trying to force him to speak.

"I need to see you, Tess. I need to talk to you. Could we meet for lunch?"

"Tomorrow?"

"Better make it Friday."

"Just lunch?" She was pressing him as she never did, unable to hide her desperation.

"I can't leave Jude for long. She needs me now. It'll have to just be lunch. The Italian place?"

Tess felt a wave of pure hatred for Jude. She wanted to

tell Gordon that she needed him just as much, or more than, his wife did; that she was in far more trouble than Jude with her mere, commonplace miscarriage.

"That's fine," she said, and made her voice throb with sympathy as she told Gordon how sorry she was to hear about Jude. "Let me know if there's anything at all I can do—tell her that."

"I'll see you on Friday," he said.

Gordon didn't waste any time on Friday. As soon as they had ordered, he came right to the point.

"This has affected Jude much more than I could have dreamed. I'd hardly come to terms with the idea that she was pregnant, and she's responding as if she'd lost an actual baby instead of only . . . I've told her we'll start another just as soon as we can, but she seems to think she's doomed to lose that one, too." He had been looking into her eyes as he spoke, but now he dropped his gaze to the white tablecloth. "Maybe Jude has always been a little unstable, I don't know. Probably it's something hormonal, and she'll get back to normal soon. But whatever . . . it seems to have affected her mind. And she's got this crazy idea that the miscarriage is somehow *your* fault." He looked up with a grimace, to see how she responded.

Tess said quietly, "I'm sorry."

"Maybe she's always been jealous of you on some level—no, I can't believe that. It's the shock and the grief, and she's fixed on you . . . I don't know why. I'm sure she'll get over it. But right now there's no reasoning with her. She won't even consider the idea of seeing you— don't try to call her—and—" He sighed deeply. "She doesn't want me to see you, either. She wanted me to tell you, today, that it's all over."

"Just like that."

"Oh, Tess." He looked at her across the table, obviously pained. She noticed for the first time the small lines that had appeared around his eyes. "Tess, you know I love you. It's not that I love Jude any more than I love you. I'd never agree to choose between you.''

"That's exactly what you're doing."

"I'm not. It's not forever. But Jude is my wife—I have a responsibility to her. You've always known that. She can't cope right now, that's all. I've got to go along with her. But this isn't the real Jude—she's not acting like herself at all.''

"Of course she is," said Tess. "She's always been erratic and illogical and acted on emotion.''

"If you saw her, if you tried to talk to her, you'd realize. She just won't—or can't—listen to reason. But once she's had time to recover, I know she'll realize how ridiculous she was. And once she's pregnant again, she'll be back to normal, I'm certain.''

Tess realized she wasn't going to be able to eat her lunch. Her stomach was tight as a fist.

Gordon said, "This won't last forever, I promise. But for now, we're just going to have to stop seeing each other.''

No apologies, no softening of the blow. He was speaking to her man-to-man, Tess thought. She wondered what he would do if she burst into tears or began shouting at him.

"Why are you smiling?" he asked.

"I didn't know I was. Do we have to stop all contact with each other? Do I pretend you've dropped off the face of the earth, or what?''

"I'll phone you. I'll keep in touch. And I'll let you know if anything changes—when something changes.''

Tess looked at her watch. "I have to get back and supervise some tests.''

"I'll walk you—''

"No, stay, finish your food," she said. "Don't get up." She had suddenly imagined herself clinging to him on a street corner, begging him not to leave her. She didn't want to risk that, yet she could not kiss him casually, as if she would be seeing him again in a few hours or days. As she came around the table, she put her hand on his face for just a moment, then left without looking back.

As a child, Tess had been mad about horses, going through the traditional girlish phase of reading, talking, drawing and dreaming of them, begging for the impossible, a horse of her own. For her ninth birthday her parents had enrolled her for riding lessons. For half a year she had learned to ride, but after her mother's death Tess had refused to have anything more to do with horses, even had a kind of horror of them. She had only one memento from that phase of her life: the blue-glazed, ceramic head of a horse. In her youth she'd kept it hidden away, but now she took pleasure in it again, in its beauty, the sweeping arch of the sculpted neck and the deep, mottled color. It was a beautiful object, nothing like the nightmare.

Tess sat alone in her apartment sipping bourbon and Coke and gazing at the horse head, now and again lifting it to touch its coolness to her flushed cheek.

You didn't kill your mother, she told herself. Wishing the baby would not be born is not the same thing as *making* it not be born. You weren't—aren't—responsible for your dreams. And dreams don't kill.

Outside, the day blued towards night and Tess went on drinking. She felt more helpless and alone than she had ever before felt as an adult, as if the power to rule her own life had been taken from her. She was controlled, she thought, by the emotions of others: by Jude's fear, by Gordon's sense of responsibility, by her own childish guilt.

But Tess did not allow herself to sink into despair. The next morning, although hungover and sad, she knew that life must go on. She was accustomed, after all, to being alone and to taking care of herself. She knew how to shut out other thoughts while she worked, and she made an effort to schedule activities for her non-working hours so that dinner out, or a film, or drinks with friends carried her safely through the dangerous, melancholy hour of blue.

Over the next six weeks, Gordon spoke to her briefly three times. Jude seemed to be getting better, he said, but she was still adamant in her feelings towards Tess. Tess could never think of anything to say to this, and the silence stretched between them, and then Gordon stopped calling. After three months, Tess began to believe that it was truly over between them. And then Gordon came to see her.

He looked thin and unhappy. At the sight of him, Tess forgot her own misery and only wanted to comfort him. She poured him a drink and hovered over him, touching his hair shyly. He caught her hand and pulled her down beside him on the couch, and began to kiss and caress her rather clumsily. She was helping him undress her when she realized he was crying.

"Gordon! Darling, what's wrong?" She was shocked by his tears. She tried to hold him, to let him cry, but understood he didn't want that. After a minute he blew his nose and shook his head hard, repudiating the tears.

"Jude and I," he began. Then, after a pause, "Jude's left me."

Tess felt a shocking sense of triumph, which she repressed at once. She waited, saying nothing.

"It's been hell," he said. "Ever since the miscarriage. That crazy idea she had, that you were somehow responsible for it. She said it was because you didn't mind sharing me with her, but that a baby would have changed things— you would have been left out of the cozy family group. I told her that you weren't like that, you weren't jealous, but she just laughed at me, and said men didn't understand."

She must go carefully here, Tess thought. She had to admit her responsibility and not let Gordon blame Jude too much, but she didn't want Gordon thinking she was mad.

"Gordon," she said. "I *was* jealous—and I was very afraid that once you were a father, things would change and I'd be left out in the cold."

He dismissed her confession with a grimace and a wave of his hand. "So what? That doesn't make any difference. Even if you'd wanted her to have a miscarriage, you didn't make it happen. You couldn't. Jude seems to think that you wished it on her, like you were some kind of a witch. She's crazy, that's what it comes down to."

"She might come back."

"No. It's over. We'd talked about a trial separation, and we started seeing a marriage counselor. It made it worse. All sorts of things came up, things I hadn't thought were problems. And then she found somebody else—she's gone off with somebody else. She won't be with him for long, but she won't come back."

Tess had thought for a long time that the breakup of Gordon and Jude would inevitably lead to the breakup between Gordon and herself, and so for the next few months she was tense, full of an unexamined anxiety, waiting for this to happen. Gordon, too, was uneasy, unanchored without his wife. Unlike Tess, he did not enjoy living alone, but he made a great effort to ration his time with Tess, not to impose upon her. They tried to go on as they always had, ignoring the fact that Jude was no longer there to limit the time they spent together. But when Tess finished her doctorate, they had to admit to the inevitability of some major, permanent change in their relationship. Tess could stay on in New Orleans, teaching English as a foreign language and scraping a living some-how, but that wasn't what she wanted. It wasn't what she had worked and studied for, and so she tried to ignore the feeling of dread that lodged in her stomach as she sent out her CV and searched in earnest for a university that might hire her. She had always known this time would come. She didn't talk about it to Gordon. Why should she? It was her life, her career, her responsibility. She would make her plans, and then she would tell him.

An offer came from a university in upstate New York. It wasn't brilliant, but it was better than she'd expected: a heavy teaching schedule, but with a chance of continuing her own research.

She told Gordon about it over dinner in a Mexican restaurant.

"It sounds good, just right for you," he said, nodding.

"It's not perfect. And it probably won't last. I can't count on more than a year."

"You're good," he said. "They'll see that. You'll get tenure."

"Maybe I won't want it. I might hate it there."

"Don't be silly." He looked so calm and unmoved that Tess felt herself begin to panic. Didn't he care? Could he really let her go so easily? She crunched down hard on a tortilla chip and almost missed his next words. ". . . scout around," he was saying. "If I can't find anything in Watertown, there must be other cities close enough that we could at least have weekends together."

She stared, disbelieving. "You'd quit your job? You'd move across the country just because I'm . . ."

"Why not?"

"Your job . . ."

"I'm not in love with my job," he said.

Tess looked into his eyes and felt herself falling. She said, "Upstate New York is not the most exciting place—"

"They need accountants there just like everywhere else," he said. "I'll find a job. I'm good. Don't you believe me?" He grinned at her with that easy arrogance she'd always found paradoxically both irritating and attractive.

"Are you sure?" she asked.

"I'm sure about this: I'm not letting you go without a fight. If you're not sure about me, better say so now, and we can start fighting." He grinned again, and, beneath the table, gripped her knees between his. "But I'm going to win."

Six months later they were living together in a small, rented house in Watertown, New York. But, although living together, they saw less of each other than they had in New Orleans. Unable to find a job actually in Water-town, Gordon spent at least three hours on the road every day, travelling to and from work. He left in the mornings while Tess still slept, and returned, exhausted, in time for a late dinner and then bed. It was a very different life they led than the one they'd known in New Orleans. They had left behind all those restaurant meals, the easy socializing in French Quarter bars, the flirtations with other people, the long, sultry evenings of doing very little in the open air. The days this far north were short, the nights long and cold. Because Tess didn't like to cook, and Gordon had time for it only on the weekends, they ate a lot of frozen convenience foods, omelets and sandwiches. They watched a lot of television, complaining about it and apologizing to each other. They planned to take up hobbies, learn sports, join local organizations, but when the weekends came, almost always they spent the two days at home, in bed, together.

Her own happiness surprised Tess. She had always be-lieved that she would feel suffocated if she lived with a man, but now whenever Gordon was out of the house she missed him. Being with him, whether talking, making love, or simply staring like twin zombies at the flickering screen, was all she wanted when she wasn't working. She couldn't believe that she had imagined herself content with so little for so long—to have shared Gordon with another woman without jealousy. She knew she would be jealous, now, if Gordon had another lover, but she also knew she had nothing to worry about. She had changed, and so had he. When he asked her to marry him, she didn't even hesitate. She knew what she wanted.

Within four months of the marriage Tess was pregnant.

It wasn't planned—and yet it wasn't an accident, either. She had been careful for too many years to make such a simple mistake, and in Gordon's silence was his part of the responsibility. Without a word spoken, in one shared mo-ment, they had decided. At least, they had decided not to decide, to leave it to fate for once. And afterward Tess was terrified, waking in the middle of the night to brood on the mistake she was making, wondering, almost until the very last month, if she couldn't manage to have an abortion, after all.

Gordon did everything he could to make things easier for her. Since he couldn't actually have the baby for her, he devoted himself to her comfort. And except for the physical unpleasantness of being pregnant, and the middle of the night terrors, Tess sometimes thought, as she basked in the steady glow of Gordon's attentive love, that this might be the happiest time of her life.

In the months before the baby was born, they decided that Gordon's continuing to commute to work wouldn't be possible. Instead, he would set up on his own as an accountant and work from home. It might be difficult for the first few years, but Gordon had a few investments here and there, and at a pinch they could scrape by on Tess's salary. Gordon said, with his usual self-confidence, that he could make far more money self-employed than anyone ever did as an employee, and Tess believed him. Things would work out.

Her labor was long and difficult. When at last the baby was placed in her arms, Tess looked down at it, feeling exhausted and detached, wondering what this little creature had to do with her. She was glad when Gordon took it away from her. Lying back against the pillows she watched her husband.

His face changed, became softer. Tess recognized that rapturous, melting expression, because she had seen it occasionally, during sex. She had never seen him look at anyone else like that. She burst into tears.

Gordon was beside her immediately, pushing the baby at her. But she didn't want the baby. She only wanted Gordon, although she couldn't stop crying long enough to tell him. He held her as she held the baby, and gradually his presence calmed her. After all, the baby was *theirs*.

She and Gordon belonged to each other more certainly now than ever before. No longer merely a couple, they were now a family. She knew she should be happy.

She tried to be happy, and sometimes she was, but this baby girl, called Lexi (short for Alexandra), made her feel not only love but also fear and frustration and pain. Motherhood was not as instinctive as she had believed it would be, for Gordon was clearly better at it than she was, despite her physical equipment. Breast-feeding, which Tess had confidently expected to enjoy, was a disaster. No one had told her, and she had never dreamed, that it would *hurt*. And her suffering was in vain. Lexi didn't thrive until they put her on the bottle. Watching Gordon giving Lexi her late-night feed while she was meant to be sleeping, Tess tried not to feel left out.

It was a relief, in a way, to be able to go back to work after six weeks: back to her own interests, to her students and colleagues, doing the things she knew she was good at. But it wasn't quite the same, for she missed Lexi when she wasn't around. Always, now, she felt a worrying tug of absence. For all the problems, she couldn't wish Lexi away. She only wished that loving Lexi could be as simple and straightforward as loving Gordon. If only she could explain herself to Lexi, she thought, and Lexi explain herself to Tess—if only they shared a language.

When she said this to Gordon one evening after Lexi had been put to bed, he laughed.

"She'll be talking soon enough, and then it'll be Why? Why? Why? all the time, and demanding toys and candy and clothes. Right now, life is simple. She cries when she wants to have her diaper changed, or she wants to be fed, or she wants to be burped or cuddled. Then she's happy."

"But you have to figure out what she wants," Tess said. "She can't tell you—that's my point. And if you do the wrong thing, she just goes on crying and getting more and more unhappy. I'm no more complex than Lexi, really. I have the same sorts of needs. But I can tell you what I want. If I started crying now, you'd probably think I wanted my dinner. But what I really want is a cuddle.''

He looked at her tenderly and left his chair to join her on the couch. He kissed her affectionately.

She kissed him more demandingly, but he didn't respond.

"You'll have to do better than that,'' she said. "Or I'll start crying.''

"I was thinking about dinner.''

"Forget about dinner. Why don't you check to see if my diapers need changing?''

He laughed. Maybe he laughed too loudly, because a moment later, like a response, came Lexi's wail.

"Leave her,'' said Tess. "She'll fall back to sleep.''

They sat tensely, holding each other, waiting for this to happen. Lexi's cries became louder and more urgent.

Tess sighed. The moment had passed, anyway. "I'll go,'' she said. "You fix dinner.''

Time alone with Gordon was what Tess missed most. Their desires, and the opportunity to make love, seldom meshed. As Lexi approached her first birthday she seemed to spend even more time awake and demanding attention. This affected not only her parents' relationship but also Gordon's fledgling business. He was floundering, distracted by the demands of fatherhood, unable to put the time and energy he needed into building up a list of clients. Time was all he needed, Tess thought, and he must have that time. She thought it all through before approaching him about it, but she was certain that he would agree with her. He would be reasonable, as he always was. She didn't expect an argument.

"Day-care!'' he repeated, pronouncing it like an obscenity. "Leave Lexi in some crummy nursery? Are you kidding?''

"Why are you so sure it would be crummy? I'm not proposing we look for the cheapest place we can find—of course, we'll look around and see what's available, and choose the best we can afford.''

"But why?"

"Because there's no way we can afford a full-time babysitter—you know that."

"We don't need a full-time babysitter. We've got me."

"That's what I mean. You're not being paid to look after Lexi, but while you're taking care of her you can't make a living."

He stared at her. She couldn't read his expression; he was miles away from her. "I see. I've had my chance, and I've failed, so now I have to get a real job."

"No!" She clutched his hand, then lowered her voice. "For heaven's sake, Gordon, I'm not criticizing you. And I'm not saying you should go to work for some company . . . I believe in you. Everything you said about being able to make a lot of money in a few years, I'm sure that's true. I know you'll make a success of it. Only . . . you need time. You can't be out meeting people, or writing letters, or balancing books if you have to keep breaking off to get Lexi her rattle. Your work needs attention just as much as she does . . . you have to be able to really commit yourself to it."

"You're right," he said in his usual, reasonable tone. He sighed, and Tess's heart lifted as he said, "I've been thinking about it a lot, and coming to the same conclusion. Well, not quite the same conclusion. You're right that I can't get much work done while I'm looking after Lexi— weekends aren't enough. But why do we have to pay someone else to look after Lexi? We can manage ourselves— we just need to be a little more flexible. We could divide up the week between us. You don't have classes on Tuesdays and Thursdays. If you stayed home then, and took responsibility for the weekends, too—why are you shaking your head?"

"Just because I don't have classes on Tuesdays and Thursdays doesn't mean I don't have work to do. I have to be around to supervise, and advise, and there's my research. When am I ever going to get my book written if I don't have some time to myself? We can't manage by ourselves. There's no shame in that. It's why day-care centers exist. We both have to make a living, and for that we need—''

"What about what Lexi needs?''

"Gordon, she'll get plenty of attention. We're not going to deprive her of anything—''

"We're going to deprive ourselves, though.'' He was almost vibrating with intensity. "Look, one of the greatest experiences in the world is bringing up a child. Teaching her, watching her change and grow every day. I don't want to miss out on that. Maybe in a couple of years, but not now. We can manage. So what if we're not rich? There are things more important than money and careers. If you spent more time with her yourself you'd know what I mean.''

"You think I don't spend enough time with her?'' Tess said quietly.

"I didn't say that.''

"But it's what you think. You think I'm selfish, or that my job is more important to me. It's not that. I love Lexi very much. I love her as much as you do. But I won't—I can't—let her absorb me. I miss her whenever I'm away from her, but I know I can't let my whole life revolve around her. You can't hold on to her forever. Eventually she'll have to grow up and leave us.''

"For God's sake, she's not even a year old! You're talking like I'm trying to stop her from going to college or something.''

"She may be a baby, but she's still a person. She has a life apart from you and me—she has to. And so do we. Not just individually, but as a couple. Or aren't we a couple anymore? Are we only Lexi's parents? I *miss* you, Gordon; I feel like—'' She stopped, because if she said anything more she knew she would be crying.

"Let's go to bed,'' Gordon said, not looking at her. "Let's not argue. We'll talk about it later.''

They went to bed and made love and, for a little while, Tess felt they had reached an understanding, had confirmed the love they still had for each other.

But then the nightmare came.

Lying in bed, drowsily aware of Gordon's close, sleeping warmth, Tess heard the window fly open. When she opened her eyes, she saw, as she had known she would, the familiar, bone-white head of the mare staring in at her, waiting for her.

Her heart sank. I won't move, she thought. I won't go. I will wake myself. But she struggled in vain to open her eyes, or to close them, or even to turn her head so that the creature would be out of her sight. She felt the bitter chill of the winter night flooding the bedroom, and she began to shiver. I must close the window, she thought, and as she thought that, she realized she was getting up and walking toward the creature who had come for her.

Tess stared at the horse, recognizing the invitation in the toss of the pale head. She tried to refuse it. I don't wish anyone any harm, she thought. I love my daughter. I love my husband. I don't want you. Go away.

But she could not wake, or speak, or do anything but walk in slow, somnambulist fashion toward the window, outside of which the nightmare ran in place on the wind.

I don't want to hurt anyone—I won't! Oh, please, let me wake!

But it was her own body that carried her, despite her mental protests, to the window and onto the sill. And as she struggled against the dream, almost crying with frustration, she flung herself through the open window, into the cold night, upon the nightmare's back.

And then she was clinging desperately to the creature's neck, feeling herself slipping on its icy back, as it mounted the sky. This ride was nothing like the last one. She was terrified, and she knew she was in imminent danger of falling, if not of being thrown. Whatever she had once known of riding had vanished. The muscles in her thighs

ached, and the cold had numbed her fingers. She didn't
think she would be able to hang on for very long, particularly not if the mare continued to leap and swerve and
climb so madly. Closing her eyes, Tess tried to relax, to
let instinct take over. She pressed her cheek against the
mare's neck and breathed in the smell of blood. Choking
back her revulsion, she struggled to sit upright, despite the
pressure of the wind. Neck muscles knotted and moved
within her embrace, and the mare's long head turned back,
one wild eye rolling to look at her.

Tess felt herself slipping, sliding inexorably down. Unless the mare slowed her pace she would fall, she thought.
She struggled to keep her grip on the creature's twisting
neck, and because she still could not speak, sent one final,
pleading look at the mare to ask for mercy. And just
before the nightmare threw her, their eyes met, and Tess
understood. Within the nightmare's eye she saw her daughter's cold, blue gaze: judgmental, selfish, pitiless.

From Another Country

THAT SUMMER ALIDA became aware of death in much the same way she had been aware of sex in her teens: it was everywhere around her, experienced by others, it was inevitable and terrifying and she could not stop thinking about it.

She was a woman of thirty years, unmarried, childless. She had never lost anyone close to her. And in that summer the doctors found an inoperable, malignant tumor in her father's brain.

Sitting with her father, Alida longed to ask him about the experience of dying, but she could not, any more than she had ever been able to ask him, when she was younger, about sex. There were certain mysteries parents would never reveal to their children. Even to ask him about pain seemed disrespectful. She saw him every weekend, and usually one evening during the week as well, and when she visited she tried to be cheerful and ordinary, and to anticipate his needs, giving him the pills before he asked for them. They said little to each other. Their closest moments, then as always, were in watching television, sharing the same vicarious experience, her laugh echoing his.

And then she saw death, before her very eyes.

She was in Holborn underground station, waiting for a train after a weary day at work. The platform was hot and crowded, and Alida stared at a particular man simply because he happened to be in her line of sight. Her thoughts were on other things—her father, a new pair of shoes, an argument at work—but she absorbed the fact that this dark-haired, dark-skinned man in early middle age was wearing a suit that looked too heavy for the weather and was fanning himself erratically with a folded *Financial Times*.

She saw him hit himself in the face with the paper as he dropped it, and as the paper fell, he fell, too, heavily and clumsily, his arms and legs jerking stiffly, out of control. He was probably dead by the time he hit the ground. Alida didn't need a doctor's pronouncement to confirm her impression: she seemed to know it instinctively, with the same certainty that she knew she was alive.

Although he was a stranger, his death made a powerful impression on her. That night she couldn't fall asleep: she kept seeing his death, as if the darkness of her room was a screen for the film of her memories. She noticed new details—the pattern on his tie, the scuff marks on his shoes—and saw all the other individuals who made up the crowd in which he died. There was a girl in a pink dress and white cloth boots reading *The Clan of the Cave Bear*; two dirty, spiky-haired teenagers in black leather holding hands; a cluster of American women talking loudly about *Cats*; a man with one gold earring; a couple of sober, dark-suited businessmen, one of whom carried a bright blue plastic briefcase; an Oriental woman with two doll-like children; a man in black—

A man in black who had not been there before, and was no longer there after, the death.

Alida sat up in bed, struggling to breathe, closing her eyes the better to see.

A man in black.

Close to the man who had died. She saw his hand come out; he had touched the man who died. When? Before or after the paper fell? Could it have been coincidence? Just a man in a black suit among so many others in gray or blue or brown—

Except that she couldn't see his face, as she could see the faces of all the others. And after the death, he was gone. Gone utterly, as if he had never been.

No matter how she struggled, she could not see his face, nor where he went after the death. When at last, near morning, she slept, it was to dream about the man in black, standing in the crowded underground station, watching her, watching her father fall before her and die.

The following week, Alida decided to alter her usual habit of visiting her parents on Saturday, and instead went to see some friends who were fixing up an old house in Stoke Newington.

It was a warm, sunny day, and as she stepped off the bus at the request stop on Newington Church Street, Alida noticed how many people were out: clumps of drably dressed teenagers lounging against the buildings, women in brilliant saris flowing along like the personification of summer, geriatric couples moving at a snail's pace, young mothers trying to keep their children close at hand. The street rose and curved, and the pavements were narrow. As Alida dodged and moved along, she occasionally was forced off the curb into the road, which made her nervous, for the traffic moved swiftly, and the drivers, as they rounded the curve, did not slow down or seem aware of the need for special care.

Ten yards ahead, by the tobacconist's shop before the bend in the road, a golden retriever was lying on the pavement, and a woman with a baby in a pushchair had paused to talk to two young men, creating a bottleneck that might be dangerous if some impatient pedestrian stepped off the curb into the road at the wrong moment. But it wasn't the awareness of possible danger that made Alida feel suddenly cold, made her clench her teeth and walk more quickly as she rubbed bare arms prickling with gooseflesh—it was the sight of the man in black waiting just beyond the woman, baby, men and dog.

She didn't for a moment believe she was mistaken, that he might have been some other man in an ordinary black suit, because it was by some sense other than sight that she recognized him. In fact, from this distance she could not even see his face, which was somehow—mysteriously, in the open air and bright sunlight—in shadow.

She began to walk even more quickly, almost running, in her determination to reach him before he could disappear, determined to see his face and find him ordinary.

Beside her, below her line of sight, someone else was moving: a child. And she heard a woman's voice, sharp but tired, calling behind her: "Gavin!"

Alida realized that she was going to have to jog down into the street for a moment: either that or trip over the dog, or risk losing sight of her quarry as she pushed past the people in her way. The risk of the traffic seemed preferable.

Something brushed past her hip. Still thinking of the dog, she glanced down and saw a red-haired child, perhaps three years old, running past and giggling. From behind, sounding more despairing, the woman's voice again: "*Gav*-in!"

The man in black stepped forward, now, like the child, actually standing in the street. His arms were outstretched, and he bent his knees, lowering himself, reaching for the child who, seemingly unaware, was running directly toward him.

Alida was staring straight at the man in black now, and still she could not see his face. There was a glare of sunlight reflecting off the windows of an approaching car, and it dazzled her.

Later she went over and over it in her mind, trying to figure out why she had done what she did.

She had known, on the instant of seeing the man in black stretching out his arms, that the child was doomed. Young Gavin was obviously about to die—probably to be hit by a car rounding the bend.

It would have been a normal response, not even heroic, to have grabbed the child, to have scooped him into her arms and pulled him back to safety and to the gratitude of his mother. It would have been the act of a moment, the obvious thing to do, to have thrown herself at the child. But she had not.

Instead, against all reason, Alida had flung herself at the man in black, had thrown herself into his waiting, outstretched arms, and taken the embrace that was meant for the child.

The next thing she knew was pain. A blinding agony that lanced all through her, stretched her joints out of socket and broke every bone, took even her scream and shattered it inside her agonized eardrums. She was ripped apart and thrown back together into a shuddering, wracked heap that knew not even its own name.

"Are you all right, love?"

Opening her eyes was like ripping skin off a barely healed wound; her throat was too raw for a moan. Alida realized that she was alive. She was standing on Newington Church Street, her back against a wall, and before her was a little white-haired lady—hairnet protecting her fresh perm, blue dress buttoned up to the neck, handbag square and glossy as the Queen's—gazing at her with concern.

Alida looked down at herself and saw that she was whole, with no signs of blood or bruising, even her clothes—flowered print skirt and sleeveless pullover—undisturbed.

"What happened?" she asked and clenched her teeth and rocked against the wall as an aftershock of pain ripped through her.

"I don't know my love, I'm sure. I happened to notice you, and you were backing up to the wall as if you couldn't stand properly on your own, and you had a look on your face . . . it was the look that worried me . . .''

"Not . . . a car didn't hit me?'' Alida looked out at the road, past the woman's emphatic negative, to where the multicolored traffic glittered in the sun and surged ceaselessly past.

She saw the yellow dog panting in the sunlight, still blocking the door to the tobacconist's shop, although the two young men and the woman with the pushchair had moved on out of sight. She forced herself away from the wall, far enough to look around the bend, and was rewarded by the sight of Gavin's red curls. The little boy's hand was firmly in his mother's grip as they walked away.

As for the man in black—

The pain that was her memory of him was so sudden and sharp that she bit her tongue, finding the taste of blood a relief.

"I'll be all right," she said to the woman who was still worrying about her. "It's over now."

"Maybe it was the heat," said the old woman. "I'd see a doctor, though, just to make sure. It might be your heart, and you can't be too careful."

But Alida knew it wasn't the heat, and it wasn't her heart. It was death, and she had survived it.

She walked on, moving slowly, for the intensity of the experience had left her feeling almost boneless. As she came to the old churchyard, she went in and sank onto a low stone bench to rest. She couldn't face her friends just yet: they would know by looking at her that something had happened, and she didn't know how she could explain it to them. She wasn't sure she wanted to tell anyone, for she expected disbelief, and she did not want to be made to doubt her own experience.

She had seen Death. She had felt it, gone through, and survived.

Despite the warmth of the day, Alida shivered. The agony was still there, on the edge of her consciousness, dangerous even to think about. And yet—she had come through. Death, like pain, was comprehensible; it had a place in the world like that other mystery, sex. And, like sex, it was both simpler and more momentous than she had imagined in her innocence.

She felt almost pleased with herself, with her new maturity. After a few more moments of reflection she was able to stand up, smooth down her skirt, and go to see her friends as if she was the same person they had always known.

She thought that was the end of it. She had satisfied her curiosity and cured her obsession; she had come to terms with her own mortality and that of others and need no longer dream of death.

But death had not finished with her. On the bus that evening, going home, she saw the man in black perched on a seat beside a frail old woman. His face was turned away to the window, as if he was watching the passing scene. Later, she saw him huddled in a doorway between two shabby tramps with a bottle of wine, and another day he leaned solicitously over a baby in a pram, and dogged the footsteps of a heavyset young man. Death was everywhere, and no matter how she tried, Alida could not blind herself to his dark presence. Even when she did not see the man in black she sensed him near.

She was sitting at her father's bedside, knitting a sweater while he slept fitfully, when a chill premonition of pain made her look up.

Death came in sideways, his face turned away from her. He crept in like a crab, presenting the smooth black cloth on his back, his face against the pale green wallpaper as if he expected to merge with it unnoticed.

The tenor of her father's breathing changed, becoming rasping and shallow, and Alida opened her mouth to call her mother, but no sound emerged. The ball of wool rolled under the bed as she lurched to her feet, and she found her legs too weak to carry her to safety, weak with that

remembered, crippling pain. She stared at the intruder as
he sidled along the wall, aware that in another moment he
would reach the headboard, and then he would be able to
lean down to touch her father.

There was no conscious decision. She was thinking of
escape, of the pain she could not bear to experience again,
and not of self-sacrifice. But she could not stand by and
watch her father suffer. It was almost an instinctive, physical response, to push Death away—

So she flung herself across the bed, threw herself for the
second time into Death's outstretched arms, taking the
embrace meant for someone else. And embrace him she
did, rather than push him away; clutched him tight as if he
were a long-lost lover.

His whole body was charged. As she embraced him, she
felt her flesh sear wherever his touched it. It was as if a
powerful electric current ran from him to her, melding
their two beings into one. She felt him imprinted upon her
surface, and then etching deeper. She felt the flesh melting
from her bones, dripping off like hot fat, sizzling. She felt
his arms binding her like chains heated white hot, searing
through her arms, her ribs, reaching her interior, where her
heart burst into flame.

Yet she was still alive. Alida realized she had emerged
from the other side of pain, and did not understand how,
when her flesh had been melted away and her bones gone
to ash, mere consciousness could have survived. She became aware of her aching body, which lay across the foot
of her father's bed. She felt it begin to heal, felt her blood
cool and flow again, felt her bones reconstitute themselves, felt her raw, liquid flesh solidify, and at last she
raised herself up, looking timidly around the room.

There was no sign of the man in black. As for her
father, he was sleeping peacefully, breathing regularly,
and looked better than he had for days. The terrifying
translucent quality she had noticed about his face was
gone, leaving him her familiar, living father. She had

taken his death, she thought, and they had both survived. She closed her eyes on tears of joy.

As the days passed, Alida's father grew stronger. He began to eat more, and no longer complained of pain. The doctors were wary of offering hope and seemed to view the idea of total remission as skeptically as they would the miracle Alida knew had occurred. But she knew the truth. She had won him back from death. The immediate danger had passed, and now he would live to be an old man.

Alida's pleasure in this was complicated by what it told her about herself, and she withdrew from family and friends to brood on it.

She had saved her father, as well as a stranger's child, from death, and she did not doubt that she had the power to do the same thing for others. It was an awesome responsibility, a godlike role she had not asked for and did not want. Was she meant to be a new savior, meant to suffer and die a thousand times to redeem the lives of others? Was she to give up any life of her own and travel around the country foiling Death on highways and in hospitals? Yet even if she had wanted that, Alida knew she could not conquer Death. She could only save a few out of the millions he marked each year for his own, and that was as it should be. She would gladly suffer again if need be to save her mother, or a friend, or some innocent child, but why should she help the very old, or the wicked, to evade their rightful deaths?

Alida decided to trust to chance and her own instincts. She would not go in search of Death, but she would use her ability when she felt she must.

In the days and the weeks that followed this decision, Alida continued to catch glimpses of the man in black, but never more than that: a sighting across a crowded street or in a passing car, or a premonitory shudder as a stranger brushed past. She thought she should have been happy in her freedom: she wasn't being forced to make a decision; she didn't have to die again. But she was restless and on edge, sleeping badly, skipping meals, always waiting for and wondering about the next death.

She began dreaming of death again, but this time it was not the loss or recovery of loved ones that she lived through in her sleep; now she dreamed of the man in black. Now when she slept she found herself pushing impatiently through the darkness, pulling at his arm, pressing herself against him, struggling to see his face. In her dreams pain was transformed to pleasure, and instead of fearing the agony, she longed for his embrace. Gradually this longing crept into her waking hours and she had to recognize that the lives she might save did not matter to her. All she wanted was Death.

But Death, it seemed, did not want her. Although she had felt earlier that it was her obsession with death that had drawn the man in black to her, and made it possible for her to see him when others did not, her desire no longer worked such magic. She thought perhaps it was having the opposite effect, that her very eagerness might be foiling her: Death might see her not as a lover but as a threat, a dangerous rival who stole his chosen victims.

She began to haunt the casualty wards of hospitals, but although she often sensed the presence of Death, she was never able to draw close enough to touch. She stopped going to work, preferring to roam the streets at all hours of the day and night. Yet no matter how often she saw that familiar black suit it would vanish as soon as she attempted to follow. She read about deaths in the papers and heard of them on the news: starvation in Africa, a car bomb in Ireland, a machine-gun maniac in Los Angeles, and all the obituaries, all the private little deaths that took place out of her presence, beyond her reach. So many died, so many who did not have to. Why wasn't she allowed to intervene? Why couldn't she find someone who was about to die? Only her dreams gave her any relief, and they were few and far between as she found it harder and harder to sleep.

Alida did not realize quite how desperate her mood had become until one morning in the bathroom she found herself staring at the blood welling from a cut on her finger—a cut she'd made in a futile, half-conscious, attempt to extract the blade from a disposable plastic razor.

The pain scarcely registered, but the sight of the bright red blood recalled her to herself, and she stared at the mirror, seeing for the first time how pale and haggard and thin she had become. How near death she looked.

And her eyes shifted from her own face to look beyond. She couldn't even hold her own gaze; she was always looking for the man in black, always trying to see that still unseen, unknown face. Everything she did was an attempt to call him back to her, but she knew she must not take her own life unless she really was giving up. Because she didn't want to die—she wanted Death, and to survive death, again and again.

Twice before she had managed it; how hard could it be to find someone else who was about to die? Alida did not realize she'd made up her mind to attempt murder until she actually had her victim in range, directly in front of her and too close to the edge of the station platform, a hot wind presaging the arrival of a train. Alida had taken one step forward, and brought her hands up to push, when from the corner of one eye, amid the crowds, she saw the unmistakable black suit drawing near.

Horror froze her, as she understood what she had meant to do. Death vanished. She could not act. Around her, people pushed and shoved and clambered into the train, leaving her behind, alone with herself and her desire.

No, not desire: she had to recognize now that it had taken on the force of an addiction. It was a need that had set her at odds with herself, that had taken over her life, her mind and her will.

But not entirely. She could still think, and she could refuse to give in. She would change. She had to.

Trembling but determined, Alida rose out of the underground onto the gray city street, thinking of how she would forget her two deaths and concentrate on living. She was too much alone, she decided; she needed to spend more time with her friends, and to find a lover.

She imagined a man in her arms again, in the warm privacy of her bed, wrapping her legs around him and pressing her mouth to his, holding him close, forcing him to be still, feeling his poor, feeble attempts to get away, feeling the power tear through him, ripping him out of life—

It took an act of considerable will to stop that chain of thoughts, and Alida could do nothing about the fact that her heart was pounding and her breath coming in short gasps of excitement—or was it fear? Alida didn't know what to think. She had become a stranger to herself. She didn't dare to think about what she wanted. It was as if she contained two people, and the desires of each one were incomprehensible, and dangerous, to the other.

She went on walking because it was the easiest thing to do, and because it seemed safe. It might even do some good, she thought, to walk until her mind was emptied by exhaustion. She was scarcely aware of where she went, or of the passage of time. She crossed the Thames and continued traveling southward, moving at a steady pace, untiring. She had no destination in mind, but gradually she realized that she would soon be in her parents' neighborhood. The light was failing—it would be dinnertime; and her mother always made more than enough. She was not hungry, but Alida snatched at the idea of a meal with her parents as at an anchor to normality. They would be pleased to see her, and for a little while she might seem to be her old self again.

Her parents lived on a quiet side road, in one of a row of large but slightly shabby terraced houses. Turning the corner, Alida at once made out the familiar figure of her father. No longer restricted to his bed, he was standing now and very slowly, carefully sweeping the dead leaves from the crazy-paving that he had laid down in place of the front garden the summer that Alida was fourteen.

She felt an overpowering rush of love at the sight of him. It seemed that in that one moment, as she saw him moving slowly in the twilight, she recalled all that he had been to her through thirty years, the whole sound and sight and feel and smell and meaning of him in her life. She began to walk more quickly, wondering if the sound of her heels clicking against the pavement would make him turn, anticipating the slow, pleased smile that would spread across his worn face at the sight of her, savoring his surprise.

Then something other than daughterly affection made her heart beat faster as she glimpsed something—someone—beyond her father, behind him, half-hidden by the shadow of the arched entrance to the front door. The man in the black suit.

There could be no doubt. His utter stillness sent a chill through her. And then, almost as if he were signaling his contempt for her, a black-suited, pale-fingered arm was outstretched. It fell just short of her father's stooping shoulders, but if he moved so much as a step back, those fingers would touch him. And there was nothing Alida could do about it. She could not reach Death first, as she had done before. This time, her father stood between her and Death.

Her only hope was to make her father come forward, out of Death's reach, toward her. If she could warn him in time, call him to her—

She screamed, calling him by the infantile name she'd ceased using years before, two syllables he had not heard for fifteen years. Perhaps he didn't understand, perhaps he only recognized the terror and the longing in a woman's scream.

The sound made him turn to look, and Alida came running, moving toward him faster than she had ever moved in her life. She saw the expression on his face change, and with part of her mind she wondered what he saw to make him look so terrified. Whatever it was, it made him step backward, almost stumbling away from her.

Backward, within easy reach—and yet the man in black did not take him. As she knocked open the little iron gate and flung herself forward, Alida did not even wonder why.

Then her arms were around her father and she was holding him tight, feeling him die.

This death was not like the other two, the ones she had received secondhand, charged and painful from the hands of the man in black. For this death was hers, and she gave it.

She felt his bones shatter like glass beneath the pressure of her arms, and when she put her lips to his it was to suck out his last, shuddering breath. She lanced his soul and let out the life, and pumped his body full of death, and then she let it fall.

No pain, this time, but only an exquisite relief, a rich, heady pleasure. She stood, breathing hard, watching the shadowed entranceway, waiting for the man in black to come out.

When he did, when he stepped into the failing light and showed himself to her, she saw that he had the ordinary face of a stranger. He was a mortal man once again, having passed the burden or the gift of death to Alida.

She reached out with long, cool fingers to caress the human face before her. She closed his eyes and gave him the rest he had been longing for. Letting his body fall beside that of the man who had once been Alida's father, Death vanished about her business.

The Dragon's Bride

the black notebook

I DON'T REMEMBER anything at all about two months of my life, the two most important months of my life.

The summer that I was twelve I was sent to England. That time is gone. How can I get it back? The memory must be there, hidden away in my mind, if I could only get to it. I must remember it before it is too late.

The one thing I do remember, without any hesitation, is the day I returned.

My mother picked me up at the airport. She was alone. She didn't say anything about my father, and I think I was afraid to ask. When we got home, I realized that everything was different. Everything had changed, even the smell of the house and the way the light came through the windows. Yet there was nothing I could put my finger on. The same furniture occupied the same places, but it was as if everything I knew had been taken away and replaced by exact replicas. It looked the same but I knew it was not. It wasn't mine any more. I did not belong. And my father was gone.

I woke up in the middle of the night. The house was

dark and silent, and I knew it would be hours before I could watch TV or go outside. I got up anyway. I decided to unpack my suitcase.

Because my aunt, unlike my mother, had not packed for me, my clothes were a jumble. I tried to be neat as I put them away, and as I was shaking the creases out of a red sundress, something small and hard flew out of its folds, hit the floor, and rolled under the bed.

I went after it, scrabbling until my fingers closed on something I could pull out into the light.

It was made of some light, reddish metal, round and flat, about the size of a quarter. I thought it was a button or a medallion, although there were no holes or pins. It was in the shape of a dragon, intricately detailed, the working so fine that I could see each individual scale, and the tiny slits of closed eyes. It slept curled around itself, nose to arrow-pointed tail. It was odd and very beautiful, and I could not remember ever having seen it before.

Then it came to life. The eyes opened, flashing like points of fire, and the dragon uncoiled. I was almost hypnotized by the sight of it as it flowed like quicksilver through my hands. Then it wrapped itself around my ring finger, caught its tail in its mouth, and froze. It was cold again, hard and solid, as if it had never been alive or known another form, as if it had never been anything but a finger ring of some light, strong, red-gold material, fashioned in the likeness of a serpent or dragon swallowing its own tail.

I must have stared at it for a full minute, trying to make sense of what had happened. I didn't want to touch it. I kept my fingers spread as widely apart as they would go, and I stared at it, trying to will it back to life, trying to will it to vanish from my hand. Finally, frightened but determined, I took hold of it between the thumb and forefinger of my right hand and tried to take it off.

It wouldn't budge, not even to be twisted. It seemed to have grown into my flesh and become a part of my hand.

Soon I became hysterical, rubbing my hand along the carpet and then smashing it against the wall, screaming. My mother found me like that, my left hand torn and bloody. Before the doctor arrived to give me a shot, I had broken two of my fingers. I guess I was lucky that was all. If my mother hadn't stopped me, I might have cut the finger off.

I don't know why it scared me so much. It hasn't worried me for years. I wouldn't think about it at all, if it weren't for this letter from my aunt, calling me back to England. My time has come. I need more time.

* * *

The Golden Bough was his excuse, but Fitz didn't pretend even to himself that the attraction was intellectual. One sight of her tall, slim figure, her glossy auburn hair, and the endearingly awkward way she wrapped one long leg around the other, perching like a stork as she read, and Fitz knew he had to talk to her even if the book in her hand had been by Judith Krantz.

He said, "There's an illustrated edition on the remainder table."

She looked up, startled, and stumbled slightly as she came down on two legs. She had slanting gray eyes, a small nose, pale skin: a pretty but unremarkable face. He guessed her age at twenty-two, five years younger than he was.

Fitz gestured at her book. "It doesn't cost much more than that one, and it's worth it for the illustrations. It's also got bigger print, so it's easier to read in hardcover. If you're planning on reading it, that is. I don't think anybody does read it these days; it's become a part of the collective unconscious. You keep it on the shelf and absorb it by osmosis, you know? I must have had my copy for ten years—bought it when I was reading *The Waste Land* in high school, probably even listed it in the bibliography to my term paper, but I never actually read the thing. I'd open it at random, read a few lines, and feel like I'd learned something.''

"That's how I read,'' she said. "When there's something I really want to know, and I don't know how to find it, I go to a library, or a bookstore, and I just take books off shelves and open them and . . . I find things. It doesn't always work, but a lot of the time it does. It's the only way to find out some things.''

There was something faintly Southern in her voice, and the intensity of her gaze hooked him. He liked the way she talked to him, as if they weren't strangers, as if they already shared something.

"What are you trying to find out?''

"Well, if I knew *that* . . .'' She shrugged. "Right now, I'm looking up dragons. I want to find out the *truth* about dragons. Most of what I've found so far is useless.''

"What sort of dragons?''

"The kind they have—or had, or might have—in England.''

Inwardly, Fitz was groaning. Dragons and unicorns and knights in armor—he loathed that sort of cheap, ready-made fantasy. Still, she had been looking in *The Golden Bough* and not on the science fiction shelves. "You mean as in St. George and?''

"I guess so. Did he rescue a maiden?''

"Undoubtedly. They always did, didn't they? Not much of a story without the princess bride.''

"But why? Why the connection between virgins and dragons? In here''—she waved the book—''he connects dragons with water spirits, and says maidens were sacrificed to ward off floods. Did they have to be virgins? Would the dragon refuse the sacrifice if they weren't virgins?''

"Well, sexist attitudes in a sexist society,'' Fitz said. "Isn't there some connection between human sacrifice and sacred marriage? If the women were given to dragons as brides, of course they'd have to be virgins. The dragon could be expected to be pretty pissed if he got damaged goods, so to speak. Hey, *I* didn't make it up. I guess it was a pretty sexist assumption in the first place, that the dragon would be male. If I remember right, Jung saw the dragon as an archetypal female image. It represented the devouring aspect of the mother, and the maiden held captive by it was some aspect of the hero, so by killing the dragon he was setting *himself* free.''

Her gray eyes were wide. ''The dragon is a symbol for the mother?''

''Well, that's just one interpretation. You can make these things mean whatever you want.''

She was abruptly cold, remote from him. ''No you can't. It's not a game. Things have meanings from within—you can't just stick labels on the outside and switch them around. Who is this Young? What did he write?''

''Carl Gustav Jung.'' He spelled the last name. ''They've probably got his books over in the psychology section. I don't know where I read that about the dragon, but it was probably in something *about* Jung, rather than by him, knowing my habits.''

''Can you remember anything else about dragons?''

''Oh, bits and pieces. I read a lot—about everything and anything. My mind is a vast warehouse of trivial information, as one of my professors once told me. I'd never make an expert—my mind could never settle on any one subject for long enough. What's your particular interest in dragons?''

She looked down. ''It's complicated.''

''The most interesting things are. Have you had dinner? There's a Greek place right around the corner. We could talk there . . . of shoes, and ships, and sealing wax, of cabbages, and . . . dragons.''

She smiled. He admired what it did to her face. ''I don't even know your name.''

''Fitz. Officially, Lawrence Fitzgerald, but only my mother ever calls me Lawrence.''

"I'm Isobel." She replaced *The Golden Bough* carefully on the shelf. "No one's ever tried to pick me up before."

"Really? Well, there's always a first time. I've never rescued a maiden from a dragon."

This made her face go grave again. "Would you, if you had the chance? Would you rescue me?"

"I'd do everything in my power,' he said. "Just give me a sword."

They left the bookstore together, as Fitz had somehow known they would. He'd always had luck with women, although he was not a handsome man. He was short, his colorless hair was thinning, and his nose, as his sister had been the first to point out, looked rather like a potato. But, as his sister also admitted, he had beautiful, puppy-dog brown eyes, and a sweet nature. "You look so harmless," she said. "They think they're safe with you, and then, before they know it, they're hooked. And then you meet someone else, and, all unintentionally on your part, hearts get broken."

Fitz didn't like being told he looked harmless, but certainly he meant no harm. He thought that women liked him because he liked them. Hearts got broken only because being in love with one woman had never stopped him from falling in love with another.

"Do you like Greek food?" he asked Isobel at the door of the restaurant. "If you don't, we can go somewhere else."

"I don't know. I've never had it."

"Never? You must be new to New York."

She nodded. "I got here today."

"From?"

"Virginia."

"Ah." He said hello to Milo, the owner's son. Milo looked at Isobel, gave Fitz a knowing look, and conducted them to a table at the back. There was much discussion over the menu, as Fitz explained everything and Isobel made her choice. Milo brought the usual bottle of retsina without being asked, and took their order. Then they were alone together. Fitz looked across the table at Isobel and sighed happily. He loved beginnings. He decided Isobel was prettier than he had thought in the bookstore. He had been too taken by her body then to really notice her face.

He raised his glass to hers. "Destruction to dragons," he said.

"What do you think dragons are, really?" she asked.

"Tell you the truth, Isobel, I've never given the subject a lot of thought. In the Bible the dragon is the devil, the old serpent. In China, the dragon symbolized leadership—only the Emperor could use the dragon sign. I read something once that speculated that those old stories of dragons terrorizing populations and being slain might have some basis in fact . . . that there might have been some sort of large land reptile—a cross between a crocodile and a gila monster—which survived in Europe into the Middle Ages, or later. A leftover dinosaur." He grinned. "That idea has an appeal to me—I always liked dinosaurs. It seemed so unfair that *all* of them should have been wiped out so many centuries before I was even born."

Her hands on the table top tugged and worried at each other. "You really think there might be an actual dragon somewhere? Not just an idea, or a symbol, but a real live animal, in a cave, incredibly old . . ."

"Now? Today?" He shrugged. "Well, maybe. We never know as much as we think we do. Even though the world seems smaller now, there's still Bigfoot, and the Loch Ness monster, so why not something like a dragon hidden away in a cave? Why should that be any stranger than an alligator, or one of those giant snakes? Imagine what one of those big tortoises would look like without a shell. Drink your wine—I want to know what you think of it."

She sipped obediently, and looked startled. "Ooh." She took another taste.

"Like it?"

She nodded. "I think so. It's like—pine trees."

"Have you ever seen something you thought might be a dragon?" Fitz asked.

She put the glass down, then seemed to make an effort to hold on to it. "I don't know. I don't remember. I might have, when I was a kid."

"In Virginia?"

Isobel shook her head. "In England. But I don't remember! I don't remember what happened to me there, at all. And now I'm supposed to go back there—my aunt wants me to go visit her, and I'm afraid to. I want to know why I'm afraid. It has something to do with a dragon, but—that might just be a symbol. I thought it probably had to be a symbol—but a symbol for what? The devil, I thought, but . . . maybe it could be symbolic *and* real? Do you think there could be, somewhere in England, in a cave, a creature hundreds of years old? Just a few people know about it, and they keep it a secret and they look after it. They take care of it . . . maybe they even worship it because it has some kind of power. Or they think it does. There might be a whole kind of religion built up around it, and there always has to be someone, kind of like a high priestess . . ."

Fitz waited, but she seemed to have come to a stop. He tore off a piece of pita bread and scooped up some taramasalatta. "You . . . remember something like this?"

"No. I told you, I don't remember anything. Two months in England, staying with my aunt, and I can't remember a thing. Except that I'm scared to go back there. That's a sort of story that I made up . . . I guess I made it up . . . how could it be true?"

"Why do you feel you have to go back to England?"

"It's not just a matter of feeling. I should be there now—or at least on my way. I just graduated from college, and my aunt sent me a ticket to London. I didn't want it. My mother pressured me—I thought she'd be on my side, but she insisted I had to go. She's her sister, you see, but they haven't seen each other for years. Or even talked. There was a falling out, and I guess now, after all these years, they're thinking about making up. But I don't see why I have to be in on it, why I have to be the go-between. Let my mother go herself if she wants. She wants me to be the peace offering. Or the sacrifice.''

''The maiden to the dragon?''

Her shoulders relaxed. ''I thought if I ever said that to anyone they'd think I was crazy.''

''You don't seem crazy to me. It was probably a good thing for you to stand up to your mother and refuse—''

''But I didn't stand up to her. I ran away. I was supposed to change planes, but instead I just walked out of the airport. My bags were checked through, so I had to let them go. They're on their way to Gatwick right now, and my mother and my aunt both think I'm on my way, too. I just couldn't do it. I didn't have any reason I could give them, but I knew I needed more time to think things through.''

The main course arrived then, providing a natural, and needed, break. Fitz watched Isobel closely. It was true, as he had said, that she didn't seem crazy to him. Of course, he was no expert, but he'd met people he thought were neurotic or disturbed, and he didn't put Isobel in that class. He'd noticed her nervous habit of tugging at one of her fingers—all right, she was nervous—and he didn't know what dragons could possibly have to do with an unhappy childhood experience, or with her relationship with her mother, but he was intrigued by her as well as attracted. He wanted to know more.

Over dinner he asked her about herself, and she told him she had been an art major in college. She had worked part-time and summers in the past as a waitress, but she didn't know what she was going to do about getting a real job, or where she would go. She thought she'd like to do something in design.

He told her about growing up in New Jersey, wanting to be an astronaut, a baseball player, or Ernest Hemingway.

In college he couldn't choose between anthropology, history, or dropping out to become Robert Stone. Instead, he got a job delivering telephone books, happened to be in the right place at the right time to hear about a job writing copy for an in-house publication, and got it.

"Do you write anything else?"

"When I'm inspired," he said. "*Not* very often." He signaled Milo for another bottle of retsina.

"Oh, no," said Isobel when the bottle arrived.

"Why not? I thought you liked it."

"I do, but I'm not used to drinking so much." She pressed her hands against flushed cheeks. "I've had enough—more than enough."

"No more," Fitz said to Milo. "Two Greek coffees." He looked across at Isobel when Milo had gone. "You don't have to stay sober," he said. "I'm a gentleman. You can trust me to put you in a cab and send you back to your hotel."

"I don't have a hotel," she said. "I hoped I could go home with you."

Fitz nodded slowly. "Of course you can. I'd better warn you, though, that it's a one-room, one-bed apartment, and I'm not sure I could be a gentleman all night."

"I want to sleep with you."

Her words were electric. Fitz wanted to look serious, romantic, or sexy, but couldn't help grinning like a kid. He reached across the table and took her hand.

With a gasp, she jerked it away.

Fitz stared at her.

"I'm sorry," she said breathlessly.

"Don't apologize. You don't have to apologize. I just thought you meant—"

"I *did* mean it. I'm funny about that hand, that's all. It's silly." She drew a deep breath and thrust her left hand at him, like someone daring fire.

Cautiously, he put out his hand and touched hers, let it rest on his palm. He ran his thumb across the backs of her fingers. For no reason, he suddenly shivered. It was a soft, lovely hand, there was nothing wrong with it at all, but Fitz was glad that the arrival of the coffee gave him an excuse to let it go.

* * *

the black notebook

I can't even remember what she looks like. My mother doesn't have any pictures of her, except one, of the two of them, taken when they were teenagers, and that isn't much good because my aunt has her face half turned away. My father took that picture when he met them, on vacation in England.

I used to think that they had both been in love with him, and that my father had chosen my mother, and that was the reason for the strain between them. Now I think that the choice was made not by my father, but by the two girls. They must have agreed between them that one should go and one should stay; one would have a husband and a normal sort of life and the other—

There is one way I can remember what my aunt looks like. If I stare at myself in the mirror long enough, her face starts coming through. I've never been able to do it for very long because I'm terrified she'll take control. More proof, if I needed it, that she's a witch. What exactly does she want with me? And how can I fight her?

More questions than answers, but I've thought of this: If my father saved my mother, why shouldn't a man save *me*? A woman can't have two husbands.

* * *

His apartment was an embarrassment. It stank of cats, the bed hadn't been turned back into a sofa that morning, and there were dirty clothes, papers and magazines strewn everywhere. He hadn't expected, when he went out for an evening browse, to be bringing anyone back with him.

"I'm sorry about the mess," he said. "I'd say it's not usually like this, but you wouldn't believe me. Let me just feed the cats and clean up a little . . . Would you like some coffee, or tea, or . . . There's probably some beer or orange juice in the fridge."

"I'm fine," she said.

"Well . . . make yourself at home, if you can stand the thought. Look at the books or something. I won't be long."

He was nervous. He hadn't been so nervous with a woman since he was nineteen. He didn't know what it was, but there was something wrong.

As he fed the cats, and changed the litter in their box, Fitz tried to figure it out. It wasn't just that Isobel was strange—he'd known lots of strange ladies—but that he didn't believe she really wanted to go to bed with him. Attracted as he was to her, he could sense no answering spark. Something else was going on; something else was driving her.

When he came out of the tiny kitchen he found Isobel waiting for him. She wasn't examining the books that lined every wall, as most of his visitors did. She was simply standing beside the untidy wreckage of his bed, doing nothing at all but waiting for him.

"I'm sorry it's such a mess," he said. "It won't take me long to get some of it cleared away."

Watching him as if he were an animal who might run away, Isobel stretched out her hand and let it rest on his arm. "Kiss me," she said.

He could not refuse her, and as soon as he took her in his arms, his nervousness melted away. He thought that she would melt, too, but she was like a statue, as if she didn't know how to kiss and was watching things happening to her body from some distance.

"What's wrong?"

"Nothing."

"Relax . . . Why don't we sit down? It might be easier." He was used to kissing taller women, but perhaps she felt awkward bending to meet him, he thought.

They perched on the edge of the bed, and Fitz kissed her without pressure, without too much intensity, holding himself back. He cuddled and nuzzled her gently, in a friendly sort of way, and he thought she was beginning to relax. His hand slipped to her breast, and immediately she was tense again. Fitz cursed himself, and moved the offending hand: Oops, sorry, just passing through, didn't mean any harm.

"Do you want me to take off my clothes?"

He drew back to look at her. "Why do I have the feeling we're not watching the same movie here?"

"You want to make love to me, don't you?"

"There's no hurry," he said. "Why don't we just neck for a little while, get to know each other? We don't have to go any further if you don't want."

"But I do."

He held her hands in both of his. "You need a place to stay the night, you've got it. We can share the bed, or you can have my sleeping bag on the floor. There is no price for this service. You don't have to have sex with me."

"But I want to."

"Sure."

"Don't you like me?" Tears welled up in her gray eyes.

"God, yes, of course I do! Isobel, please don't cry." His chest ached; he thought he might cry himself. "I think you're wonderful, I think you're gorgeous. I don't know what you want with me, though. I can't believe it's sex. You're so tense—"

"I'm tense."

"Yes, you're tense, you're not enjoying this, so why—"

She began to tremble. "I want to! But I don't know how!"

Suddenly he understood. He almost laughed at his own

stupidity, but he didn't want to hurt her. "You're a virgin."

She nodded.

"Sweetheart, that's no crime. You should have said—well, I guess you did, only I was too dumb to take it in. I guess I couldn't believe anyone as lovely as you could still be—I'm flattered you chose me for your first."

"You're not going to send me away?"

"I'm not going to send you away. We're going to make love. But that's something two people do. This isn't an endurance test, and it isn't something I know about and you don't. I want your first time to be as good for you as—as it always should be. But you've got to tell me what you like, and what you don't like, and if you're tense because I'm hurting you, or just because you're nervous."

"I thought—from books—that the first time always hurt."

"Well. It might. But I don't think it has to. Anyway, that's only part of it, penetration. The other stuff should just feel good."

He couldn't tell if she believed him, and he wondered what sort of upbringing she'd had. How innocent was she? Had she never had a boyfriend, never made out in the back seat of a car, never touched herself in bed at night to make herself feel good? If not, what had stopped her? Fitz had no experience with virgins at all. He was feeling nervous again. There were so many things that could go wrong, and it was all his responsibility.

"I don't suppose you're on the Pill? I've got some contraceptives. Wait—I'll be right back."

When he returned from the bathroom, Isobel had undressed and was lying curled on top of the sheets. The sight of her slim, pale body—the fact that she hadn't covered herself—and the frightened, expectant look on her face caused him to feel a rush of tenderness for her. He wanted to protect her. By the time he had taken off his own clothes and joined her on the bed, Fitz felt as if *he* were the virgin.

"Aren't you cold?" he asked. "Let's get under the covers." The room was warm and stuffy, but he was trembling. He took her in his arms, and the feel of her naked flesh, and the faint, warm scent of her, aroused him unbearably. He had an erection such as he remembered from adolescence, so hard it was painful. If he did anything at all but hold her, he thought, he would explode.

Isobel was no longer the girl he'd met in the bookstore, a girl he'd had dinner with and been attracted to like so many others. She had become a stranger when she took off her clothes. Now he didn't know who she was. She was a fantasy, unattainable and forbidden. Her breasts were soft and strange against his chest. So this was what women were like, under their clothes. His sister raised her dress, to show him. He was afraid to look at her, and dying to know more. He was afraid she would wake up and push him away; he was afraid his father would come in. He had no right to be here; he would be punished.

She moved; he felt her thighs against his. "Kiss me," she said.

Fitz groaned as, helplessly, out of control, he came.

In agony and pleasure he pressed himself against her, and then, abruptly, it was over.

He felt an immediate repulsion, from her and from himself. He pushed himself away from her, turned his back, and reached for the tissues to clean himself. Every muscle was trembling in the aftermath of intensity, but what shook him more profoundly was the loathing he felt. He didn't even want to look at her. He didn't understand what had happened to him, but somehow he blamed her. It was as if she had taken control of him, demonstrated her power over him, and then let him go.

Gradually, though, he calmed, and his feelings began to seem like something from a bad dream: they weren't real, after all, they had nothing to do with the real Isobel. It wasn't fair to blame her for feelings she had, quite innocently, stirred up in him.

Fitz rolled back and put his arm around her, and kissed her on the mouth. "Sorry about that," he said.

She looked wary and confused. "What happened?"

"I got a little too excited. That's never happened to me before, I don't—" He stopped. She didn't want an explanation, only reassurance, and the best way to give her that was not in words.

He began to make love to her, without passion, but skillfully. Having no desire himself, he concentrated on creating it in her, relying on past experience and alert to her every response. As he kissed and touched and stroked and watched her, he was aware of her reactions almost before she was herself. He found the tiny sparks of her desire and fanned them to flames. He opened her with his mouth and felt her melt on his tongue. Her body changed, reshaped by his hands. What had been a hundred separate nerves leaping beneath her flesh combined in one strong, steady pulse, and her urgency transmitted itself to him. He forgot about being gentle, and he didn't know, or care, as he thrust into her, whether the sound she made was of pain or satisfaction. The virgin was gone. She twisted beneath him and wrapped her legs around his waist as if from old experience, and her excitement drove him on; she was exciting him now, and he was indifferent to her pleasure, lost in his own. He had a sense of being watched, of others, nearby, encouraging him. He closed his eyes to focus on this sensation, and he was deep beneath the earth, in a cave. She was squirming beneath him and he was stabbing her with his sword—he was killing the dragon *for* her, to prove his love, while she, the princess, watched him. She beckoned to him, the princess, and raised her dress, offering him his reward. The cave was hot and moist around them, she was hot and moist, embracing him, and then he felt the dragon moving, still alive, and he tried to free himself, but she held him tight, and it was too late.

As he came he shouted. The orgasm seemed to empty

him of everything, pain, pleasure, memory, desire, under-standing. He lay, stunned, on top of her, unable to move, staring at the closely woven blue threads of the pillowcase as he waited for his personality to come back from wher-ever it had gone.

* * *

the black notebook

There wasn't any blood. And it didn't hurt. No blood, no pain. What does *that* mean?

Oh, God, I know what it means. I feel sick. I wasn't a virgin.

There's never been a man—not in my memory, but maybe out of it? In England, when I was twelve? How could she?

I remember something about blood. I thought that my period must have started while I was in England, because I don't remember the first time—and that's supposed to be one of the things every woman remembers. I just remem-ber that I hadn't got what my mother called "the curse" before I went to England, but after I was home again and had started seventh grade, there was a big blue box of sanitary napkins in my bathroom cupboard, and I could count on getting excused from gym a couple of days every month.

Now I think that the blood I remember—or almost remember—wasn't just from my first period. I was raped. My aunt gave me to her master. The devil—or the dragon. That was the betrothal. Now she wants me to go back, to be married to him.

While Fitz was making love to me, I kept seeing drag-ons and snakes, huge serpents coiling and uncoiling in the air above us. It didn't matter whether my eyes were open or closed. I felt their flickering tongues touch me, like ice sometimes and sometimes like fire. But they couldn't hurt me, not with Fitz there to protect me.

I thought that Fitz would change everything for me, but now I don't know. The ring is still on my finger. Whatever is waiting for me in England still waits.

* * *

Fitz thought that she would be gone when he got back from work, that she would vanish like a dream. He couldn't concentrate on his work, and twice he tried to phone her. But was his telephone ringing in an empty apartment, or was she simply too shy to answer? Daydreams drifted through his mind, as he imagined searching all New York City for her, even flying to England to track her down. He realized he didn't even know her last name, and it was all he could do not to leap up and run home immediately. As it was, he left half an hour early, claiming he had to take his cat to the vet.

She was still there, curled, like one of his cats, on the sofa. Unlike the cats, she was reading a book, which she put down when she saw Fitz.

He went to her, sank onto the sofa beside her, took her in his arms and began kissing her. The whole day, he felt now, could only have led to this. Neither of them said a word, but there was no mistaking her response, the way her body leaped to meet his, and soon they had discarded their clothes and were making love on the sofa.

When they had finished, and Fitz had moved off her, he had a sense of disorientation when he turned to kiss her again and saw the flushed, young, pretty face of a stranger. Who was she? What was their connection? He felt remote from her and yet concerned, as if they were strangers who had experienced some shared disaster beyond their control, like a flood or an earthquake. It was that which made him say, "Are you all right?"

"I didn't know it would be like that," she said dreamily. "I didn't know it would be that . . . powerful."

"What's your name?" he asked suddenly.

"What?"

"You never told me your last name."

"Mannering. Does sex change you?"

"Everything changes you. Meeting you changed me."

"I mean, maybe it's not so much about virginity—maybe virginity is just a symbol, and what's important is the connection to someone else. If my father had fallen in love with my aunt instead . . . She can't make me do something I don't want to do; I don't see how she can."

"No."

"I'm going to call my mother tonight; I really have to."

Fitz felt a premonition of loss. "Don't," he said. "Don't go to England, don't go home, just stay here with me. I'll help you find a job."

The telephone rang.

After a while Isobel said, "Shouldn't you answer it?"

"I'm not interested. I don't want to talk to anyone but you."

When the telephone had stopped ringing, Isobel said, "I have to call my mother, it's not fair. She's probably worried about me. I'm sure my aunt would have phoned her when I didn't turn up. I have to tell her that I'm going to stay here."

"As long as that's what you're going to tell her." He kissed her for some time, then they got up and dressed.

"I'll go out and get us some food while you call your mother," Fitz said. "You like Chinese? Anything in particular?"

But as soon as he was on the street, the fear came back, the fear that had haunted him all day while he was away from her. What if she left? What if her mother talked her into leaving? What if she simply left without saying goodbye? How would he ever find her again? The worry buzzed at his mind like a fly, and he couldn't swat it away. Logic didn't help. He knew it was an unreasonable fear; more than that, it wasn't his sort of fear. It wasn't like him to be so obsessive, so possessive, about anyone. Who was she? he asked himself, as he began, quite unconsciously, to run.

She was huddled on the floor beside the telephone, crying. Fitz stared, unaware of the cats who cried and stroked themselves against his legs. "Isobel—"

"Oh, Fitz, she's dead!"

"Your mother?" He dropped to the floor and cradled her in his arms.

"My aunt." She sniffed, then wiped her eyes and blew her nose. "I'm all right. I hardly knew her—I'm not upset about that. It was my mother, really, hearing her, hearing—" Her voice quavered and broke, but she recovered. "She sounded so . . . angry, at me. Almost like she blamed me."

"That's crazy. How could it be your fault?"

Isobel shook her head. "I think she was mad at me for something that happened a long time ago, something I forgot." She stared at the floor and sighed shakily. "My father. I thought he left while I was away in England. But he went with me to England. Why don't I remember that? And then he didn't come back. I knew all the time that there was something between my mother and my aunt about my father, but I thought it was over when he married my mother and took her to the States. It wasn't. He left my mother for her. And because, when he left her, he was with me, and because I came back without him, I think . . . she somehow blames me."

"That's crazy."

Isobel shook her head. "I understand it. Anyway, now I *have* to go. He's probably still there. He's sure to turn up at the funeral. My mother thinks it's the least I can do for her."

Fitz felt lost. He didn't know what he could say.

Then Isobel gripped his hand. "But I'm still scared! I

have to go, I can't keep running, but—Fitz, will you come with me?''

''To England?''

''Please.''

Fitz wanted to be cool about it, to look reliable and responsible, a man of the world who would protect Isobel from all dangers. But he couldn't stop grinning.

* * *

the black notebook

I thought at first it was too *neat*. It had to be planned, to get me over there, it had to be a trap, her ''death.'' But if I know it's a trap, doesn't that give me an advantage?

Anyway, I want to fight. I don't want to run away anymore. I want to find out what it is I'm afraid of, what it is I've forgotten. I want to find out what, besides her house, she has left me as my inheritance. And maybe I'll find my father.

* * *

Five days later, they were in England, driving southwest into a fairy-tale landscape of gentle green hills and valleys, thatched cottages, and picturesque villages. The sky was gray and heavy, the air misty, the weather more like March than June, but Fitz was enchanted. Isobel was silent and tense, anticipating something she would not talk about. The funeral was over—it had taken place before they arrived, so there was no cause for hurry. But Isobel was driven. She wouldn't agree to even one night in London first, but had insisted on renting a car and driving directly from Gatwick down to the county of Devon where her aunt's house—now *her* house—was. Fitz could only hope that when they arrived and found no danger Isobel would relax. Otherwise their vacation together wasn't going to be much fun.

It was nearly four when they arrived in Tavistock, an old-fashioned–looking gray-stone town of narrow, hilly streets, nestled on the edge of Dartmoor. The solicitor—Fitz loved the word and corrected Isobel when she referred to him as a lawyer—who was handling the estate had his office there. Fitz parked the rented car in the Victorian square and, as he got out, gazed around with a hungry curiosity. He'd still seen nothing of England except through the car windows, and he wanted to explore. The town was full of people, and except for a few youths with backpacks, they didn't look like tourists. He turned to Isobel and saw that she was shivering, holding herself and looking unhappy.

He put his arms around her. "Guess you should have brought your winter coat, huh? Where's your sweater?"

Unexpectedly, she clung to him. "Oh, Fitz, you won't leave me?"

"Sweetheart, of course I won't!"

"Whatever happens . . . no matter what I do, or how I change . . . you'll still love me? You'll stay with me?"

"Of course I will. I didn't come here to abandon you in England." He stroked her back, then slipped his hand beneath her shirt to feel her silken-smooth skin. His feeling of protectiveness changed to one of pure desire. He thought of how long it had been since they had made love—a longer stretch of abstinence than at any time since they had met. Six hours or more on the crowded plane, five hours driving, add a few hours in airports on both sides of the ocean, and altogether it added up to a very long day and night during which time they had been constantly together, but never alone. He kissed her urgently, and although she responded, he felt she was holding back, put on edge, perhaps, by being in public.

"Let's find a hotel," he said.

She pushed him away. "The lawyer—"

"The solicitor can wait."

"I don't want to put it off till tomorrow. Not after we've come so far. *We* can wait. It won't take long, just to sign some papers and get a key."

The experiences of the past week made him believe that if he persisted, he could make her change her mind. But was it worth it? Not if she was going to spend the rest of the night worrying about it. This was the reason they had come, after all.

"All right," he said. "Let's get it over with."

Fitz had hoped for ancient, Dickensian law chambers and was disappointed by the reality of airy white rooms that smelled of fresh paint on the ground floor of a gray house halfway up a hill of similar houses. Isobel had hinted at the idea of a conspiracy to get her to England, but Fitz could not believe that the solicitor—a young man in a three-piece suit who seemed bored by the whole business and had apparently had little contact with Isobel's aunt—could have been involved in anything of the kind. As he was showing them out, within twenty minutes of their arrival, Isobel finally asked, in a roundabout way, if he had any news of her father.

"It was my understanding that Miss Ward lived alone, and always had since the death of her mother," he said. "No one has contacted me in regard to you, Miss Mannering. My only instructions were those left in the will. But if you would like me to make inquiries . . ."

"No, no, I was only wondering . . . was there anyone, any stranger, at the funeral?"

"I didn't attend the funeral myself. The person to ask about that would be Mrs. Teggs, or her daughter, at Trescott Farm. They were your aunt's nearest neighbors and saw her every day. It was the daughter who found her body."

"I'll talk to them," Isobel said. "Thank you."

The solicitor had given them explicit directions to the house, with a map of the area. It seemed to be in an isolated spot, by itself on the moor, the nearest neighbor the farm more than half a mile away.

"What did your aunt do?" Fitz asked, as they walked back to the car.

"Besides practice witchcraft? I don't know. She might have had some inherited money; I think my mother's got some kind of trust fund. It's not much, but . . . if she lived frugally enough she might not have had to work."

"Do you really think she was a witch?"

"Yes. Oh—I don't know. There was something strange about her. If not witchcraft, some pagan religion, maybe. I'm sure she had powers . . . and I'm sure she believed in them."

They reached the car, and Fitz hesitated as he reached for the keys. "Are you sure you want to go straight there? We could stay the night here, rest, get over our jet lag—"

"Fitz, the whole reason I'm *here* is to go there. I can still—even though I know she's dead, I can almost feel her waiting for me, and until I see for myself, I can't think about anything else." She was shaking again, and this time he knew it wasn't from the cold. But when he tried to hold her she fended him off. "Don't! Don't distract me. Just drive."

So he did. They were both silent as Fitz concentrated on steering through the winding, narrow streets of the town, and then through country lanes less crowded but no less winding. At first, high green hedges on either side hid whatever view there might have been, but as the road climbed higher they emerged onto the moor and its inspiring, if bleak, open vistas. Fitz was impressed. Here England seemed a much larger, more ancient place. The bare, rocky landscape, the treeless spaces startlingly broken by the odd-shaped juttings of rock called tors, were very different from the misty green watercolor scenes they had driven through earlier. There was no coziness here. If this land belonged in a fairy tale, it was not a comforting one.

The directions to the house were easy to follow. After a time they turned off the main road onto a smaller one, which led down into a valley. They drove over a small stone bridge across a stream and saw the wooden sign to Trescott Farm pointing down an unpaved track.

The sign reminded Fitz of something the solicitor had said, and he asked, "How did your aunt die?"

"She killed herself."

"Why didn't you tell me that before?"

"Didn't I? I thought I did. I guess because you didn't ask."

He had been thinking of Isobel's aunt as an old woman, like his father's sister. He had imagined disease and a hospital bed, and knowing the details had not seemed necessary. Suicide made it a very different story. For the first time Fitz wondered if Isobel might actually be in some danger.

"There it is," Isobel said suddenly, sharply. "There's the house!"

The witch's house. A small, white-washed thatched cottage with windows like blank eyes. Fitz had already noticed the importance the English gave to gardens, and it seemed odd that this little house had none, not even a few flowers, a vine or a window box to brighten it up. The inhabitant had been dead little more than a week, but the house looked as if it had been deserted for years. Behind the house the land rose sharply, a bare, high hill. Beside the house, to the left, was a small wood of twisted, stunted trees. Between the wood and the house there was a sort of driveway, a roughly pebbled area, and Fitz pulled off the track onto this. As he did, he thought he caught a glimpse of someone running away through the trees, but when he turned to look, with the branches and the shifting light it was impossible to be sure.

Trying to shrug off his uneasiness, Fitz asked Isobel, "Recognize it?"

"Yes," she said, staring at the house. "That's it ex-

actly. I recognize it, like a face, but I can't place it. I still
don't remember it—but I *know* it. Let's go in. Don't lose
me, all right?''

He squeezed her hand.

The black-painted door stuck slightly; Fitz had to give it
a sharp tug to open it. Inside, the air was chilly and
smelled of damp.

Isobel made a small sound. ''It smells the same,'' she
said. She held tightly to his hand.

The room they were in was low-ceilinged but light, with
white walls and a pale carpet. The furniture, stripped pine
and flower-printed fabrics, looked fairly new and somehow contradicted the uncared-for aspect of the exterior.
Someone had chosen each piece to match her taste.

''This way,'' said Isobel, opening the door to the right.
''Her bedroom.''

The furniture was older in this room, probably inherited.
A high, narrow bed, a wardrobe, chest of drawers, dressing table and rocking chair all in a dark, reddish wood.
But there was a boldly striped bedspread, yellow and gray,
which matched the curtains and the Indian rug on the
floor. Fitz looked at Isobel, who was staring blankly into
the age-spotted mirror on the dressing table. He looked
around at the white walls where a few small pictures hung.
They had elaborate, heavy frames and were so dark that he
couldn't make out their subject matter. He moved closer to
the nearest and discovered a small portrait of a young
woman. He thought it must be a very old picture, although
he couldn't identify the period. The subject had a high
forehead revealed by an elaborate peaked hat that covered
her hair, and she wore a high-necked dress studded with
pearls. Her face was pretty, but also disturbing. Her slanting gray eyes reminded him of Isobel, but her tiny mouth
was pursed in an unpleasant way: she might be about to
smile, or to bite, he thought. There was something in her
lap, just visible at the bottom of the canvas. He leaned
closer, and saw that it was some sort of ugly animal.

Probably it was meant to be a dog, although he'd never seen a dog with such a boneless-looking body.

"Hey, Iso—"

Turning, he saw that she was still staring into the mirror. She had gone very pale, and her eyes were wide and unseeing. "Isobel," he said sharply, and gave her hand a tug.

She fell into his arms with a gasp and a shudder, and clung to him.

"She's not dead, Fitz! I can feel it!"

"She *is* dead," Fitz said. He rubbed her back. "There was a funeral. She was buried."

"Oh, her *body*—"

"You talking about her ghost? You think this house is haunted?" He meant to be rational, and he'd never had any experience he would have classed as supernatural, but Fitz had the feeling now that Isobel could, all too easily, convince him of any crazy thing about this house and her undead dead aunt.

"I'm haunted," she muttered against his neck. Then she straightened up and pulled away. "I don't know what I think. Come on, let's go upstairs. Upstairs was my room."

She opened a door—Fitz had thought it was a closet—and revealed a staircase. The unpainted wooden steps were difficult to climb, being both steep and curving, but they did not go very far. They ended in a tiny hall with three doors, one leading to a bathroom. Isobel opened one of the other doors to a bedroom furnished with twin beds, dresser, writing table and chair, and book case. The colors were bright and cheerful.

"She didn't change anything," Isobel said in a wondering tone. "Nine years, and it's just the same. Even the books she bought for me. Almost as if she was expecting me to come back . . . the twelve-year-old me. How lonely she must have been."

"What's in the other room?"

"Nothing." She seemed absorbed in the titles of the books on the bookshelves.

"Nothing at all?"

"It's empty."

Fitz went to see for himself. Heavy brown curtains at the windows, but nothing else, not even a light shade, or a rug to cover the plain, worn floorboards.

The empty room disturbed him. He closed the door on it and returned to Isobel. "Why?"

She shrugged. Straightening up, she dusted her hands. "I guess she didn't need it. She was living by herself. I guess the rooms downstairs were enough. You can see she didn't use this room."

"You'd think she could have used it for something, if only for storage. I mean, I live alone, basically in one room, but if I had more rooms I could fill them up."

She smiled affectionately; he guessed she was remembering his apartment. "Not everybody collects as much paper as you do, Fitz."

He grinned back at her. "Their loss," he said. He put his arms around her. "Feeling better?"

"I was happy in this room, I can remember that much."

He kissed her. She broke it off before he could make more of it. "Let's bring our stuff in from the car before it gets dark."

"It won't be dark for hours."

"I know. Let's do it now, and then find out how to get this place warm."

"I'd rather find out how to get *you* warm."

She blushed. "You already know how. Come on. First things first."

"My feelings exactly." He sighed elaborately and let her go.

After he had carried their luggage upstairs, Fitz joined Isobel in the kitchen. This large room at the back of the house seemed by far the oldest, and the least touched by individual personality or the passage of time. And it was warm. The old-fashioned, fuel-burning stove was giving off a steady heat.

Isobel said, "Mrs. Teggs lit the fire earlier today, and she left us eggs and milk, bread and butter and cheese. I saw the note on the table with the loaf of bread when I came in. Wasn't that *nice*? Aren't people *nice*?"

Fitz nodded dubiously. He couldn't imagine being pleased if one of his neighbors in New York turned the heating on and left him a bag of groceries. He'd wonder what they wanted in return. "So she's got a key?"

"I guess so. Well, they're the only neighbors, after all; it makes sense. If she ever needed anything, or had to go away, or— "

"Or killed herself."

"That wasn't here," Isobel said quickly.

"Where was it?"

She looked confused. "I don't know—nobody said anything, nobody told me, but—I'm sure she didn't kill herself in this house." She turned away, busying herself with looking in cupboards. "I don't know about you, but I'm hungry. I could make us omelets."

Fitz sat down at the big, scarred wooden table, resting his face in his hands, feeling how tired he was. He wasn't aware of being hungry, but food might perk him up, he thought. He wished they were in a London hotel, sitting in a nice restaurant, holding hands and waiting to be served. He didn't want to be in this house, but he didn't know how to say so. Now that they were here, it seemed such an effort to go away again. He realized that he had been expecting Isobel to insist on leaving, to feel uncomfortable in the house where her aunt had lived and died. He had expected to present the rational argument for at least spending the night, and then he would have allowed himself to be swayed, to give in to her wishes and take her away somewhere, anywhere. He didn't want to admit that he was afraid. He didn't have any reason for being afraid.

It was still light outside when they had finished eating

and went up to bed. Fitz had no idea what time it was. His watch had stopped, and there didn't seem to be any clocks in the house.

They pushed the twin beds together, but decided it was too much trouble to remake them. Although they felt cold and slightly damp, at least the sheets smelled clean. Fitz thought he might be too tired to do anything but fall asleep, but when Isobel slipped naked beneath the sheets and pressed against him, Fitz responded immediately. They made love as if asleep, slowly, langorously, without words, eyes half closed, and fell asleep, deeply contented, still joined.

Hours later he woke in darkness, to a woman's naked body pressed demandingly against his, and a hand stroking his cock. He reached for her, and she caught his hand and pulled it down, between her legs. She was very wet, and very certain of what she wanted, instructing him just how, and when, and where to touch her by the pressure of her own fingers. This assertiveness was new, and Fitz found it exciting. He was still more than half asleep and thought it possible that either he, or Isobel, or both of them were dreaming. But it made no difference. He simply relaxed and let her take control. She had far more energy than he did, changing position, gliding over him, rubbing against him while he lay passively and let her move him as she wished. Eventually she mounted him, and rode him to some private, demanding rhythm of her own. As he ran his hands over her, fondling her breasts, and feeling the flexing muscles in her stomach and thighs, his only regret was that he could not see her. But the sound that she made when she came was vivid enough to bring back a week's worth of erotic memories, and triggered his own orgasm.

She collapsed onto him, but only for a moment; then she raised herself off of him and got out of bed. Fitz made a small sound of protest, but was too drained to do anything else. It would have been nice to have her snuggle close to him, but already he was falling back to sleep.

Then a scream jolted him awake.

"Isobel!"

Silence. Heart pounding, Fitz got up into darkness, feeling, through his fear, as stiff and uncoordinated as if he had been given a stranger's body. "Isobel?"

He made his way to the door and then he saw her, standing naked and streaked with blood in the bathroom.

A huge mirror hung on the wall above the bathtub, and Isobel was staring at her reflection as if hypnotized. Her hands were crimson; her thighs, stomach and breasts all daubed with blood; there were even streaks of it on her face.

Shocked and queasy, Fitz caught his hand in his mouth, and realized that it, too, was dark with dried blood. He looked down, saw the blood on his own thighs, matting his pubic hair, staining his penis, and he breathed more easily as he understood.

"It's only your period," he said, and touched her shoulder.

She cried out, and flinched away, still staring at herself. "The blood," she said.

"It doesn't matter—we can clean it off. You're *not* hurt, are you? It *is* only—"

"It's happened before," she said hopelessly. "It will happen again. It always happens."

"What happens, sweetheart?" He put his arms around her from behind and held her tightly, and stared up at the mirror over her shoulder.

"I looked in the mirror and I didn't see me. I saw *her*. All covered with blood. With my father. And I *remembered*." She shut her eyes. Fitz felt the shudder go through her.

"What?" he asked.

"I look just like her," she whispered. "All in blood." She shuddered, and rubbed hard at her face, as if trying to rub the blood off.

"It's all right," he said. "It's only your period. I'll

clean you off." He let go of her, took a hand towel and wet it at the sink, and began, very gently, to clean her face.

"She might be my mother, you know," Isobel said. "That might be why I look so much like her. That might be why I see her face in the mirror. If she was my real mother."

When he had finished washing her face and breasts, Fitz knelt on the cold floor and cleaned the blood from her stomach, her thighs, her legs. So much blood. Even knowing what it was, knowing it was normal and not alarming, he felt sickened by it. How did women stand it, month after month without control? He wished he could take a shower, but his choice was either a bath or a wash at the sink. He began to run water in the sink.

Isobel was still standing and staring in the mirror. There was a fresh trickle of blood running down her leg.

"Isobel, for heaven's sake—" He grasped her by the arms and made her look at him. "Would you put a Tampax in and go to bed, please?"

She stared as if she'd never seen him before. "What did I say?" she asked.

"Huh?"

"What did I say, while I was looking in the mirror? I've forgotten again. What did I remember?"

She seemed wide-awake now, but desperate.

Fitz sighed. "You didn't say a whole lot. Something about blood. And you said you'd seen your aunt with your father. And that you looked just like your aunt, covered in blood. And that maybe your aunt was your real mother and that was why you looked like her."

"What about my aunt and my father? What else did I say?"

"Nothing. Just that you'd seen them. Don't you remember?"

"No. I've forgotten again."

* * *

the black notebook

I could just go away. Fitz would be happy to take me. I would be safe, then. I know that. Nobody but me made me come here. I don't have to stay. But if I go away, I'll never remember what happened. I'll never know—and knowing is somehow very important. Maybe it's dangerous, but if you don't take risks you might as well be dead. I'm not going to run away.

It's like sex. I used to be so afraid of it. I was running for years and I didn't realize it. I used to think there was a sort of curse on me, a mark like the ring but which others could see, which my aunt had put on me to keep me a virgin. I was afraid of what might happen—I didn't *know* what might happen—so I kept myself away from any chance of it . . . until I was more afraid of something else.

Sex is a power, like knowledge. And it can destroy people—but I don't have to let it destroy me. And I don't have to let this other power, what my aunt knew, destroy me—even if, in the end, it destroyed her. I'm going to learn how to use it.

* * *

Fitz was eager to get away the next morning, to drive down to Cornwall, or to Wales, or London, to see castles or villages or Stonehenge—whatever Isobel wanted, anything to get their vacation off to a good start.

But Isobel would not leave.

"You go by yourself," she said. "Go somewhere and come back tonight—then you won't have to pay for a hotel."

"I know I said I was broke, but I'm not *that* broke," he said. "Anyway, I don't want to go by myself. We can come back here tonight if you want, but you're coming with me. I didn't come on this vacation by myself."

"I'm not ready to leave. I need to do some thinking.

I've come all this way; I can't turn my back on it now. I want to remember what happened to me when I was a kid. I want to remember my aunt. I have to stay here."

She was no longer the terrified girl who had clung to him in Tavistock and begged him not to leave her. In a pale pink sweater, tight black jeans and running shoes she was cool, self-contained, remote, and more desirable than ever. Fitz reached for her, but she pushed his hands away.

"Don't," she said angrily. "Don't try to seduce me."

"And I thought you liked it."

"Not when you're trying to use sex to change my mind."

"Not at all. But if we're going to stay here all day we might as well have a good time. I'd rather make love with you than see all the sights of England, anyway."

"I told you, I need to think. I'm staying here for a reason. That's no reason for *you* to stay, too. You'd just be bored. There's nothing here for you."

"There's you." He wanted to touch her again—he *knew* he could melt her, given the chance—but at the look she gave him he did not dare. "Do you remember asking me not to leave you?"

She closed her eyes. "Yes." Then she opened them. "I'm not asking you to leave me now. But that doesn't mean you have to be with me every minute, does it? I don't need a bodyguard."

"Are you sure?"

"Yes."

He thought of how she had been, standing in the bathroom and staring, terrified, at herself in the mirror. "Let me stay," he said. "Just in case you do need me. Don't worry about me being bored."

Isobel shrugged, irritated but resigned. "All right. I was going to walk down to Trescott Farm and thank Mrs. Teggs. And I thought her daughter might be able to tell me something. Do you want to come?"

"Sure. It's a nice day for a walk."

Although it was cool, the sun was out, promising later warmth, and the air tasted fresh and green. On the road, Isobel took his hand, and Fitz felt his spirits lift. He gazed up at the moor and thought that even staying close to the house there would probably be plenty to see. He'd lived in cities all his life, and this was such a change from anything he'd ever known. It was so quiet: he could hear nothing but the sound of the wind, and the occasional harsh cry of a rook. He wondered again what Isobel's aunt had done all by herself out here. It seemed she hadn't even owned a car, and the nearest village was three miles away. Had she walked down this narrow road every day, as they were doing now?

They reached the farm, entering the yard through a broken-down wooden gate. The farmhouse didn't wear the aura of eternity that the cottage had: it was just an ordinary house, painted green, with a slate roof. There was a girl in a dirty yellow sweater and a flowered skirt sitting on the front steps as if waiting for them.

At the sight of her, the hairs rose on the back of Fitz's neck and he felt a total, inexplicable antipathy toward her. He sometimes reacted negatively to people he didn't know, but seldom so strongly. He felt threatened and defensive, like a dog in someone else's territory. He put his arm protectively around Isobel, but she shrugged him off, and walked toward the girl, smiling.

"Are you Donna? You don't remember me, of course . . . You were probably only four or five when I was here last."

The girl nodded, standing up. She had a flat, freckled face and a blank expression. "You're Isobel." She turned to yell up at the house, "Mum! She's here!" Then, to Isobel: "We thought you'd be here today. I stayed home from school on purpose. Mum says, Will you come in for a cup of tea?"

"Yes, thank you. This is my friend Fitz."

Donna gave no sign of having noticed. "Come in," she

said, and went up the steps to open the door. Isobel started after, but Fitz caught her arm.

"I don't like this," he said, low-voiced. "I don't want to go in there."

"Then don't," she said coldly, pulling away. He had to follow her inside.

There was the sound of frying and the smell of hot grease. Mrs. Teggs was a plump, plain woman who embraced Isobel and exclaimed over her. Introduced to Fitz she smiled shyly and nodded at him, not quite meeting his eye. More than anything, Fitz was uneasily aware of Donna's presence. There was nothing obviously threatening about her—she was just a rather slatternly-looking teenager leaning against a wall and chewing a fingernail—but Fitz would not have turned his back on her.

Mrs. Teggs offered them "a good cooked breakfast," which to Fitz's dismay, Isobel accepted with alacrity. He refused everything but tea and watched in disbelief as Isobel tucked into fried eggs, sausage, bacon and fried bread—all of it dripping with grease—with undisguised appetite. He didn't even like his tea, which was served to him in a cup with a film of grease on the rim and half-full of milk.

While they ate, Isobel asked a few questions and Mrs. Teggs responded with a flood of reminiscences about her friend Agnes, Isobel's aunt. To Fitz it sounded like a collection of platitudes and told him nothing about the actual woman. What had she done? Who had she been? And why had she killed herself? He didn't interrupt, though. He pretended to drink his cold, milky tea, and divided his attention between Donna and Isobel, watching one with suspicion, the other with baffled love.

When she had finished eating, Isobel said, "May I use your bathroom, please?"

"Of course, love," said Mrs. Teggs. "Donna will show you where it is. More tea, Mr. Fitzgerald?"

Feeling helpless, Fitz watched them go. He shook his

head at the proffered teapot and then, although he trusted this woman little more than her daughter, asked, "Do you know why she killed herself?"

Mrs. Teggs looked at the tablecloth as she replied. "She had cancer. It wasn't the pain—she was a brave woman—but it was her independence. She was that independent, she wouldn't want to live if she couldn't look after herself. She would have died in the end. She chose to go a few months sooner, and be no trouble to anyone."

"But—couldn't she have hung on for a few more weeks? She killed herself at the time she was expecting her niece to come visit her. Don't you think that's strange?"

"I don't know, Mr. Fitzgerald. I wouldn't presume to judge."

Isobel and Donna came back into the room. Fitz stood up, to forestall the possibility that they might stay any longer. But Isobel seemed ready to leave. She bent and kissed Mrs. Teggs on the cheek. "Thank you for everything. It was really nice to hear you talk about my aunt—I know you must have been a wonderful friend to her."

"And I hope I may be to you as well, my dear. You must let me know if there's anything I can do for you, anything at all."

"Thank you."

"Thank you for the tea," Fitz said. Outside, he said nothing to Isobel until they had left the farmyard and were out of sight of the farmhouse. Only then did he feel free of Donna's baleful gaze. "What did that girl say to you?"

She stopped walking. "What is *wrong* with you today?"

"Wrong with me?"

"You sit there glaring at poor Donna, and acting like you think Mrs. Teggs is going to poison you, and now you interrogate me!"

"I wasn't—"

"Maybe they're not the most fascinating, sophisticated

people—unlike your friends in New York—but they're my neighbors, and I need to be on good terms with them.''

"Your neighbors—you sound like you're planning to stay.''

"Maybe I will. It *is* my house.'' Then she shrugged. "And maybe I won't. That's not the point. The point is, you're acting like a jealous dog, growling when anybody so much as looks at me. And I don't like it.''

This was so true he couldn't even defend himself. They walked the rest of the way back in silence and Fitz struggled to understand his own feelings.

Partly as a peace offering to her, partly to prove to himself that he could, Fitz ignored his instincts and his desires and told Isobel that he was going out for a drive, just to get a feel for the country and to see what there was to see. He'd be back before dark, and he would bring something for dinner. He was still hoping, even as he started the car, that she would change her mind and rush out after him, but the empty windows of the house seemed to be the only eyes that watched him go.

His hands were sweating, and he had to keep clearing his throat. Fitz told himself it was driving on the wrong side of the road that made him uneasy, but the images that came unwanted to his mind all involved Isobel. Isobel clinging to him and begging him not to leave her. Isobel covered with blood and screaming. Isobel under attack from something he couldn't see—

He couldn't see the road; his vision swam with tiny pinpoints of light, and his heart was in his throat. Fitz stopped the car. There was nowhere to pull over, but neither was there any traffic. He hadn't even reached the main road yet. He put his head against the steering wheel and trembled, and tried to will his heart and breathing back to normal.

"Oh, God,'' he said. "Oh, Isobel.''

As soon as he gave in and decided to turn back he felt calmer.

* * *

the black notebook

The cave is where it began and the cave is where it ended.

As soon as Donna told me she had found Aunt Agnes' body in a cave, I knew. And then I forgot again. But something happened to me in that cave when I was twelve. The answer is there.

It's up on the moor, behind the house. I don't know if I could find it by myself, but Donna will take me there.

The problem is Fitz, who won't let me out of his sight. He prowls around like some weird kind of watchdog. As long as he is here, I can't find out what I want to know. He keeps me tied down to his reality so I can't find my own.

Sometimes I'm grateful for him. As long as he is here to save me, nothing *too* bad can happen—but nothing too good, either.

I think that because my aunt died, I'm safe, at least for a while. I'm no longer needed as a sacrifice. I can take her place.

I have to get to the cave. I have to know. I have to find the dragon.

If only Fitz would go away, just for a little while . . .

* * *

Fitz put the notebook down. He was shaking. He looked at his watch, although it was still not going, wondering how long he had been out, how much a head start she had on him. He didn't waste any more time. He went out and began to climb the sloping hill at the back of the house, up toward the moor. He didn't know how he was going to find the cave, but there was no need to worry. He had not gone far before he saw Donna, her yellow sweater like a marking flag.

He was trembling again, or perhaps he had never stopped shaking. It was anger, not fear, and it was directed at Donna.

"Where is she?" he shouted. "Where did she go? What have you done?"

The girl gaped at him, her face flat and stupid. When he reached her, Fitz grabbed her by the arm. "Where is Isobel?"

Instead of answering, she let herself fall against him. He was very aware of her small, soft breasts, and the warmth and pressure of her thighs beneath the thin skirt. The fact that she had given him an erection made him even angrier, and he held her by the arms with bruising force, holding her away from him as he shouted. "Don't pretend you don't understand! I know all about it! Tell me where she is! Show me the cave!"

She nodded, and made an effort to take his hand, her fingers pulling weakly at his. Because he still had hold of her other arm, Fitz allowed her to loosen his grasp. He let her take hold of his hand, expecting that she would lead him to Isobel. He was shocked when she suddenly thrust herself at him again, tugging his hand to her crotch.

He pushed her off, so violently that she fell down. Her skirt rode up. She was naked underneath. She had sparse, reddish pubic hair. She made no move to cover herself, or to rise. Instead, she opened her legs, showing him more.

Fitz was violently, horribly aroused. He wanted to throw himself on top of her. He wanted to rape her. Would it be rape, when she would welcome it?

With an effort, he turned his head, forcing himself to look away. "Get up," he said. His voice sounded strange to him, not like his own. "For God's sake, get up."

He felt her hand on his ankle, and held himself still, knowing that if he kicked out as he wanted to do, she would fall, and this time he might not be able to stop himself from falling on top of her. He made himself stand like a rock as she pulled herself up. He said, his voice very controlled, "Donna, you must show me where Isobel is. It could be dangerous. You don't want Isobel to be hurt, do you? You must help me."

She was rubbing herself against him like an animal. She had found his erection, and swiftly, skillfully, undid his pants to set it free. He didn't stop her. He couldn't. Now her mouth was on him, and he was in an agony of pleasure. He grabbed her hair, but only to pull it back from her face, the better to see what she was doing to him. He didn't know how much longer his legs would hold him up. He thought of how she had sprawled on the ground, opening her legs to his gaze, showing him everything, and he wanted to see her like that again.

"Take your clothes off," he said.

As she moved away from him he saw her face, blank and round as the moon, and he hated her. He wanted to hurt her. As she took her sweater off, arms crossed in front of her breasts, temporarily helpless, he attacked. Shoving her on to the ground, Fitz pushed her skirt up, brutally parted her legs, and thrust into her.

She let out a thin, high scream, like a rabbit caught in a trap. He was fiercely glad he had hurt her, but her pain triggered his pleasure. He managed only a few short, savage strokes inside her and then he was coming, helpless to stop or prolong the final moment.

He pulled out as soon as he was finished. Her clammy flesh sickened him. He wanted to be away. There was blood on her thighs, blood on his cock, he saw, as he cleaned himself with his handkerchief. He threw the soiled cloth on top of her. He didn't wait to see what she would do. He wanted to forget what had happened, and he knew he never would.

He had to find Isobel. If anything happened to her, if he was too late, he would never forgive Donna—or himself. He was to blame, after all. What sort of hero was he, to rape a virgin when he should be saving his own princess from the dragon?

"Isobel!" he called, his voice high and desperate. "Isobel!" He expected no reply. He began to run. He had no idea where he was going. He could only hope that because Donna had been here, the cave was nearby.

Then he saw it: a rocky outcrop, the dark entrance to a cave. He stopped just outside, a sudden dread keeping him from entering. "Isobel? Are you in there? Please tell me you're all right!"

He had no light, not even a box of matches, and he couldn't guess if this might be the entrance to a cavern, or a tunnel deep into the earth. But he had no choice. He had to go in after her; he had to find her. There had never been any other option. Fitz breathed deeply, trying to calm himself, and then dropped to his hands and knees. He had never had any particular fear of the dark, nor of small spaces, but now, together, they terrified him.

"Isobel," he said, "I'm coming in," and pushed himself, headfirst, through the narrow entrance. His shoulders cleared the sides easily. Dry leaves crunched to ash beneath his hands and knees. Inside, although he moved at once to the side, not to block any light from the entrance, the darkness was profound. He closed his eyes in despair, and saw no difference when he opened them again.

"Isobel." He spoke quietly, but the air seemed to vibrate around the name. He could feel it on his skin. For the first time he had some sense of the space he was in, and he thought, with a glimmer of hope, that it was not so very large, probably no bigger than one of the rooms in Isobel's house.

He was about to speak again—the sound of his own voice was somehow encouraging—when he heard something else.

Something moved. And he knew he wasn't alone in the cave.

But whatever moved was certainly not Isobel. It wasn't human. It was the sound of something moving without legs, something coiling and uncoiling, something writhing on the ground. In the inky blackness he could almost see it: a gigantic snake or worm stirring in its corner, roused to wakefulness by his voice.

But Isobel, too, must be here, and she was in greater danger than he was. He had come here to save her, and he would, even if he had no sword or any sort of weapon. Almost sick with fear, Fitz forced himself to move, to take one crouching step forward, his hand outstretched. And so he found Isobel.

Touching her, he realized she was lying on her back. She made no response when he ran his hands over her body. He was shocked to find she was naked, but as far as his hands could discover she was uninjured, and her heart was beating, and she was breathing steadily. He kissed her, and felt a pulse in her neck. Was she sleeping, unconscious, or pretending?

Fitz was afraid to speak again, afraid to make too much noise or do anything that might disturb the creature he had heard. He had to get Isobel out. When she did not respond to his shaking, he took hold of her shoulders and dragged her as best he could to the exit, wincing at the thought of unseen rocks on her tender flesh. He climbed out first, and then pulled her through, his heart beating madly with the terror that something from the other side would pull her back.

He could see no injuries in the daylight, no obvious bumps or bruises on her head that might have made her unconscious. He wondered where her clothes were, but if they were in the cave he wasn't going back for them. Donna had apparently vanished, to his relief.

The sweat was drying on him, making him shiver, and he knew he had to get Isobel inside and warm. Staggering under her weight, he carried her down to the house.

The first thing was to call a doctor—but there was no telephone in the house.

He remembered now that he had commented on that to Isobel: another oddity about her aunt's reclusive life. There might be a phone at Trescott Farm, but he wasn't ever going back there if he could help it. No, he had best get Isobel out of here. He'd take her to Tavistock, or to Plymouth—anywhere with a lot of people and a hospital.

Dressing her was more difficult than he had expected. He settled on a gray track suit and didn't bother about underwear or shoes. He bundled the rest of her clothes and his into their suitcases, and after he had settled Isobel in the car, he put their luggage in the trunk and got behind the wheel.

Then the car wouldn't start.

It was completely dead. The ignition made a clicking sound. The engine did nothing. Fitz got out and had what he knew would be a useless look under the hood. He was completely ignorant about cars. He'd been driving since high school, but he'd never owned a car. He closed the hood and got behind the wheel again. Turned the key. Click. Again. Click. He did everything he could think of, and then he rested his head against the steering wheel and tried not to cry.

He carried Isobel back into the house and put her to bed in her aunt's old room: he couldn't face trying to negotiate those winding stairs with her in his arms. Then he began a methodical search of the house. He found no first-aid books or medical texts of any kind, no liquor, no drugs of any kind unless some unlabeled jars of herbs in the kitchen might qualify. He wished he had asked *how* Isobel's aunt had killed herself. He wondered if Isobel had swallowed sleeping pills. He couldn't find any bump or bruise to indicate that she might have struck her head. If she had taken pills the empty bottle might be up in the cave—on the other hand, Donna might have taken it away.

Standing at the foot of the bed he stared at Isobel and tried to will her eyes open. She looked so peaceful, as if only sleeping. Her breathing seemed regular, and her skin felt warm enough. Maybe she *would* wake up in a few hours; maybe she *would* be all right.

But how could he risk it? How could he stay here beside her, doing nothing, when she might, for all he knew, be dying?

He couldn't.

Yet he could not leave her.

Again and again Fitz went to the front door, opened it, stepped outside. Once he was halfway to Trescott Farm before his nerve broke and he ran all the way back. More than once he got to the road, where he moved indecisively back and forth, hating himself for being unable to act. He sat on the living room floor and looked at a map and figured he could reach the nearest village in less than an hour, walking and running, if only he could make up his mind.

He heated some milk, added a lot of sugar to it, and tried to get Isobel to drink it. He didn't force it, fearful of choking her, but he propped her up in bed, soaked a cloth in the warm, sweet drink, and brushed her lips and tongue with it.

He talked to her. He chafed her hands between his own, rubbed her feet, and piled on more blankets to keep her warm. He stared out the front window and prayed for a passing car, even for Mrs. Teggs.

Nothing happened. Isobel didn't wake up, but she did not, so far as he could tell, get worse. When it grew dark, Fitz made himself a pallet on the floor beside her bed, and lay down to rest, listening to the even, steady music of her breathing. He didn't expect to sleep, but he did.

This time when he went to the cave, he took a light, and a sword to kill the dragon. The first thing he saw in the cave was a four-poster bed. Isobel was lying on it, naked. Her eyes were closed, but he didn't think she slept. She was on her back. Her legs were spread wide, and her arms thrown above her head. Her face was flushed and on it that look of abandonment, of sheer, greedy sexual pleasure that he had often seen. She was moving her hips as if in sexual intercourse, but she was alone. Fitz shone the light caressingly along her body and caught a glistening motion in her pubic hair. He leaned closer, steadying the beam, and froze in horror. He saw a snake moving in and out of her vagina.

If he tried to kill it with his sword he would be more likely to hurt *her*. Yet to leave the snake unharmed was unthinkable. Even if it were not poisonous, even if she were in no immediate danger, the sight of it horrified and disgusted him. He couldn't allow it to continue, no matter what danger he put himself in. He dropped his sword, therefore, and reached out, bare-handed. He grabbed the snake as it emerged, and he pulled it from her body. But as he did so, he heard Isobel cry out in anguish, and the snake sank its teeth into his hand.

Fitz woke. The throbbing in his hand faded and vanished: only a dream pain. He was disoriented for a moment. Knowing that he was not in the cave of his dream, he didn't know where he really was. Then he remembered, and sat up, listening for Isobel's breathing.

"Isobel?"

He held his breath, and he heard something moving.

It was a boneless, legless sound: the sound of some large creature moving after the fashion of a worm or a snake. He had heard that sound before, in the cave; whatever monster had been in the cave was now in the room with them.

Fitz tried to remember where the nearest light was, and the door, but he couldn't even tell from what corner of the small dark room the sound had come.

He got up slowly, trying to be quiet, and climbed onto the bed. He bent his head until his lips encountered Isobel's head on the pillow. He felt her smooth hair, her cheek, and then felt her eyelash flutter against his face. Awake!

"Iso—"

Her mouth met his, her tongue flickered against his lips, and he almost forgot his fear as they kissed. Perhaps it had been a dream; perhaps it was *all* a dream.

She raised her arms to embrace him, and the covers slipped down. She was naked. He felt her bare arms and breasts, and it seemed to him that she was glowing with heat. He stroked her face and kissed her more passionately.

Outside, a cloud drifted away, and the silvery light of the full moon shone through the window. Isobel's face was mysterious and beautiful in that light, and the gleam in her eyes excited him. He remembered how she had looked in his dream, and it seemed to him that her face wore the same smile now.

"Let me in," he said, giving a tug to the blanket. She smiled, and slipped to the side, away from him, and drew back the covers to welcome him in.

He gathered her into his arms, and reached out with his legs to catch hers, wanting to embrace her with his whole body.

But where her legs should have been was the smooth, scaly body of a gigantic snake, two feet across, at least, and unmistakable. The monster was in bed with them.

Fitz shouted. The thing coiled itself about his legs, trapping him. He struggled to break away, but it was too powerful. And still Isobel held him in her arms as if nothing else were happening, and she smiled.

She smiled.

"Isobel," he said. He could barely speak. Helplessly, he wet himself. There were tears in his eyes. It was Isobel who was wrapped about him, holding his legs in what could become a crushing trap; he knew that, and yet he didn't believe it. "Please—let me go."

"Don't you want to make love to me?" she asked.

He did want to, and it horrified him that he could desire her and fear her at the same time. "Let me go."

"No, Fitz, I'm never going to let you go." Her lower half gave him a squeeze that made him scream; he was certain he felt a bone break.

The instinct for survival won over the love her face still

inspired in him. His hands were free, and he grabbed her throat and began to strangle her.

The smile on her face did not change, but her neck did. The soft, warm skin became cool and slickly scaled, and it expanded in his grasp. As her neck lengthened, becoming her body, her face was still recognizably her own. He felt her breasts flattening against his chest and her arms shrinking away to nothing, and the moonlight showed him what he did not want to see. Her eyes went on watching him with undiminished intelligence as she squeezed him harder and harder. Her smile widened and her lips vanished. He didn't know if he heard his own bones cracking, or if it was the sound her jaws made as her mouth opened before his face. Her mouth was bigger than his face, bigger than his head, and he felt the searing heat of her breath as he screamed for the last time into her mouth, down her endless throat, as it closed over his head.

*   *   *

the black notebook

There wasn't much of him left, but I buried his bones at the back of the cave, beside the bones of my father.

CLIVE
BARKER

for Mary

I long to talk with some old lover's ghost
Who died before the god of Love was born.
                    John Donne, *Love's Deitie*

The Hellbound Heart

ONE

So intent was Frank upon solving the puzzle of Lemarchand's box that he didn't hear the great bell begin to ring. The device had been constructed by a master craftsman, and the riddle was this—that though he'd been told the box contained wonders, there simply seemed to be no way into it, no clue on any of its six black lacquered faces as to the whereabouts of the pressure points that would disengage one piece of this three-dimensional jigsaw from another.

Frank had seen similar puzzles—mostly in Hong Kong, products of the Chinese taste for making metaphysics of hard wood—but to the acuity and technical genius of the Chinese the Frenchman had brought a perverse logic that was entirely his own. If there was a system to the puzzle, Frank had failed to find it. Only after several hours of trial and error did a chance juxtaposition of thumbs, middle and last fingers bear fruit: an almost imperceptible click, and then—victory!—a segment of the box slid out from beside its neighbours.

There were two revelations.

The first, that the interior surfaces were brilliantly polished. Frank's reflection—distorted, fragmented—skated across the lacquer. The second, that Lemarchand, who had been in his time a maker of singing birds, had constructed the box so that opening it tripped a musical mechanism, which began to tinkle a short rondo of sublime banality.

Encouraged by his success, Frank proceeded to work on the box feverishly, quickly finding fresh alignments of fluted slot and oiled peg which in their turn revealed further intricacies. And with each solution—each new half twist or pull—a further melodic element was brought into play—the tune counterpointed and developed until the initial caprice was all but lost in ornamentation.

At some point in his labors, the bell had begun to ring—a steady somber tolling. He had not heard, at least not consciously. But when the puzzle was almost finished—the mirrored innards of the box unknotted—he became aware that his stomach churned so violently at the sound of the bell it might have been ringing half a lifetime.

He looked up from his work. For a few moments he supposed the noise to be coming from somewhere in the street outside—but he rapidly dismissed that notion. It had been almost midnight before he'd begun to work at the birdmaker's box; several hours had gone by—hours he would not have remembered passing but for the evidence of his watch—since then. There was no church in the city—however desperate for adherents—that would ring a summoning bell at such an hour.

No. The sound was coming from somewhere much more distant, through the very door (as yet invisible) that Lemarchand's miraculous box had been constructed to open. Everything that Kircher, who had sold him the box, had promised of it was true! He was on the threshold of a new world, a province infinitely far from the room in which he sat.

Infinitely far; yet now, suddenly near.

The thought had made his breath quick. He had anticipated this moment so keenly, planned with every wit he possessed this rending of the veil. In moments they would be here—the ones Kircher had called the Cenobites, theologians of the Order of the Gash. Summoned from their experiments in the higher reaches of pleasure, to bring their ageless heads into a world of rain and failure.

He had worked ceaselessly in the preceding week to prepare the room for them. The bare boards had been meticulously scrubbed and strewn with petals. Upon the west wall he had set up a kind of altar to them, decorated with the kind of placatory offerings Kircher had assured him would nurture their good offices: bones, bonbons, needles. A jug of his urine—the product of seven days' collection—stood on the left of the altar, should they require some spontaneous gesture of self-defilement. On the right, a plate of doves' heads, which Kircher had also advised him to have on hand.

He had left no part of the invocation ritual unobserved. No cardinal, eager for the fisherman's shoes, could have been more diligent.

But now, as the sound of the bell became louder, drowning out the music box, he was afraid.

Too late, he murmured to himself, hoping to quell his rising fear. Lemarchand's device was undone; the final trick had been turned. There was no time left for prevarication or regret. Besides, hadn't he risked both life and sanity to make this unveiling possible? The doorway was even now opening to pleasures no more than a handful of humans had ever known existed, much less *tasted*—pleasures which would redefine the parameters of sensation, which would release him from the dull round of desire, seduction and disappointment that had dogged him from late adolescence. He would be transformed by that knowledge, wouldn't he? No man could experience the profundity of such feeling and remain unchanged.

The bare bulb in the middle of the room dimmed and brightened, brightened and dimmed again. It had taken on the rhythm of the bell, burning its hottest on each chime.

In the troughs between the chimes the darkness in the room became utter; it was as if the world he had occupied for twenty-nine years had ceased to exist. Then the bell would sound again, and the bulb burn so strongly it might never have faltered, and for a few precious seconds he was standing in a familiar place, with a door that led out and down and into the street, and a window through which—had he but the will (or strength) to tear the blinds back—he might glimpse a rumor of morning.

With each peal the bulb's light was becoming more revelatory. By it, he saw the east wall flayed; saw the brick momentarily lose solidity and blow away; saw, in that same instant, the place beyond the room from which the bell's din was issuing. A world of birds was it? Vast black birds caught in perpetual tempest? That was all the sense he could make of the province from which—even now—the hierophants were coming—that it was in confusion, and full of brittle, broken things that rose and fell and filled the dark air with their fright.

And then the wall was solid again, and the bell fell silent. The bulb flickered out. This time it went without a hope of rekindling.

He stood in the darkness, and said nothing. Even if he could remember the words of welcome he'd prepared, his tongue would not have spoken them. It was playing dead in his mouth.

And then, light.

It came from *them*: from the quartet of Cenobites who now, with the wall sealed behind them, occupied the room. A fitful phosphorescence, like the glow of deep-sea fishes: blue, cold, charmless. It struck Frank that he had never once wondered what they would look like. His imagination, though fertile when it came to trickery and theft, was impoverished in other regards. The skill to picture these eminences was beyond him, so he had not even tried.

Why then was he so distressed to set eyes upon them?

Was it the scars that covered every inch of their bodies, the flesh cosmetically punctured and sliced and infibulated, then dusted down with ash? Was it the smell of vanilla they brought with them, the sweetness of which did little to disguise the stench beneath? Or was it that as the light grew, and he scanned them more closely, he saw nothing of joy, or even humanity, in their maimed faces: only desperation, and an appetite that made his bowels ache to be voided.

"What city is this?" one of the four enquired. Frank had difficulty guessing the speaker's gender with any certainty. Its clothes, some of which were sewn *to* and *through* its skin, hid its private parts, and there was nothing in the dregs of its voice, or in its willfully disfigured features that offered the least clue. When it spoke, the hooks that transfixed the flaps of its eyes and were wed, by an intricate system of chains passed through flesh and bone alike, to similar hooks through the lower lip, were teased by the motion, exposing the glistening meat beneath.

"I asked you a question," it said. Frank made no reply. The name of this city was the last thing on his mind.

"Do you understand?" the figure beside the first speaker demanded. Its voice, unlike that of its companion, was light and breathy—the voice of an excited girl. Every inch of its head had been tattooed with an intricate grid, and at every intersection of horizontal and vertical axes a jeweled pin driven through to the bone. Its tongue was similarly decorated. "Do you even know who we are?" it asked.

"Yes." Frank said at last. "I know."

Of course he knew; he and Kircher had spent long nights talking of hints gleaned from the diaries of Bolingbroke and Gilles de Rais. All that mankind knew of the Order of the Gash, he knew.

And yet . . . he had expected something different. Expected some sign of the numberless splendours they had access to. He had thought they would come with women, at least; oiled women, milked women; women shaved and

muscled for the act of love: their lips perfumed, their
thighs trembling to spread, their buttocks weighty, the way
he liked them. He had expected sighs, and languid bodies
spread on the floor underfoot like a living carpet; had
expected virgin whores whose every crevice was his for
the asking and whose skills would press him—*upward,
upward*—to undreamed-of ecstasies. The world would be
forgotten in their arms. He would be exalted by his lust,
instead of despised for it.

But no. No women, no sighs. Only these sexless *things*,
with their corrugated flesh.

Now the third spoke. Its features were so heavily
scarified—the wounds nurtured until they ballooned—that
its eyes were invisible and its words corrupted by the
disfigurement of its mouth.

"What do you want?" it asked him.

He perused this questioner more confidently than he had
the other two. His fear was draining away with every
second that passed. Memories of the terrifying place beyond
the wall were already receding. He was left with these
decrepit decadents, with their stench, their queer defor-
mity, their self-evident frailty. The only thing he had to
fear was nausea.

"Kircher told me there would be five of you," Frank
said.

"The Engineer will arrive should the moment merit,"
came the reply. "Now again, we ask you: *What do you
want?*"

Why should he not answer them straight? "Pleasure,"
he replied. "Kircher said you know about pleasure."

"Oh we do," said the first of them. "Everything you
ever wanted."

"Yes?"

"Of course. Of course." It stared at him with its all-
too-naked eyes. "What have you dreamed?" it said.

The question, put so baldly, confounded him. How could
he hope to articulate the nature of the phantasms his libido

had created? He was still searching for words when one of
them said:

"This world . . . it disappoints you?"

"Pretty much," he replied.

"You're not the first to tire of its trivialities," came the
response. "There have been others."

"Not many," the gridded face put in.

"True. A handful at best. But a few have dared to use
Lemarchand's Configuration. Men like yourself, hungry
for new possibilities, who've heard that we have skills
unknown in your region."

"I'd expected—" Frank began.

"We *know* what you expected," the Cenobite replied.
"We understand to its breadth and depth the nature of your
frenzy. It is utterly familiar to us."

Frank grunted. "So," he said, "you know what I've
dreamed about. You can supply the pleasure."

The thing's face broke open, its lips curling back: a
baboon's smile. "Not as you understand it," came the
reply.

Frank made to interrupt, but the creature raised a silenc-
ing hand.

"There are conditions of the nerve endings," it said,
"the like of which your imagination, however fevered,
could not hope to evoke."

". . . yes?"

"Oh yes. Oh most certainly. Your most treasured depravity is child's play beside the experiences we offer."

"Will you partake of them?" said the second Cenobite.

Frank looked at the scars and the hooks. Again, his
tongue was deficient.

"*Will you?*"

Outside, somewhere near, the world would soon be
waking. He had watched it wake from the window of this
very room, day after day, stirring itself to another round of
fruitless pursuits, and he'd known, *known*, that there was
nothing left out there to excite him. No heat, only sweat.

No passion, only sudden lust, and just as sudden indifference. He had turned his back on such dissatisfaction. If in doing so he had to interpret the signs these creatures brought him, then that was the price of ambition. He was ready to pay it.

"Show me," he said.

"There's no going back. You do understand that?"

"*Show me.*"

They needed no further invitation to raise the curtain. He heard the door creak as it was opened, and turned to see that the world beyond the threshold had disappeared, to be replaced by the same panic-filled darkness from which the members of the Order had stepped. He looked back towards the Cenobites, seeking some explanation for this. But they'd disappeared. Their passing had not gone unrecorded however. They'd taken the flowers with them, leaving only bare boards, and on the wall the offerings he had assembled were blackening, as if in the heat of some fierce but invisible flame. He smelled the bitterness of their consumption; it pricked his nostrils so acutely he was certain they would bleed.

But the smell of burning was only the beginning. No sooner had he registered it than half a dozen other scents filled his head. Perfumes he had scarcely noticed until now were suddenly overpoweringly strong. The lingering scent of filched blossoms; the smell of the paint on the ceiling and the sap in the wood beneath his feet—all filled his head. He could even smell the darkness outside the door, and in it, the ordure of a hundred thousand birds.

He put his hand to his mouth and nose, to stop the onslaught from overcoming him, but the stench of perspiration on his fingers made him giddy. He might have been driven to nausea had there not been fresh sensations flooding his system from each nerve ending and taste bud.

It seemed he could suddenly feel the collision of the dust motes with his skin. Every drawn breath chafed his lips; every blink, his eyes. Bile burned in the back of his throat, and a morsel of yesterday's beef that had lodged between his teeth sent spasms through his system as it exuded a droplet of gravy upon his tongue.

His ears were no less sensitive. His head was filled with a thousand dins, some of which he himself was father to. The air that broke against his eardrums was a hurricane; the flatulence in his bowels was thunder. But there were other sounds—innumerable sounds—which assailed him from somewhere beyond himself. Voices raised in anger, whispered professions of love, roars and rattlings, snatches of song, tears.

Was it the world he was hearing—morning breaking in a thousand homes? He had no chance to listen closely; the cacophony drove any power of analysis from his head.

But there was worse. The eyes! Oh god in heaven, he had never guessed that they could be such torment; he, who'd thought there was nothing on earth left to startle him. Now he reeled! Everywhere, *sight*!

The plain plaster of the ceiling was an awesome geography of brush strokes. The weave of his plain shirt an unbearable elaboration of threads. In the corner he saw a mite move on a dead dove's head, and wink its eyes at him, seeing that he saw. Too much! *Too much*!

Appalled, he shut his eyes. But there was more *inside* than out; memories whose violence shook him to the verge of senselessness. He sucked his mother's milk, and choked; felt his sibling's arms around him (a fight, was it, or a brotherly embrace? Either way, it suffocated). And more; so much more. A short lifetime of sensations, all writ in a perfect hand upon his cortex, and breaking him with their insistence that they be remembered.

He felt close to exploding. Surely the world outside his head—the room, and the birds beyond the door—they, for all their shrieking excesses, could not be as overwhelming as his memories. Better that, he thought, and tried to open his eyes. But they wouldn't unglue. Tears or pus or needle and thread had sealed them up.

He thought of the faces of the Cenobites: the hooks, the chains. Had they worked some similar surgery upon him, locking him up behind his eyes with the parade of his history?

In fear for his sanity, he began to address them, though he was no longer certain that they were even within earshot.

"*Why*?" he asked. "Why are you doing this to me?"

The echo of his words roared in his ears, but he scarcely attended to it. More sense impressions were swimming up from the past to torment him. Childhood still lingered on his tongue (milk and frustration) but there were adult feelings joining it now. He was grown! He was moustached and mighty, hands heavy, gut large.

Youthful pleasures had possessed the appeal of newness, but as the years had crept on, and mild sensation lost its potency, stronger and stronger experiences had been called for. And here they came again, more pungent for being laid in the darkness at the back of his head.

He felt untold tastes upon his tongue: bitter, sweet, sour, salty; smelled spice and shit and his mother's hair; saw cities and skies; saw speed, saw deeps; broke bread with men now dead and was scalded by the heat of their spittle on his cheek.

And of course there were women.

Always, amid the flurry and confusion, memories of women appeared, assaulting him with their scents, their textures, their tastes.

The proximity of this harem aroused him, despite circumstances. He opened his trousers and caressed his cock, more eager to have the seed spilled and so be freed of these creatures than for the pleasure of it.

He was dimly aware, as he worked his inches, that he must make a pitiful sight: a blind man in an empty room, aroused for a dream's sake. But the wracking, joyless orgasm failed to even slow the relentless display. His knees buckled, and his body collapsed to the boards where his spunk had fallen. There was a spasm of pain as he hit the floor, but the response was washed away before an-other wave of memories.

He rolled onto his back, and screamed; screamed and begged for an end to it, but the sensations only rose higher still, whipped to fresh heights with every prayer for cessation he offered up.

The pleas became a single sound, words and sense eclipsed by panic. It seemed there was no end to this, but madness. No hope but to be lost to hope.

As he formulated this last, despairing thought, the torment stopped.

All at once; all of it. Gone. Sight, sound, touch, taste, smell. He was abruptly bereft of them all. There were seconds then, when he doubted his very existence. Two heartbeats, three, four.

On the fifth beat, he opened his eyes. The room was empty, the doves and the piss-pot gone. The door was closed.

Gingerly, he sat up. His limbs were tingling; his head, wrist and bladder ached.

And then—a movement at the other end of the room drew his attention.

Where, two moments before, there had been an empty space, there was now a figure. It was the fourth Cenobite, the one that had never spoken, nor shown its face. Not *it*, he now saw: but *she*. The hood it had worn had been discarded, as had the robes. The woman beneath was gray yet gleaming, her lips bloody, her legs parted so that the elaborate scarification of her pubis was displayed. She sat on a pile of rotting human heads, and smiled in welcome.

The collision of sensuality and death appalled him. Could he have any doubt that she had personally dispatched these victims? Their rot was beneath her nails, and their tongues—twenty or more—lay out in ranks on her oiled thighs, as if awaiting entrance. Nor did he doubt that the brains now seeping from their ears and nostrils had been driven to insanity before a blow or a kiss had stopped their hearts.

Kircher had lied to him—either that or he'd been horribly deceived. There was no pleasure in the air; or at least not as humankind understood it.

He had made a mistake opening Lemarchand's box. A very terrible mistake.

"Oh, so you've finished dreaming," said the Cenobite, perusing him as he lay panting on the bare boards. "Good."

She stood up. The tongues fell to the floor, like a rain of slugs.

"Now we can begin," she said.

TWO

1

"It's not quite what I expected," Julia commented as they stood in the hallway. It was twilight; a cold day in August. Not the ideal time to view a house that had been left empty for so long.

"It needs work," Rory said. "That's all. It's not been touched since my grandmother died. That's the best part of three years. And I'm pretty sure she never did anything to it towards the end of her life."

"And it's yours?"

"Mine and Frank's. It was willed to us both. But when was the last time anybody saw big brother?"

She shrugged, as if she couldn't remember, though she remembered very well. A week before the wedding.

"Someone said he spent a few days here last summer. Rutting away, no doubt. Then he was off again. He's got no interest in property."

"But suppose we move in, and then he comes back, wants what's his?"

"I'll buy him out. I'll get a loan from the bank and buy him out. He's always hard up for cash."

She nodded, but looked less than persuaded.

"Don't worry," he said, going to where she was standing and wrapping his arms around her. "The place is ours, doll. We can paint it and pamper it and make it like heaven."

He scanned her face. Sometimes—particularly when doubt moved her, as it did now—her beauty came close to frightening him.

"Trust me," he said.

"I do."

"All right then. What say we start moving in on Sunday?"

2

Sunday.

It was still the Lord's Day up this end of the city. Even if the owners of these well-dressed houses and well-pressed children were no longer believers, they still observed the sabbath. A few curtains were twitched aside when Lewton's van drew up, and the unloading began; some curious neighbors even sauntered past the house once or twice, on the pretext of walking the hounds; but nobody spoke to the new arrivals, much less offered a hand with the furniture. Sunday was not a day to break sweat.

Julia looked after the unpacking, while Rory organized the unloading of the van, with Lewton and Mad Bob providing the extra muscle. It took four round-trips to transfer the bulk of the stuff from Alexandra Road, and at the end of the day there was still a good deal of bric-a-brac left behind, to be collected at a later point.

About two in the afternoon, Kirsty turned up on the doorstep.

"Came to see if I could give you a hand," she said, with a tone of vague apology in her voice.

"Well, you'd better come in," Julia said. She went back into the front room, which was a battlefield in which only chaos was winning, and quietly cursed Rory. Inviting the lost soul round to offer her services was his doing, no doubt of it. She would be more of a hindrance than a help;

her dreamy, perpetually defeated manner set Julia's teeth
on edge.

"What can I do?" Kirsty asked. "Rory said—"

"Yes," said Julia. "I'm sure he did."

"Where is he? Rory, I mean."

"Gone back for another vanload, to add to the misery."

"Oh."

Julia softened her expression. "You know it's very
sweet of you," she said, "to come round like this, but I
don't think there's much you can do just at the moment."

Kirsty flushed slightly. Dreamy she was, but not stupid.

"I see," she said. "Are you sure? Can't . . . I mean,
maybe I could make a cup of coffee for you?"

"Coffee," said Julia. The thought of it made her realize
just how parched her throat had become. "Yes," she
conceded. "That's not a bad idea."

The coffeemaking was not without its minor traumas.
No task Kirsty undertook was ever entirely simple. She
stood in the kitchen, boiling water in a pan it had taken a
quarter of an hour to find, thinking that maybe she shouldn't
have come after all. Julia always looked at her so strangely,
as if faintly baffled by the fact that she hadn't been smothered at birth. No matter. *Rory* had asked her to come,
hadn't he? And that was invitation enough. She would not
have turned down the chance of his smile for a hundred
Julias.

The van arrived twenty-five minutes later, minutes in
which the women had twice attempted, and twice failed, to
get a conversation simmering. They had little in common.
Julia the sweet, the beautiful, the winner of glances and
kisses, and Kirsty the girl with the pale handshake, whose
eyes were only ever as bright as Julia's before or after
tears. She had long ago decided that life was unfair. But
why, when she'd accepted that bitter truth, did circumstance insist on rubbing her face in it?

She surreptitiously watched Julia as she worked, and it
seemed to Kirsty that the woman was incapable of ugli-

ness. Every gesture—a stray hair brushed from the eyes with the back of the hand, dust blown from a favorite cup—all were infused with such effortless grace. Seeing it, she understood Rory's doglike adulation, and understanding it, despaired afresh.

He came in, at last, squinting and sweaty. The afternoon sun was fierce. He grinned at her, parading the ragged line of his front teeth that she had first found so irresistible.

"I'm glad you could come," he said.

"Happy to help—" she replied, but he had already looked away, at Julia.

"How's it going?"

"I'm losing my mind," she told him.

"Well, now you can rest from your labors," he said. "We brought the bed this trip." He gave her a conspiratorial wink, but she didn't respond.

"Can I help with unloading?" Kirsty offered.

"Lewton and M.B. are doing it," came Rory's reply.

"Oh."

"But I'd give an arm and a leg for a cup of tea."

"We haven't found the tea," Julia told him.

"Oh. Maybe a coffee, then?"

"Right," said Kirsty. "And for the other two?"

"They'd kill for a cup."

Kirsty went back to the kitchen, filled the small pan to near brimming, and set it back on the stove. From the hallway she heard Rory supervising the next unloading.

It was the bed, the bridal bed. Though she tried very hard to keep the thought of his embracing Julia out of her mind, she could not. As she stared into the water, and it simmered and steamed and finally boiled, the same painful images of their pleasure came back and back.

3

While the trio were away, gathering the fourth and final load of the day, Julia lost her temper with the unpacking.

It was a disaster, she said; everything had been parcelled up and put into the tea chests in the wrong order. She was having to disinter perfectly useless items to get access to the bare necessities.

Kirsty kept her silence, and her place in the kitchen, washing the soiled cups.

Cursing louder, Julia left the chaos and went out for a cigarette on the front step. She leaned against the open door, and breathed the pollen-gilded air. Already, though it was only the twenty-first of August, the afternoon was tinged with a smoky scent that heralded autumn.

She had lost track of how fast the day had gone, for as she stood there a bell began to ring for Evensong: the run of chimes rising and falling in lazy waves. The sound was reassuring. It made her think of her childhood, though not—that she could remember—of any particular day or place. Simply of being young, of mystery.

It was four years since she'd last stepped into a church: the day of her marriage to Rory, in fact. The thought of that day—or rather, of the promise it had failed to fulfil—soured the moment. She left the step, the chimes in full flight, and turned back into the house. After the touch of the sun on her upturned face, the interior seemed gloomy. Suddenly she tired to the point of tears.

They would have to assemble the bed before they could put their heads down to sleep tonight, and they had yet to decide which room they would use as the master bedroom. She would do that now, she elected, and so avoid having to return to the front room, and to ever-mournful Kirsty.

The bell was still pealing when she opened the door of the front room on the second floor. It was the largest of the three upper rooms—a natural choice—but the sun had not got in today (or any other day this summer) because the blinds were drawn across the window. The room was consequently chillier than anywhere else in the house; the air stagnant. She crossed the stained floorboards to the window, intending to remove the blind.

At the sill, a strange thing. The blind had been securely *nailed* to the window frame, effectively cutting out the least intrusion of life from the sunlit street beyond. She tried to pull the material free, but failed. The workman, whoever he'd been, had done a thorough job.

No matter; she'd have Rory take a claw hammer to the nails when he got back. She turned from the window, and as she did so she was suddenly and forcibly aware that the bell was still summoning the faithful. Were they not coming tonight? Was the hook not sufficiently baited with promises of paradise? The thought was only half alive; it withered in moments. But the bell rolled on, reverberating around the room. Her limbs, already aching with fatigue, seemed dragged down further by each peal. Her head throbbed intolerably.

The room was hateful, she'd decided; it was stale, and its benighted walls clammy. Despite its size, she would not let Rory persuade her into using it as the master bedroom. Let it rot.

She started towards the door, but as she came within a yard of it, the corners of the room seemed to creak, and the door slammed. Her nerves jangled. It was all she could do to prevent herself from sobbing.

Instead she simply said, "Go to hell," and snatched at the handle. It turned easily (why should it not? yet she was relieved) and the door swung open. From the hall below, a splash of warmth and ochre light.

She closed the door behind her and, with a queer satisfaction the root of which she couldn't or wouldn't fathom turned the key in the lock.

As she did so, the bell stopped.

4

"But it's the biggest of the rooms . . ."

"I don't like it, Rory. It's damp. We can use the back room."

"If we can get the bloody bed through the door."

"Of course we can. You know we can."

"Seems a waste of a good room," he protested, knowing full well that this was a *fait accompli*.

"Mother knows best," she told him, and smiled at him with eyes whose luster was far from maternal.

THREE

1

The seasons long for each other, like men and women, in order that they may be cured of their excesses.

Spring, if it lingers more than a week beyond its span, starts to hunger for summer to end the days of perpetual promise. Summer in its turn soon begins to sweat for something to quench its heat, and the mellowest of autumns will tire of gentility at last, and ache for a quick sharp frost to kill its fruitfulness.

Even winter—the hardest season, the most implacable—dreams, as February creeps on, of the flame that will presently melt it away. Everything tires with time, and starts to seek some opposition, to save it from itself.

So August gave way to September and there were few complaints.

2

With work, the house on Lodovico Street began to look more hospitable. There were even visits from neighbors, who—after sizing up the couple—spoke freely of how happy they were to have number fifty-five occupied again. Only one of them made any mention of Frank, referring in passing to the odd fellow who'd lived in the house for a few weeks the previous summer. There was a moment of embarrassment when Rory revealed the tenant to have been his brother, but it was soon glossed over by Julia, whose power to charm knew no bounds.

Rory had seldom made mention of Frank during the years of his marriage to Julia, though he and his brother were only eighteen months apart in age, and had, as children, been inseparable. This Julia had learned on an occasion of drunken reminiscing—a month or two before the wedding—when Rory had spoken at length about Frank. It had been melancholy talk. The brothers' paths had diverged considerably once they'd passed through adolescence, and Rory regretted it. Regretted still more the pain Frank's wild life-style had brought to their parents. It seemed that when Frank appeared, once in a blue moon, from whichever corner of the globe he was presently laying waste, he only brought grief. His tales of adventures in the shallows of criminality, his talk of whores and petty theft, all appalled their parents. But there had been worse, or so Rory had said. In his wilder moments Frank had talked of a life lived in delirium, of an appetite for experience that conceded no moral imperative.

Was it the tone of Rory's telling, a mixture of revulsion and envy, that had so piqued Julia's curiosity? Whatever the reason, she had been quickly seized by an unquenchable curiosity concerning this madman.

Then, barely a fortnight before the wedding, the black sheep had appeared in the flesh. Things had gone well for him of late. He was wearing gold rings on his fingers, and his skin was tight and tanned. There was little outward sign of the monster Rory had described. Brother Frank was smooth as a polished stone. She had succumbed to his charm within hours.

A strange time ensued. As the days crept toward the date of the wedding she found herself thinking less and less of her husband-to-be, and more and more of his brother. They were not wholly dissimilar; a certain lilt in their voices, and their easy manner, marked them as siblings. But to Rory's qualities Frank brought something his brother would never have: a beautiful desperation.

Perhaps what had happened next had been inevitable; and no matter how hard she'd fought her instincts, she would only have postponed the consummation of their feelings for each other. At least that was how she tried to excuse herself later. But when all the self-recrimination was done with, she still treasured the memory of their first—and last—encounter.

Kirsty had been at the house, hadn't she?, on some matrimonial business, when Frank had arrived. But by that telepathy that comes with desire (and fades with it) Julia had known that today was the day. She'd left Kirsty to her listmaking or suchlike, and taken Frank upstairs on the pretext of showing him the wedding dress. That was how she remembered it—that he'd asked to see the dress—and she'd put the veil on, laughing to think of herself in white, and then he'd been at her shoulder, lifting the veil, and she'd laughed on, laughed and laughed, as though to test the strength of his purpose. He had not been cooled by her mirth however; nor had he wasted time with the niceties of a seduction. The smooth exterior gave way to cruder stuff almost immediately. Their coupling had had in every regard but the matter of her acquiescence, all the aggression and the joylessness of rape.

Memory sweetened events of course, and in the four years (and five months) since that afternoon, she'd replayed the scene often. Now, in remembering it, the bruises were trophies of their passion, her tears proof positive of her feelings for him.

The day following, he'd disappeared. Flitted off to Bangkok or Easter Island, some place where he had no debts to answer. She'd mourned him, couldn't help it. Nor had her mourning gone unnoticed. Though it was never explicitly discussed, she had often wondered if the subsequent deterioration of her relationship with Rory had not started there: with her thinking of Frank as she made love to his brother.

And now? Now, despite the change of domestic interiors, and the chance of a fresh start together, it seemed that events conspired to remind her again of Frank.

It wasn't just the gossip of the neighbors that brought him to mind. One day, when she was alone in the house and unpacking various personal belongings, she came across several wallets of Rory's photographs. Many were relatively recent: pictures of the two of them together in Athens and Malta. But buried amongst the transparent smiles were some pictures she couldn't remember ever having seen before (had Rory kept them from her?); family portraits that went back decades. A photograph of his parents on their wedding day, the black and white image eroded over the years to a series of grays. Pictures of christenings, in which proud godparents cradled babies smothered in the family lace.

And then, photographs of the brothers together; as toddlers, with wide eyes; as surly schoolchildren, snapped at gymnastic displays and in school pageants. Then, as the shyness of acne-ridden adolescence took over, the number of pictures dwindled—until the frogs emerged, as princes, the other side of puberty.

Seeing Frank in brilliant color, clowning for the camera, she felt herself blushing. He had been an exhibitionist youth, predictably enough, always dressed *à la mode*. Rory, by comparison, looked dowdy. It seemed to her that the brothers' future lives were sketched in these early portraits. Frank the smiling, seductive chameleon; Rory the solid citizen.

She had packed the pictures away at last, and found, when she stood up, that with the blushes had come tears. Not of regret. She had no use for that. It was *fury* that made her eyes sting. Somehow, between one breath and the next, she'd lost herself.

She knew too, with perfect certainty, when her grip had first faltered. Lying on a bed of wedding lace, while Frank beset her neck with kisses.

3

Once in a while she went up to the room with the sealed blinds.

So far, they'd done little decorating work on the upper floors, preferring to first organize the areas in public gaze. The room had therefore remained untouched. *Unentered*, indeed, except for these few visits of hers.

She wasn't sure why she went up, nor how to account for the odd assortment of feelings that beset her while there. But there was something about the dark interior that gave her comfort; it was a womb of sorts, a dead woman's womb. Sometimes, when Rory was at work, she simply took herself up the stairs and sat in the stillness, thinking of nothing; or at least nothing she could put words to.

These sojourns made her feel oddly guilty, and she tried to stay away from the room when Rory was around. But it wasn't always possible. Sometimes her feet took her there without instruction so to do.

It happened thus that Saturday, the day of the blood.

She had been watching Rory at work on the kitchen door, chiselling several layers of paint from around the hinges, when she seemed to hear the room call. Satisfied that he was thoroughly engrossed in his chores, she went upstairs.

It was cooler than usual, and she was glad of it. She put her hand to the wall, and then transferred her chilled palm to her forehead.

"No use," she murmured to herself, picturing the man at work downstairs. She didn't love him; no more than he, beneath his infatuation with her face, loved her. He chiselled in a world of his own; she suffered here, far removed from him.

A gust of wind caught the back door below. She heard it slam.

Downstairs, the sound made Rory lose his concentration. The chisel jumped its groove and sliced deeply into

the thumb of his left hand. He shouted, as a gush of color
came. The chisel hit the floor.

"Hell and damnation!"

She heard, but did nothing. Too late, she surfaced through
a stupor of melancholy to realize that he was coming
upstairs. Fumbling for the key, and an excuse to justify her
presence in the room, she stood up, but he was already at
the door, crossing the threshold, rushing towards her, his
right hand clamped ineptly around his left. Blood was
coming in abundance. It welled up between his fingers and
dribbled down his arm, dripping from his elbow, adding
stain to stain on the bare boards.

"What have you done?" she asked him.

"What does it look like?" he said through gritted teeth.
"Cut myself."

His face and neck had gone the color of window putty.
She'd seen him like this before; he had on occasion passed
out at the sight of his own blood.

"Do something," he said queasily.

"Is it deep?"

"I don't know!" he yelled at her. "I don't want to
look."

He was ridiculous, she thought, but this wasn't the time
to give vent to the contempt she felt. Instead she took his
bloody hand in hers and, while he looked away, prized the
palm from the cut. It was sizable, and still bleeding profusely. Deep blood, dark blood.

"I think we'd better take you off to the hospital," she
told him.

"Can you cover it up?" he asked, his voice devoid of
anger now.

"Sure. I'll get a clean binding. Come on—"

"No," he said, shaking his ashen face. "If I take a
step, I think I'll pass out."

"Stay here then," she soothed him. "You'll be fine."

Finding no bandages in the bathroom cabinet the equal
of the staunching, she fetched a few clean handkerchiefs

from his drawer and went back into the room. He was leaning against the wall now, his skin glossy with sweat. He had padded in the blood he'd shed; she could taste the tang of it in the air.

Still quietly reassuring him that he wouldn't die of a two-inch cut, she wound a handkerchief around his hand, bound it on with a second, then escorted him, trembling like a leaf, down the stairs (one by one, like a child) and out to the car.

At the hospital they waited an hour in a queue of the walking wounded before he was finally seen, and stitched up. It was difficult for her to know in retrospect what was more comical about the episode: his weakness, or the extravagance of his subsequent gratitude. She told him, when he became fulsome, that she didn't want thanks from him, and it was true.

She wanted nothing that he could offer her, except perhaps his absence.

4

"Did you clean up the floor in the damp room?" she asked him the following day. They'd called it the damp room since that first Sunday, though there was not a sign of rot from ceiling to skirting board.

Rory looked up from his magazine. Gray moons hung beneath his eyes. He hadn't slept well, so he'd said. A cut finger, and he had nightmares of mortality. She, on the other hand, had slept like a babe.

"What did you say?" he asked her.

"The floor—" she said again. "There was blood on the floor. You cleaned it up."

He shook his head. "No," he said simply and returned to the magazine.

"Well I didn't," she said.

He offered her an indulgent smile. "You're such a

perfect hausfrau,'' he said. "You don't even know when you're doing it.''

The subject was closed there. He was content, apparently, to believe that she was quietly losing her sanity.

She, on the other hand, had the strangest sense that she was about to find it again.

FOUR

1

Kirsty hated parties. The smiles to be pasted on over the panic, the glances to be interpreted, and worst, the conversation. She had nothing to say of the least interest to the world, of this she had long been convinced. She'd watched too many eyes glaze over to believe otherwise, seen every device known to man for wheedling oneself out of the company of the dull, from "Will you excuse me, I believe I see my accountant,'' to passing out dead drunk at her feet.

But Rory had insisted she come to the housewarming. Just a few close friends, he'd promised. She'd said yes, knowing all too well what scenario would ensue from refusal. Moping at home in a stew of self-recrimination, cursing her cowardice, and thinking of Rory's sweet face.

The gathering wasn't such a torment as it turned out. There were only nine guests *in toto*, all of whom she knew vaguely, which made it easier. They didn't expect her to illuminate the room, only to nod and laugh where appropriate. And Rory—his hand still bound up—was at his most winning, full of guileless bonhomie. She even wondered if Neville—one of Rory's work colleagues—wasn't making eyes at her behind his spectacles, a suspicion that was confirmed in the middle of the evening when he maneuvered himself to her side and enquired whether she had any interest in cat breeding. She told him she hadn't, but was always interested in new experiences. He seemed delighted, and on this fragile pretext proceeded to ply her with liqueurs for the rest of the night. By eleven-thirty she was a whoozy but happy wreck, prompted by the most casual remark to ever more painful fits of giggling.

A little after midnight, Julia declared that she was tired, and wanted to go to bed. The statement was taken as a general cue for dispersal, but Rory would have none of it. He was up and refilling glasses before anyone had a chance to protest. Kirsty was certain she caught a look of displeasure cross Julia's face, then it passed, and the brow was unsullied once again. She said her goodnights, was complimented profusely on her skill with calf's liver, and went to bed.

The flawlessly beautiful were flawlessly happy, weren't they? To Kirsty this had always seemed self-evident. Tonight, however, the alcohol made her wonder if envy hadn't blinded her. Perhaps to be flawless was another kind of sadness.

But her spinning head had an inept hold on such ruminations, and the next minute Rory was up, and telling a joke about a gorilla and a Jesuit that had her choking on her drink before he'd even got to the votive candles.

Upstairs, Julia heard a fresh bout of laughter. She was indeed tired, as she'd claimed, but it wasn't the cooking that had exhausted her. It was the effort of suppressing her contempt for the damn fools who were gathered in the lounge below. She'd called them friends once, these half-wits, with their poor jokes and their poorer pretensions. She had played along with them for several hours; it was enough. Now she needed some cool place, some darkness.

As soon as she opened the door of the damp room she knew things were not quite as they had been. The light from the shadeless bulb on the landing illuminated the boards where Rory's blood had fallen, now so clean they might have been scrubbed. Beyond the reach of the light, the room bowed to darkness. She stepped in, and closed the door. The lock clicked into place at her back.

The dark was almost perfect, and she was glad of it. Her eyes rested against the night, their surfaces chilled.

Then, from the far side of the room, she heard a sound.

It was no louder than the din of a cockroach running behind the skirting boards. After seconds, it stopped. She held her breath. It came again. This time there seemed to be some pattern to the sound; a primitive code.

They were laughing like loons downstairs. The noise awoke desperation in her. What would she not do, to be free of such company?

She swallowed, and spoke to the darkness.

"I hear you," she said, not certain of why the words came, or to whom they were addressed.

The cockroach scratches ceased for a moment, and then began again, more urgently. She stepped away from the door and moved towards the noise. It continued, as if summoning her.

It was easy to miscalculate in the dark, and she reached the wall before she'd expected to. Raising her hands, she began to run her palms over the painted plaster. The surface was not uniformly cold. There was a place, she judged it to be halfway between door and window, where the chill became so intense she had to break contact. The cockroach stopped scratching.

There was a moment when she swam, totally disoriented, in darkness and silence. And then, something moved in front of her. A trick of her mind's eye, she assumed, for there was only imagined light to be had here. But the next spectacle showed her the error of that assumption.

The wall was alight, or rather something behind it burned with a cold luminescence that made the solid brick seem insubstantial stuff. *More*; the wall seemed to be coming apart, segments of it shifting and dislocating like a magician's prop, oiled panels giving on to hidden boxes whose sides in turn collapsed to reveal some further hiding place. She watched fixedly, not daring to even blink for fear she miss some detail of this extraordinary sleight-of-hand, while pieces of the world came apart in front of her eyes.

Then, suddenly, somewhere in this ever more elaborate

system of sliding fragments, she saw (or again, *seemed* to see) movement. Only now did she realize that she'd been holding her breath since this display began, and was beginning to become light-headed. She tried to empty her lungs of the stale air, and take a draught of fresh, but her body would not obey this simple instruction.

Somewhere in her innards a tic of panic began. The hocus-pocus had stopped now, leaving one part of her admiring quite dispassionately the tinkling music that was coming from the wall, the other part fighting the fear that rose in her throat step by step.

Again, she tried to take a breath, but it was as if her body had died, and she was staring out of it, unable now to breathe or blink or swallow.

The spectacle of the unfolding wall had now ceased entirely, and she saw something flicker across the brick, ragged enough to be shadow but too substantial.

It was human, she saw, or had been. But the body had been ripped apart and sewn together again with most of its pieces either missing or twisted and blackened as if in a furnace. There was an eye, gleaming at her, and the ladder of a spine, the vertebrae stripped of muscle, a few unrecognizable fragments of anatomy. That was it. That such a thing might live beggared reason—what little flesh it owned was hopelessly corrupted. Yet live it did. Its eye, despite the rot it was rooted in, scanned her every inch, up and down.

She felt no fear in its presence. This thing was weaker than her by far. It moved a little in its cell, looking for some modicum of comfort. But there was none to be had, not for a creature that wore its frayed nerves on its bleeding sleeve. Every place it might lay its body brought pain: this she knew indisputably. She pitied it. And with pity came release. Her body expelled dead air, and sucked in living. Her oxygen-starved brain reeled.

Even as she did so it spoke, a hole opening up in the flayed ball of the monster's head and issued a single, weightless word.

The word was:
"Julia."

2

Kirsty put down her glass, and tried to stand up.

"Where are you going?" Neville asked her.

"Where do you think?" she replied, consciously trying to prevent the words from slurring.

"Do you need any help?" Rory inquired. The alcohol made his lids lazy, and his grin lazier still.

"I am house-trained," she replied, the riposte greeted with laughter all round. She was pleased with herself; off-the-cuff wit was not her forte. She stumbled to the door.

"It's the last room on the right at the end of the landing," Rory informed her.

"I know," she said, and stepped out into the hall.

She didn't usually enjoy the sensation of drunkenness, but tonight she was reveling in it. She felt loose-limbed and light-hearted. She might well regret this tomorrow, but tomorrow would have to take care of itself. For tonight, she was flying.

She found her way to the bathroom, and relieved her aching bladder, then splashed some water onto her face. That done, she began her return journey.

She had taken three steps along the landing when she realized that somebody had put out the landing light while she was in the bathroom, and that same somebody was now standing a few yards away from her. She stopped.

"Hello?" she said. Had the cat-breeder followed her upstairs, in the hope of proving he wasn't spayed?

"Is that you?" she asked, only dimly aware that this was a singularly fruitless line of enquiry.

There was no reply, and she became a little uneasy.

"Come on," she said, attempting a jocular manner that she hoped masked her anxiety, "who is it?"

"Me," said Julia. Her voice was odd. Throaty, perhaps tearful.

"Are you all right?" Kirsty asked her. She wished she could see Julia's face.

"Yes," came the reply. "Why shouldn't I be?" Within the space of those five words the actress in Julia seized control. The voice cleared, the tone lightened.

"I'm just tired . . ." she went on. "It sounds like you're having a good time down there."

"Are we keeping you awake?"

"Goodness me, no," the voice gushed, "I was just going to the bathroom." A pause; then: "You go back down. Enjoy yourself."

At this cue Kirsty moved toward her along the landing. At the last possible moment Julia stepped out of the way, avoiding even the slightest physical contact.

"Sleep well," Kirsty said at the top of the stairs.

But there was no reply forthcoming from the shadow on the landing.

3

Julia didn't sleep well. Not that night, nor any night that followed.

What she'd seen in the damp room, what she'd heard and, finally, *felt*—was enough to keep easy slumbers at bay forever, or so she began to believe.

He was here. Brother Frank was here, in the house— and had been all the time. Locked away from the world in which she lived and breathed, but close enough to make the frail, pitiful contact he had. The whys and the wherefores of this she had no clue to; the human detritus in the wall had neither the strength nor the time to articulate its condition.

All it said, before the wall began to close on it again, and its wreckage was once more eclipsed by brick and plaster, was "*Julia*"—then, simply: "*It's Frank*"—and at the very end the word "*Blood*."

Then it was gone completely, and her legs had given way beneath her. She'd half fallen, half staggered, backward against the opposite wall. By the time she gathered her wits about her once more there was no mysterious light, no wasted figure cocooned in the brick. Reality's hold was absolute once again.

Not *quite* absolute perhaps. Frank was still here, in the damp room. Of that she had no doubt. Out of sight he might be, but not out of mind. He was trapped somehow between the sphere she occupied and some other place: a place of bells and troubled darkness. Had he died? Was that it? Perished in the empty room the previous summer, and now awaiting exorcism? If so, what had happened to his earthly remains? Only further exchange with Frank himself, or the remnants thereof, would provide an explanation.

Of the means by which she could lend the lost soul strength she had little doubt. He had given her the solution plainly.

Blood, he'd said. The syllable had been spoken not as an accusation but as an imperative.

Rory had bled on the floor of the damp room; the splashes had subsequently disappeared. Somehow, Frank's ghost—if that it was—had fed upon his brother's spillage, and gained thereby nourishment enough to reach out from his cell, and make faltering contact. What more might be achieved if the supply were larger?

She thought of Frank's embraces, of his roughness, his hardness, of the insistence he had brought to bear upon her. What would she not give to have such insistence again? Perhaps it was possible. And if it were—if she could give him the sustenance he needed—would he not be grateful? Would he not be her pet, docile or brutal at her least whim? The thought took sleep away. Took sanity and sorrow with it. She had been in love all this time, she

realized, and mourning for him. If it took blood to restore
him to her, then blood she would supply, and not think
twice of the consequences.

In the days that followed, she found her smile again.
Rory took the change of mood as a sign that she was
happy in the new house. Her good humor ignited the same
in him. He took to the redecoration with renewed gusto.

Soon, he said, he would get to work on the second
floor. They would locate the source of dampness in the
large room, and turn it into a bedroom fit for his princess.
She kissed his cheek when he spoke of this, and she said
that she was in no hurry, that the room they had already
was more than adequate. Talk of the bedroom made him
stroke her neck, and pull her close, and whisper infantile
obscenities in her ear. She did not refuse him, but went
upstairs meekly, and let him undress her as he liked to do,
unbuttoning her with paint-stained fingers. She pretended
the ceremony aroused her, though this was far from the truth.

The only thing that sparked the least appetite in her, as
she lay on the creaking bed with his bulk between her legs,
was closing her eyes and picturing Frank, as he had been.

More than once his name rose to her lips; each time she
bit it back. Finally she opened her eyes to remind herself
of the boorish truth. Rory was decorating her face with his
kisses. Her cheeks crawled at his touch.

She would not be able to endure this too often, she
realized. It was too much of an effort to play the acquies-
cent wife: her heart would burst.

Thus, lying beneath him while September's breath brushed
her face from the open window, she began to plot the
getting of blood.

FIVE

Sometimes it seemed that eons came and went while he
lingered in the wall, eons that some clue would later reveal

to have been the passing of hours, or even minutes.

But now things had changed; he had a chance of *escape*. His spirit soared at the thought. It was a frail chance, he didn't deceive himself about that. There were several reasons his best efforts might falter. Julia, for one. He remembered her as a trite, preening woman, whose upbringing had curbed her capacity for passion. He had untamed her, of course, once. He remembered the day, among the thousands of times he had performed that act, with some satisfaction. She had resisted no more than was needful for her vanity, then succumbed with such naked fervor he had almost lost control of himself.

In other circumstances he might have snatched her from under her would-be husband's nose, but fraternal politics counselled otherwise. In a week or two he would have tired of her, and been left not only with a woman whose body was already an eyesore to him, but also a vengeful brother on his heels. It hadn't been worth the hassle.

Besides, there'd been new worlds to conquer. He had left the day after to go East: to Hong Kong and Sri Lanka, to wealth and adventure. He'd had them, too. At least for a while. But everything slipped through his fingers sooner or later, and with time he began to wonder whether it was circumstance that denied him a good hold on his earnings, or whether he simply didn't care enough to keep what he had. The train of thought, once begun, was a runaway. Everywhere, in the wreckage around him, he found evidence to support the same bitter thesis: that he had encountered nothing in his life—no person, no state of mind or body—he wanted sufficiently to suffer even passing discomfort for.

A downward spiral began. He spent three months in a wash of depression and self-pity that bordered on the suicidal. But even that solution was denied him by his newfound nihilism. If nothing was worth living for it followed, didn't it, that there was nothing worth dying for either. He stumbled from one such sterility to the next, until all thoughts were rotted away by whatever opiate his immoralities could earn him.

How had he first heard about Lemarchand's box? He couldn't remember. In a bar maybe, or a gutter, from the lips of a fellow derelict. At the time it was merely a rumor—this dream of a pleasure dome where those who had exhausted the trivial delights of the human condition might discover a fresh definition of joy. And the route to this paradise? There were several, he was told, charts of the interface between the real and the realer still, made by travellers whose bones had long since gone to dust. One such chart was in the vaults of the Vatican, hidden in code in a theological work unread since the Reformation. Another—in the form of an origami exercise, was reported to have been in the possession of the Marquis de Sade, who used it, while imprisoned in the Bastille, to barter with a guard for paper on which to write *The 120 Days of Sodom*. Yet another was made by a craftsman—a maker of singing birds—called Lemarchand, in the form of a musical box of such elaborate design a man might toy with it half a lifetime and never get inside.

Stories. Stories. Yet since he had come to believe in nothing at all it was not so difficult to put the tyranny of verifiable truth out of his head. And it passed the time, musing drunkenly on such fantasies.

It was in Düsseldorf, where he'd gone smuggling heroin, that he again encountered the story of Lemarchand's box. His curiosity was piqued once more, but this time he followed the story up until he found its source. The man's name was Kircher, though he probably laid claim to half a dozen others. Yes, the German could confirm the existence of the box, and yes, he could see his way to letting Frank have it. The price? Small favors, here and there. Nothing exceptional. Frank did the favors, washed his hands, and claimed his payment.

There had been instructions from Kircher, on how best to break the seal on Lemarchand's device, instructions that were part pragmatic, part metaphysical. To solve the puzzle is to travel, he'd said, or something like that. The box, it seemed, was not just the map of the road, but the road itself.

This new addiction quickly cured him of dope and drink. Perhaps there were other ways to bend the world to suit the shape of his dreams.

He came back to the house on Lodovico Street, to the empty house behind whose walls he was now imprisoned, and prepared himself—just as Kircher had detailed—for the challenge of solving Lemarchand's Configuration. He had never in his life been so abstemious, nor so single-minded. In the days before the onslaught on the box he led a life that would have shamed a saint, focusing all his energies on the ceremonies ahead.

He had been arrogant in his dealing with the Order of the Gash, he saw that now; but there were everywhere—*in* the world and *out* of it—forces that encouraged such arrogance because they traded on it. That in itself would not have undone him. No, his real error had been the naive belief that *his* definition of pleasure significantly overlapped with that of the Cenobites.

As it was, they had brought incalculable suffering. They had overdosed him on sensuality, until his mind teetered on madness, then they'd initiated him into experiences that his nerves still convulsed to recall. They had called it pleasure, and perhaps they'd meant it. Perhaps not. It was impossible to know with these minds; they were so hopelessly, flawlessly ambiguous. They recognized no principles of reward and punishment by which he could hope to win some respite from their tortures, nor were they touched by any appeal for mercy. He'd tried that, over the weeks and months that separated the solving of the box from today.

There was no compassion to be had on this side of the Schism; there was only the weeping and the laughter. Tears of joy sometimes (for an hour without dread, a breath's length even), laughter coming just as paradoxically in the face of some new horror, fashioned by the Engineer for the provision of grief.

There was a further sophistication to the torture, devised by a mind that understood exquisitely the nature of suffering. The prisoners were allowed to see into the world they had once occupied. Their resting places—when they were not enduring pleasure—looked out onto the very locations where they had once worked the Configuration that had brought them here. In Frank's case, on to the upper room of number fifty-five, Lodovico Street.

For the best part of a year it had been an unilluminating view: nobody had ever stepped into the house. And then, *they'd* come: Rory and the lovely Julia. And hope had begun again . . .

There were ways to escape, he'd heard it whispered; loopholes in the system that might allow a mind supple or cunning enough egress into the room from which it had come. If a prisoner were able to make such an escape, there was no way that the hierophants could follow. They had to be *summoned* across the Schism. Without such an invitation they were left like dogs on the doorstep, scratching and scratching but unable to get in. Escape therefore, if it could be achieved, brought with it a *decree absolute*, total dissolution of the mistaken marriage which the prisoner had made. It was a risk worth taking. Indeed it was no risk at all. What punishment could be meted out worse than the thought of pain without hope of release?

He had been lucky. Some prisoners had departed from the world without leaving sufficient sign of themselves from which, given an adequate collision of circumstances, their bodies might be remade. He had. Almost his last act, bar the shouting, had been to empty his testicles onto the floor. Dead sperm was a meager keepsake of his essential self, but enough. When dear brother Rory (sweet butter-fingered Rory) had let his chisel slip, there was something of Frank to profit from the pain. He had found a fingerhold for himself, and a glimpse of strength with which he might haul himself to safety. Now it was up to Julia.

Sometimes, suffering in the wall, he thought she would desert him out of fear. Either that or she'd rationalize the vision she'd seen, and decide she'd been dreaming. If so, he was lost. He lacked the energy to repeat the appearance.

But there were signs that gave him cause for hope. The fact that she returned to the room on two or three occasions, for instance, and simply stood in the gloom, watching the wall. She'd even muttered a few words on the second visit, though he'd caught only scraps. The word "*here*" was amongst them. And "*waiting*," and "*soon*." Enough to keep him from despair.

He had another prop to his optimism. She was lost, wasn't she? He'd seen that in her face, when—before the day Rory had chiselled himself—she and his brother had had occasion to be in the room together. He'd read the looks between the lines, the moments when her guard had slipped, and the sadness and frustration she felt were apparent.

Yes, she was lost. Married to a man she felt no love for, and unable to see a way out.

Well, here he was. They could save each other, the way the poets promised lovers should. He was mystery, he was darkness, he was all she had dreamed of. And if she would only free him he would service her—oh yes—until her pleasure reached that threshold that, like all thresholds, was a place where the strong grew stronger, and the weak perished.

Pleasure was pain there, and vice versa. And he knew it well enough to call it home.

SIX

It turned cold in the third week of September: an Arctic chill brought on a rapacious wind that stripped the trees of leaves in a handful of days.

The cold necessitated a change of costume, and a change of plan. Instead of walking, Julia took the car. Drove down to the city center in the early afternoon and found a bar in which the lunchtime trade was brisk but not clamorous.

The customers came and went: Young Turks from firms of lawyers and accountants, debating their ambitions; parties of wine-imbibers whose only claim to sobriety was their suits; and, more interestingly, a smattering of individuals who sat alone at their tables and simply drank. She garnered a good crop of admiring glances, but they were mostly from the Young Turks. It wasn't until she'd been in the place an hour, and the wage slaves were returning to their treadmills, that she caught sight of somebody watching her reflection in the bar mirror. For the next ten minutes his eyes were glued to her. She went on drinking, trying to conceal any sign of agitation. And then, without warning, he stood up and crossed to her table.

"Drinking alone?" he said.

She wanted to run. Her heart was pounding so furiously she was certain he must hear it. But no. He asked her if she wanted another drink; she said she did. Clearly pleased not to have been rebuffed, he went to the bar, ordered doubles, and returned to her side. He was ruddy-featured, and one size larger than his dark blue suit. Only his eyes betrayed any sign of nervousness, resting on her for moments only, then darting away like startled fish.

There would be no serious conversation: that she had already decided. She didn't want to know much about him. His name, if necessary. His profession and marital status, if he insisted. Beyond that let him be just a body.

As it was there was no danger of a confessional. She'd met more talkative paving stones. He smiled occasionally—a short, nervous smile that showed teeth too even to be real—and offered more drinks. She said no, wanting the chase over with as soon as possible, and instead asked if he had time for a coffee. He said he had.

"The house is only a few minutes from here," she replied, and they went to her car. She kept wondering, as she drove—the meat on the seat beside her—why this was so very easy. Was it that the man was plainly a victim—with his ineffectual eyes and his artificial teeth—born, did he but know it, to make this journey? Yes, perhaps that was it. She was not afraid, because all of this was so perfectly predictable . . .

As she turned the key in the front door and stepped into the house, she thought she heard a noise in the kitchen. Had Rory returned home early, ill perhaps? She called out. There was no reply; the house was empty. Almost.

From the threshold on, she had the thing planned meticulously. She closed the door. The man in the blue suit stared at his manicured hands, and waited for his cue.

"I get lonely sometimes," she told him as she brushed past him. It was a line she'd come up with in bed the previous night.

He only nodded by way of response, the expression on his face a mingling of fear and incredulity; he clearly couldn't quite believe his luck.

"Do you want another drink?" she asked him, "or shall we go straight upstairs?"

He only nodded again.

"Which?"

"I think maybe I've drunk enough already."

"Upstairs then."

He made an indecisive move in her direction, as though he might have intended a kiss. She wanted no courtship, however. Skirting his touch, she crossed to the bottom of the stairs.

"I'll lead," she said. Meekly, he followed.

At the top of the steps she glanced round at him, and caught him dabbing sweat from his chin with his handkerchief. She waited until he caught up with her, and then led him halfway along the landing to the damp room.

The door had been left ajar.

"Come on in," she said.

He obeyed. Once inside it took him a few moments to become accustomed to the gloom, and a further time to give voice to his observation: "There's no bed."

She closed the door, and switched on the light. She had hung one of Rory's old jackets on the back of the door. In its pocket she'd left the knife.

He said again: "No bed."

"What's wrong with the floor?" she replied.

"The floor?"

"Take off your jacket. You're warm."

"I am," he agreed, but did nothing, so she moved across to him, and began to slip the knot of his tie. He was trembling, poor lamb. Poor, bleatless lamb. While she removed the tie, he began to shrug off his jacket.

Was Frank watching this? she wondered. Her eyes strayed momentarily to the wall. Yes, she thought; he's there. He *sees*. He *knows*. He licks his lips and grows impatient.

The lamb spoke. "Why don't you . . ." he began, "why don't you maybe . . . do the same?"

"Would you like to see me naked?" she teased. The words made his eyes gleam.

"Yes," he said thickly. "Yes. I'd like that."

"Very much?"

"Very much."

He was unbuttoning his shirt.

"Maybe you will," she said.

He gave her that dwarf smile again.

"Is it a game?" he ventured.

"If you want it to be," she said, and helped him out of his shirt. His body was pale and waxy, like a fungus. His upper chest was heavy, his belly too. She put her hands to his face. He kissed her fingertips.

"You're beautiful," he said, spitting the words out as though they'd been vexing him for hours.

"Am I?"

"You know you are. Lovely. Loveliest woman I ever set eyes on."

''That's gallant of you,'' she said, and turned back to the door. Behind her she heard his belt buckle clink, and the sound of cloth slipping over skin as he dropped his trousers.

So far and no farther, she thought. She had no wish to see him babe-naked. It was enough to have him like this—

She reached into the jacket pocket.

''Oh dear,'' the lamb suddenly said.

She let the knife lie. ''What is it?'' she asked, turning to look at him. If the ring on his finger hadn't already given his status away, she would have known him to be a married man by the underpants he wore: baggy and overwashed, an unflattering garment bought by a wife who had long since ceased to think of her husband in sexual terms.

''I think I need to empty my bladder,'' he said. ''Too many whiskies.''

She shrugged a small shrug, and turned back to the door.

''Won't be a moment,'' he said at her back. But her hand was in the jacket pocket before the words were out, and as he stepped towards the door, she turned on him, slaughtering knife in hand.

His pace was too quick to see the blade until the very last moment, and even then it was bemusement that crossed his face, not fear. It was a short-lived look. The knife was in him a moment after, slicing his belly with the ease of a blade in overripe cheese. She opened one cut, and then another.

As the blood started, she was certain the room flickered, the bricks and mortar trembling to see the spurts that flew from him.

She had a breath's length to admire the phenomena, no more, before the lamb let out a wheezing curse, and—instead of moving out of the knife's range as she had anticipated—took a step toward her and knocked the weapon from her hand. It span across the floorboards and collided with the skirting. Then he was upon her.

He put his hand into her hair and took a fistful. It seemed his intention was not violence but escape, for he relinquished his hold as soon as he'd pulled away from the door. She fell against the wall, looking up to see him wrestling with the door handle, his free hand clamped to his cuts.

She was quick now. Across to where the knife lay, up, and back toward him in one fluid motion. He had got the door open by inches, but not far enough. She brought the knife down in the middle of his pockmarked back. He yelled, and released the door handle. She was already drawing the knife out, and plunging into him a second time, and now a third and a fourth. Indeed she lost count of the wounds she made, her attack lent venom by his refusal to lie down and die. He stumbled around the room, grieving and complaining, blood following blood onto his buttocks and legs. Finally, after an age of this farcical stuff, he keeled over and hit the floor.

This time she was certain her senses did not deceive her. The room, or the spirit in it, responded with soft sighs of anticipation.

Somewhere, a bell was ringing . . .

Almost as an afterthought, she registered that the lamb had stopped breathing. She crossed the blood-spangled floor to where he lay, and said:

"Enough?"

Then she went to wash her face.

As she moved down the landing she heard the room groan—there was no other word for it. She stopped in her tracks, almost tempted to go back. But the blood was drying on her hands, and its stickiness revolted her.

In the bathroom she stripped off her flower-patterned blouse, and rinsed first her hands, then her speckled arms, and finally her neck. The dowsing both chilled and braced her. It felt good. That done, she washed the knife, rinsed the sink and returned along the landing without bothering to dry herself or to dress.

She had no need for either. The room was like a furnace, as the dead man's energies pulsed from his body. They didn't get far. Already the blood on the floor was crawling away towards the wall where Frank was, the beads seeming to boil and evaporate as they came within range of the skirting boards. She watched, entranced. But there was more. Something was happening to the corpse. It was being drained of every nutritious element, the body convulsing as its innards were sucked out, gases moaning in its bowels and throat, the skin dessicating in front of her startled eyes. At one point the plastic teeth dropped back into the gullet, the gums withered around them.

And in mere moments, it was done. Anything the body might have usefully offered by way of nourishment had been taken; the husk that remained would not have sustained a family of fleas. She was impressed.

Suddenly, the bulb began to flicker. She looked to the wall, expecting it to tremble and spit her lover from hiding. But no. The bulb went out. There was only the dim light that crept through the age-beaten blind.

"Where are you?" she said.

The walls remained mute.

"*Where are you?*"

Still nothing. The room was cooling. Her breasts had grown gooseflesh. She peered down at the luminous watch on the lamb's shrivelled arm. It ticked away, indifferent to the apocalypse that had overtaken its owner. It read 4:41. Rory would be back anytime after 5:15, depending on how dense the traffic was. She had work to do before then.

Bundling up the blue suit and the rest of his clothes, she put them in several plastic bags, and then went in search of a larger bag for the remains. She had expected Frank to be here to help her with this labor, but as he hadn't shown she had no choice but to do it herself. When she came back to the room, the deterioration of the lamb was still continuing, though now much slowed. Perhaps Frank was still finding nutriments to squeeze from the corpse, but she doubted it. More likely the pauperized body, sucked clean of marrow and every vital fluid, was no longer strong enough to support itself. When she had parcelled it up in the bag, it was the weight of a small child, no more. Sealing the bag up, she was about to take it down to the car when she heard the front door open.

The sound undammed all the panic she'd so assiduously kept from herself. She began to shake. Tears pricked her sinuses.

"*Not now* . . ." she told herself, but the feelings would simply not be suppressed any longer.

In the hallway below, Rory said: "Sweetheart?"

Sweetheart! She could have laughed, but for the terror. She was here if he wanted to find her—his sweetheart, his honeybun—with her breasts new-washed, and a dead man in her arms.

"Where are you?"

She hesitated before replying, not certain that her larynx was the equal of the deception.

He called a third time, his voice changing timbre as he walked through into the kitchen. It would take him a moment only to discover that she wasn't at the cooker stirring sauce; then he would come back and head up the stairs. She had ten seconds, fifteen at most.

Attempting to keep her tread as light as possible, for fear he heard her movements overhead, she carried the bundle to the spare room at the end of the landing. Too small to be used as a bedroom (except perhaps for a child), they had used it as a dump. Half-emptied tea chests, pieces of furniture they had not found a place for, all manner of rubbish. Here she laid the body to rest awhile, behind an upended armchair. Then she locked the door behind her, just as Rory called from the bottom of the stairs. He was coming up.

"Julia? Julia, sweetheart. Are you there?"

She slipped into the bathroom, and consulted the mirror. It showed her a flushed portrait. She picked up the blouse she'd left hanging over the side of the bath and put it on. It smelled stale, and there was undoubtedly blood spattered between the flowers, but she had nothing else to wear.

He was coming along the landing; she heard his elephantine tread.

"Julia?"

This time, she answered—making no attempt to disguise the tremulous quality of her voice. The mirror had confirmed what she feared: that there was no way she could pass herself off as undistressed. She was obliged to make a virtue of the liability.

"Are you all right?" he asked her. He was outside the door.

"No," she said. "I'm feeling sick."

"Oh, darling . . ."

"I'll be fine in a minute."

He tried the handle, but she'd bolted the door.

"Can you leave me alone for a little while?"

"Do you want a doctor?"

"No," she told him. "No. Really. But I wouldn't mind a brandy—"

"Brandy . . ."

"I'll be down in two ticks."

"Whatever madam wants," he quipped. She counted his steps as he trudged to the stairs, then descended. Once she'd calculated that he was out of earshot, she slid back the bolt and stepped on to the landing.

The late afternoon light was failing quickly; the landing was a murky tunnel.

Downstairs, she heard the clink of glass on glass. She moved as quickly as she dared to Frank's room.

There was no sound from the gloomed interior. The walls no longer trembled, nor did distant bells toll. She pushed the door open; it creaked slightly.

She had not entirely tidied up after her labors. There was dust on the floor, human dust, and fragments of dried flesh. She went down on her haunches and collected them

up diligently. Rory had been right. What a perfect hausfrau she made.

As she stood up again, something shifted in the ever-
denser shadows of the room. She looked in the direction of
the movement, but before her eyes could make sense of
the form in the corner, a voice said: "Don't look at me."

It was a tired voice—the voice of somebody used up by
events; but it was *concrete*. The syllables were carried on
the same air that she breathed.

"Frank," she said.

"Yes . . ." came the broken voice, "it's me."

From downstairs, Rory called up to her. "Are you
feeling better?"

She went to the door.

"Much better," she responded. At her back the hidden
thing said: "*Don't let him near me*," the words coming
fast and fierce.

"It's all right," she whispered to him. Then, to Rory:
"I'll be with you in a minute. Put on some music. Something soothing."

Rory replied that he would, and retired to the lounge.

"I'm only half-made," Frank's voice said. "I don't
want you to see me . . . don't want *anybody* to see me
. . . not like this . . ." The words were halting once more,
and wretched. "I have to have more blood, Julia."

"More?"

"And soon."

"How much more?" she asked the shadows. This time
she caught a better glimpse of what lay in wait there. No
wonder he wanted no one to look.

"Just *more*," he said. Though the volume was barely
above a whisper, there was an urgency in the voice that
made her afraid.

"I have to go . . ." she said, hearing music from
below.

This time the darkness made no reply. At the door, she
turned back.

"I'm glad you came," she said. As she closed the door, she heard a sound not unlike laughter behind her, nor unlike sobs.

SEVEN

1

"Kirsty? Is that you?"

"Yes? Who is this?"

"It's Rory . . ."

The line was watery, as though the deluge outside had seeped down the phone. Still, she was happy to hear from him. He called up so seldom, and when he did it was usually on behalf of both himself and Julia. Not this time however. This time Julia was the subject under discussion.

"There's something wrong with her, Kirsty," he said. "I don't know what."

"Ill, you mean?"

"Maybe. She's just so strange with me. And she looks terrible."

"Have you said anything to her?"

"She says she's fine. But she isn't. I wondered if maybe she'd spoken with you."

"I haven't set eyes on her since your housewarming."

"That's another thing. She doesn't even want to leave the house. That's not like her."

"Do you want me to . . . to have a word with her?"

"Would you?"

"I don't know if it'll do any good, but I'll try."

"Don't say anything about me talking to you."

"Of course not. I'll call in at the house tomorrow—"

("Tomorrow. It has to be tomorrow."

"Yes . . . I know."

"I'm afraid I'll lose my grip, Julia. Start slipping back.")

"I'll give you a call from the office on Thursday. You can tell me what you make of her."

(*"Slipping back?"*
"They'll know I've gone by now."
"Who will?"
"The Gash. The bastards that took me . . ."
"They're waiting for you?"
"Just beyond the wall.")

Rory told her how grateful he was, and she in turn told him that it was the least a friend could do. Then he put down the phone, leaving her listening to the rain on the empty line.

Now they were both Julia's creatures, looking after her welfare, fretting for her if she had bad dreams.

No matter, it was a kind of togetherness.

2

The man with the white tie had not bided his time. Almost as soon as he set eyes on Julia he came across to her. She decided, even as he approached, that he was not suitable. Too big; too confident. After the way the first one had fought, she was determined to choose with care. So, when White Tie asked what she was drinking, she told him to leave her be.

He was apparently used to rejections, and took it in his stride, withdrawing to the bar. She returned to her drink.

It was raining heavily today—had been raining now for seventy-two hours, on and off—and there were fewer customers than there had been the week before. One or two drowned rats headed in from the street, but none looked her way for more than a few moments. And time was moving on. It was already past two. She wasn't going to risk getting caught again by Rory's return. She emptied her glass, and decided that this was not Frank's lucky day. Then she stepped out of the bar into the downpour, put up her umbrella, and headed back to the car. As she went she heard footsteps behind her, and then White Tie was at her side and saying: "My hotel's nearby."

"Oh . . ." she said and kept on walking. But he wasn't going to be shrugged off so easily.

"I'm only here for two days," he said.

Don't tempt me, she thought.

"Just looking for some companionship . . ." he went on. "I haven't spoken to a soul."

"Is that right?"

He took hold of her wrist. A grip so tight she almost cried out. That was when she knew she was going to have to kill him. He seemed to see the desire in her eyes.

"My hotel?" he said.

"I don't much like hotels. They're so impersonal."

"Have you got a better idea?" he said to her.

She had, of course.

He hung his dripping raincoat on the hall stand, and she offered him a drink, which he welcomed. His name was Patrick, and he was from Newcastle.

"Down on business. Can't seem to get much done."

"Why's that?"

He shrugged. "I'm probably a bad salesman. Simple as that."

"What do you sell?" she asked him.

"What do you care?" he replied, razor quick.

She grinned. She would have to get him upstairs quickly, before she started to enjoy his company.

"Why don't we dispense with the small talk?" she said. It was a stale line, but it was the first thing that came to her tongue. He swallowed the last of his drink in one gulp, and went where she led.

This time she had not left the door ajar. It was locked, which plainly intrigued him.

"After you," he said, when the door swung open.

She went first. He followed. This time, she had decided, there would be no stripping. If some nourishment was soaked up by his clothes then so be it; she was not going to give him a chance to realize that they weren't alone in the room.

"Going to fuck on the floor, are we?" he asked casually.
"Any objections?"

"Not if it suits you," he said and clamped his mouth over hers, his tongue frisking her teeth for cavities. There was some passion in him, she mused; she could feel him hard against her already. But she had work to do here: blood to spill and a mouth to feed.

She broke his kiss, and tried to slip from his arms. The knife was back in the jacket on the door. While it was out of reach she had little power to resist him.

"What's the problem?" he said.

"No problem . . ." she murmured. "There's no hurry either. We've got all the time in the world." She touched the front of his trousers, to reassure him. Like a stroked dog, he closed his eyes.

"You're a strange one," he said.

"Don't look," she told him.

"Huh?"

"Keep your eyes closed."

He frowned, but obeyed. She took a step backward toward the door, and half turned to fumble in the depths of the pocket, glancing back to see that he was still blind.

He was, and unzipping himself. As her hand clasped the knife, the shadows growled.

He heard the noise. His eyes sprang open.

"What was that?" he said, reeling round and peering into the darkness.

"It was nothing," she insisted, as she pulled the knife from its hiding place. He was moving away from her, across the room.

"There's somebody—"

"*Don't.*"

"—here."

The last syllable faltered on his lips, as he glimpsed a fretful motion in the corner beside the window.

"What . . . in God's . . . ?" he began. As he pointed into the darkness she was at him, and slicing his neck open with a butcher's efficiency. Blood jumped immediately, a fat spurt that hit the wall with a wet thud. She heard Frank's pleasure, and then the dying man's complaint, long and low. His hand went up to his neck to stem the pulse, but she was at him again, slicing his pleading hand, his face. He staggered, he sobbed. Finally, he collapsed, twitching.

She stepped away from him to avoid the flailing legs. In the corner of the room she saw Frank rocking to and fro.

"Good woman, . . ." he said.

Was it her imagination, or was his voice already stronger than it had been, more like the voice she'd heard in her head a thousand times these plundered years?

The door bell rang. She froze.

"Oh Jesus," her mouth said.

"It's all right . . ." the shadow replied. "He's as good as dead."

She looked at the man in the white tie and saw that Frank was right. The twitching had all but ceased.

"He's big," said Frank. "And healthy."

He was moving into her sight, too greedy for sustenance to prohibit her stare; she saw him plainly now for the first time. He was a travesty. Not just of humanity, of life. She looked away.

The door bell was ringing again, and for longer.

"Go and answer it," Frank told her.

She made no reply.

"*Go on,*" he told her, turning his foul head in her direction, his eyes keen and bright in the surrounding corruption.

The bell rang a third time.

"Your caller is very insistent," he said, trying persuasion where demands had failed. "I really think you should answer the door."

She backed away from him, and he turned his attentions back to the body on the floor.

Again, the bell.

It was better to answer it perhaps (she was already out of the room, trying not to hear the sounds Frank was making), better to open the door to the day. It would be a man selling insurance, most likely, or a Jehovah's Witness, with news of salvation. Yes, she wouldn't mind hearing that. The bell rang again. "Coming," she said, hurrying now for fear he leave. She had welcome on her face when she opened the door. It died immediately.

"Kirsty."

"I was just about to give up on you."

"I was . . . I was asleep."

"Oh."

Kirsty looked at the apparition that had opened the door to her. From Rory's description she'd expected a washed-out creature. What she saw was quite the reverse. Julia's face was flushed; strands of sweat-darkened hair glued to her brow. She did not look like a woman who had just risen from sleep. A bed, perhaps, but not sleep.

"I just called by—" Kirsty said, "—for a chat."

Julia made a half shrug.

"Well, it's not convenient just at the moment," she said.

"I see."

"Maybe we could speak later in the week?"

Kirsty's gaze drifted past Julia to the coat stand in the hall. A man's gabardine hung from one of the pegs, still damp.

"Is Rory in?" she ventured.

"No," Julia said. "Of course not. He's at work." Her face hardened. "Is that what you came round for?" she said. "To see Rory?"

"No, I—"

"You don't have to ask my permission, you know. He's a grown man. You two can do what the fuck you like."

Kirsty didn't try to debate the point. The volte-face left her dizzied.

"Go home," Julia said. "I don't want to talk to you."

She slammed the door.

Kirsty stood on the step for half a minute, shaking. She had little doubt of what was going on. The dripping raincoat, Julia's agitation—her flushed face, her sudden anger. She had a lover in the house. Poor Rory had misread all the signs.

She deserted the doorstep and started down the path to the street. A crowd of thoughts jostled for her attention. At last, one came clear of the pack: How would she tell Rory? His heart would break, she had no doubt of that. And she, the luckless tale-teller, she would be tainted with the news, wouldn't she? She felt tears close.

They didn't come, however; another sensation, more insistent, overtook as she stepped onto the pavement from the path.

She was being watched. She could feel the look at the back of her head. Was it Julia? Somehow, she thought not. The lover then. Yes, the lover!

Safely out of the shadow of the house, she succumbed to the urge to turn and look.

In the damp room, Frank stared through the hole he had made in the blind. The visitor—whose face he vaguely recognized—was staring up at the house, at his very window, indeed. Confident that she could see nothing of him, he stared back. He had certainly set his eyes on more voluptuous creatures, but something about her lack of glamour engaged him. Such women were in his experience often more entertaining company than beauties like Julia. They could be flattered or bullied into acts the beauties would never countenance and be grateful for the attention. Perhaps she would come back, this woman. He hoped she would.

Kirsty scanned the facade of the house, but it was blank; the windows were either empty or curtained. Yet the feeling of being watched persisted; indeed it was so strong she turned away in embarrassment.

The rain started again as she walked along Lodovico

Street, and she welcomed it. It cooled her blushes, and gave cover to tears that would be postponed no longer.

3

Julia had gone back upstairs trembling, and found White Tie at the door. Or rather, his head. This time, either out of an excess of greed or malice, Frank had dismembered the corpse. Pieces of bones and dried meat lay scattered about the room.

There was no sign of the gourmet himself.

She turned back toward the door, and he was there, blocking her path. Mere minutes had passed since she'd seen him bending to drain energy from the dead man. In that brief time he had changed out of all recognition. Where there had been withered cartilage, there was now ripening muscle; the map of his arteries and veins was being drawn anew: they pulsed with stolen life. There was even a sprouting of hair, somewhat premature perhaps given his absence of skin, on the raw ball of his head.

None of this sweetened his appearance a jot. Indeed in many ways it worsened it. Previously there had been scarcely anything recognizable about him, but now there were scraps of humanity everywhere, throwing into yet greater relief the catastrophic nature of his wounding.

There was worse to come. He spoke, and when he spoke it was with a voice that was indisputably Frank's. The broken syllables had gone.

"I feel pain," he said.

His browless, half-lidded eyes were watching her every response. She tried to conceal the queasiness she felt, but knew the disguise inadequate.

"My nerves are working again," he was telling her, "and they *hurt*."

"What can I do about it?" she asked him.

"Maybe . . . maybe some bandages."

"Bandages?"

"Help me bind myself together."

"If that's what you want."

"But I need more than that, Julia. I need another body."

"Another?" she said. Was there no end to this?

"What's to lose?" he replied, moving closer to her. At his sudden proximity she became very anxious. Reading the fear in her face, he stopped his advance.

"I'll be whole soon . . ." he promised her, "and when I am . . ."

"I'd better clear up," she said, averting her gaze from him.

"When I am, sweet Julia . . ."

"Rory will be home soon."

"*Rory!*" He spat the name out. "My darling brother! How in God's name did you come to marry such a dullard?"

She felt a spasm of anger toward Frank. "I loved him," she said. And then, after a moment's pondering, corrected herself. "I thought I loved him."

His laugh only made his dreadful nakedness more apparent. "How can you have believed that?" he said. "He's a slug. Always was. Always will be. Never had any sense of adventure."

"Unlike you."

"Unlike me."

She looked down at the floor; a dead man's hand lay between them. For an instant she was almost overwhelmed by self-revulsion. All that she had done, and dreamed of doing, in the last few days rose up in front of her: a parade of seductions that had ended in death—all for this death that she had hoped so fervently would end in seduction. She was as damned as he, she thought; no fouler ambition could nest in his head than presently cooed and fluttered in hers.

Well . . . it was done.

"Heal me," he whispered to her. The harshness had gone from his voice. He spoke like a lover. "Heal me . . . please."

"I will," she said. "I promise you I will."

"And then we'll be together."

She frowned.

"What about Rory?"

"We're brothers, under the skin," Frank said. "I'll make him see the wisdom of this, the miracle of it. You don't belong to him Julia. Not anymore."

"No," she said. It was true.

"We belong to each other. That's what you want isn't it?"

"It's what I want."

"You know I think if I'd had you I wouldn't have despaired," he said to her. "Wouldn't have given away my body and soul so cheaply."

"Cheaply?"

"For pleasure. For mere sensuality. In you . . ." here he moved toward her again. This time his words held her; she didn't retreat. "In you I might have discovered some reason to live."

"I'm here," she said. Without thinking, she reached across and touched him. The body was hot, and damp. His pulse seemed to be everywhere. In every tender bud of nerve, in each burgeoning sinew. The contact excited her. It was as if, until this moment, she had never quite believed him to be real. Now it was incontestable. She had *made* this man, or remade him, used her wit and her cunning to give him substance. The thrill she felt, touching this too vulnerable body, was the thrill of ownership.

"This is the most dangerous time," he told her. "Before now, I could hide myself. I was practically nothing at all. But not anymore."

"No. I've thought of that."

"We must be done with it quickly. I must be strong and whole, at whatever cost. You agree?"

"Of course."

"After that there'll be an end to the waiting, Julia."

The pulse in him seemed to quicken at the thought.

Then he was kneeling in front of her. His unfinished hands were at her hips, then his mouth.

Forsaking the dregs of her distaste, she put her hand upon his head, and felt the hair—silken, like a baby's—and the shell of his skull beneath. He had learned nothing of delicacy since last he'd held her. But despair had taught her the fine art of squeezing blood from stones; with time she would have love from this hateful thing, or know the reason why.

EIGHT

1

There was thunder that night. A storm without rain, which made the air smell of steel.

Kirsty had never slept well. Even as a child, though her mother had known lullabies enough to pacify nations, the girl had never found slumber easy. It wasn't that she had bad dreams; or at least none that lingered until morning. It was that sleep itself—the act of closing the eyes and relinquishing control of her consciousness—was something she was temperamentally unsuited to.

Tonight, with the thunder so loud and the lightning so bright, she was happy. She had an excuse to forsake her tangled bed, and drink tea, and watch the spectacle from her window.

It gave her time to think, as well—time to turn over the problem that had vexed her since leaving the house on Lodovico Street. But she was still no nearer an answer.

One particular doubt nagged. Suppose she was wrong about what she'd seen? Suppose she'd misconstrued the evidence, and Julia had a perfectly good explanation? She would lose Rory at a stroke.

And yet, how could she remain silent? She couldn't bear to think of the woman laughing behind his back, exploiting his gentility, his naïveté. The thought made her blood boil.

The only other option was to wait and watch, to see if she could gain some incontrovertible evidence. If her worst suppositions were then confirmed, she would have no choice but to tell Rory all she'd seen.

Yes. That was the answer. Wait and watch, watch and wait.

The thunder rolled around for long hours, denying her sleep until nearly four. When, finally, she did sleep, it was the slumber of a watcher and waiter. Light, and full of sighs.

2

The storm made a ghost train of the house. Julia sat downstairs, and counted the beats between the flash and the fury that came on its heels. She had never liked thunder. She, a murderess; she, a consorter with the living dead. It was another paradox to add to the thousand she'd found at work in herself of late. She thought more than once of going upstairs, and taking some comfort with the prodigy, but knew that it would be unwise. Rory might return at any moment from his office party. He would be drunk, on past experience, and full of unwelcome fondness.

The storm crept closer. She put on the television, to block out the din, which it scarcely did.

At eleven, Rory came home, wreathed in smiles. He had good news. In the middle of the party his supervisor had taken him aside, commended him for his excellent work, and spoken of great things for the future. Julia listened to his retelling of the exchange, hoping that his inebriation would blind him to her indifference. At last, his news told, he threw off his jacket and sat down on the sofa beside her.

"Poor you," he said. "You don't like the thunder."

"I'm fine," she said.

"Are you sure?"

"Yes. Fine."

He leaned across to her and nuzzled her ear.

"You're sweaty," she said matter-of-factly. He didn't cease his overtures, however, unwilling to lower his baton now that he'd begun.

"*Please*, Rory—" she said, "I don't want this."

"Why not? What did I do?"

"Nothing," she said, pretending some interest in the television. "You're fine."

"Oh, is that right?" he said. "*You're* fine. *I'm* fine. Everybody's fucking fine."

She stared at the flickering screen. The late evening news had just begun, the usual cup of sorrows full to brimming. Rory talked on, drowning out the newscaster's voice with his diatribe. She didn't much mind. What did the world have to tell her? Little enough. Whereas she, *she* had news for the world that it would reel to hear. About the condition of the damned; about love lost, and then found; about what despair and desire have in common.

"Please, Julia"—Rory was saying—"just speak to me."

The pleas demanded her attention. He looked, she thought, like the boy in the photographs—his body hirsute and bloated, his clothes those of an adult—but still, in essence, a boy, with his bewildered gaze and sulky mouth. She remembered Frank's question: "*How could you ever have married such a dullard?*" Thinking of it, a sour smile creased her lips. He looked at her, his puzzlement deepening.

"What's so funny, damn you?"

"Nothing."

He shook his head, dull anger replacing the sulk. A peal of thunder followed the lightning with barely a beat intervening. As it came, there was a noise from the floor above. She turned her attention back to the television, to divert Rory's interest. But it was a vain attempt; he'd heard the sound.

"What the fuck was that?"

"Thunder."

He stood up. "No," he said. "Something else." He was already at the door.

A dozen options raced through her head, none of them practical. He wrestled drunkenly with the door handle.

"Maybe I left a window open," she said and got up. "I'll go and see."

"I can do it," he replied. "I'm not totally inept."

"Nobody said—" she began, but he wasn't listening. As he stepped out into the hallway the lightning came with the thunder: loud and bright. As she went in pursuit of him another flash came fast upon the first, accompanied by a bowel-rocking crash. Rory was already halfway up the stairs.

"It was nothing!" she shouted after him. He made no reply but climbed on to the top of the stairs. She followed.

"Don't . . ." she said to him, in a lull between one peal and the next. He heard her this time. Or rather, chose to listen. When she reached the top of the stairs he was waiting.

"Something wrong?" he said.

She hid her trepidation behind a shrug. "You're being silly," she replied softly.

"Am I?"

"It was just the thunder."

His face, lit from the hall below, suddenly softened. "Why do you treat me like shit?" he asked her.

"You're just tired," she told him.

"Why though?" he persisted, childlike. "What have I ever done to you?"

"It's all right," she said. "Really, Rory. Everything's all right." The same hypnotic banalities, over and over.

Again, the thunder. And beneath the din, another sound. She cursed Frank's indiscretion.

Rory turned, and looked along the darkened landing.

"Hear that?" he said.

"No."

His limbs dogged by drink, he moved away from her.

She watched him recede into shadow. Lightning, spilling through the open bedroom door, flash—lit him; then darkness again. He was walking towards the damp room. Towards Frank.

"Wait . . ." she said, and went after him.

He didn't halt, but covered the few yards to the door. As she reached him, his hand was closing on the handle.

Inspired by panic, she reached out and touched his cheek. "I'm afraid . . ." she said.

He looked round at her woozily.

"What of?" he asked her.

She moved her hand to his lips, letting him taste the fear on her fingers.

"The storm," she said.

She could see the wetness of his eyes in the gloom, little more. Was he swallowing the hook, or spitting it out?

Then: "Poor baby," he said.

Swallowed, she elated, and reaching down she put her hand over his and drew it from the door. If Frank so much as breathed now, all was lost.

"Poor baby," he said again and wrapped an embrace around her. His balance was not too good; he was a lead weight in her arms.

"Come on," she said, coaxing him away from the door. He went with her for a couple of stumbling paces, and then lost his equilibrium. She let go of him, and reached out to the wall for support. The lightning came again, and by it she saw that his eyes had found her, and glittered.

"I love you," he said, stepping across the hallway to where she stood. He pressed against her, so heavily there was no resisting. His head went to the crook of her neck, muttering sweet talk into her skin. Now he was kissing her. She wanted to throw him off. More, she wanted to take him by his clammy hand and show him the death-defying monster he had been so close to stumbling across.

But Frank wasn't ready for that confrontation, not yet.

All she could do was endure Rory's caresses and hope that exhaustion claimed him quickly.

"Why don't we go downstairs?" she suggested.

He muttered something into her neck and didn't move. His left hand was on her breast, the other clasped around her waist. She let him work his fingers beneath her blouse. To resist at this juncture would only inflame him afresh.

"I need you," he said, raising his mouth to her ear. Once, half a lifetime ago, her heart had seemed to skip at such a profession. Now she knew better. Her heart was no acrobat; there was no tingle in the coils of her abdomen. Only the steady workings of her body. Breath drawn, blood circulated, food pulped and purged. Thinking of her anatomy thus, untainted by romanticism—as a collection of natural imperatives housed in muscle and bone—she found it easier to let him strip her blouse and put his face to her breasts. Her nerve endings dutifully responded to his tongue, but again, it was merely an anatomy lesson. She stood back in the dome of her skull, and was unmoved.

He was unbuttoning himself now; she caught sight of the boastful plum as he stroked it against her thigh. Now he opened her legs, and pulled her underwear down just far enough to give him access. She made no objection, nor even a sound, as he made his entrance.

His own din began almost immediately, feeble claims to love and lust hopelessly tangled together. She half listened, and let him work at his play, his face buried in her hair.

Closing her eyes, she tried to picture better times, but the lightning spoiled her dreaming. As sound followed light, she opened her eyes again to see that the door of the damp room had been opened two or three inches. In the narrow gap between door and frame she could just make out a glistening figure, watching them.

She could not see Frank's eyes, but she felt them sharpened beyond pricking by envy and rage. Nor did she look away, but stared on at the shadow while Rory's moans increased. And at the end one moment became another, and she was lying on the bed with her wedding dress crushed beneath her, while a black and scarlet beast crept up between her legs to give her a sample of its love.

"Poor baby," was the last thing Rory said as sleep overcame him. He lay on the bed still dressed; she made no attempt to strip him. When his snores were even, she left him to it, and went back to the room.

Frank was standing beside the window, watching the storm move to the South-East. He had torn the blind away. Lamplight washed the walls.

"He heard you," she said.

"I had to see the storm," he replied simply. "I needed it."

"He almost found you, damn it."

Frank shook his head. "There's no such thing as almost," he said, still staring out of the window. Then, after a pause: "I want to be out there. I want to *have* it all again."

"I know."

"No you don't," he told her. "You've no conception of the hunger I've got on me."

"Tomorrow then," she said. "I'll get another body tomorrow."

"Yes. You do that. And I want some other stuff. A radio, for one. I want to know what's going on out there. And food: proper food. Fresh bread—"

"Whatever you need."

"—and ginger. The preserved kind, you know? In syrup."

"I know."

He glanced round at her briefly, but he wasn't seeing her. There was too much world to be reacquainted with tonight.

"I didn't realize it was autumn," he said, and went back to watching the storm.

NINE

The first thing Kirsty noticed when she came round the corner of Lodovico Street the following day was that the blind had gone from the upper front window. Sheets of newspaper had been taped against the glass in its place.

She found herself a vantage point in the shelter of a holly hedge, from which she hoped she could watch the house but remain unseen. Then she settled down for her vigil.

It was not quickly rewarded. Two hours and more went by before she saw Julia leave the house, another hour and a quarter before she returned, by which time Kirsty's feet were numb with cold.

Julia had not returned alone. The man she was with was not known to Kirsty, nor indeed did he look to be a likely member of Julia's circle. From a distance he appeared to be in middle age, stocky, balding. When he followed Julia into the house he gave a nervous backward glance, as if fearful of voyeurs.

She waited in her hiding place for a further quarter of an hour, not certain of what to do next. Did she linger here until the man emerged, and challenge him? Or did she go to the house and try to talk her way inside? Neither option was particularly attractive. She decided not to decide. Instead she would get closer to the house, and see what inspiration the moment brought.

The answer was, very little. As she made her way up the path her feet itched to turn and carry her away. Indeed she was within an ace of doing just that when she heard a shout from within.

The man's name was Sykes, Stanley Sykes. Nor was that all he'd told Julia on the way back from the bar. She knew his wife's name (Maudie) and occupation (assistant chiropodist); she'd had pictures of the children (Rebecca and Ethan) provided for her to coo over. The man seemed to be defying her to continue the seduction. She merely smiled, and told him he was a lucky man.

But once in the house, things had begun to go awry. Halfway up the stairs friend Sykes had suddenly announced that what they were doing was *wrong*—that God saw them, and knew their hearts, and found them wanting. She had done her best to calm him, but he was not to be won back from the Lord. Instead, he lost his temper and flailed out at her. He might have done worse, in his righteous wrath, but for the voice that had called him from the landing. He'd stopped hitting her instantly and become so pale it was as if he believed God himself was doing the calling. Then Frank had appeared at the top of the stairs, in all his glory. Sykes had loosed a cry, and tried to run. But Julia was quick. She had her hand on him long enough for Frank to descend the few stairs and make a permanent arrest.

She had not realized, until she heard the creak and snap of bone as Frank took hold of his prey, how strong he had become of late: stronger surely than a natural man. At Frank's touch Sykes had shouted again. To silence him, Frank wrenched off his jaw.

The second shout that Kirsty had heard had ended abruptly, but she read enough panic in the din to have her at the door and on the verge of knocking.

Only then did she think better of it. Instead, she slipped down the side of the house, doubting with every step the wisdom of this, but equally certain that a frontal assault would get her nowhere. The gate that offered access to the back garden was lacking a bolt. She slipped through, her ears alive to every sound, especially that of her own feet. From the house, nothing. Not so much as a moan.

Leaving the gate open in case she should need a quick retreat, she hurried to the back door. It was unlocked. This time, she let doubt slow her step. Maybe she should go and call Rory, bring him to the house. But by that time whatever was happening inside would be over, and she knew damn well that unless Julia was caught red-handed she would slide from under any accusation. No, this was the only way. She stepped inside.

The house remained completely quiet. There was not even a footfall to help her locate the actors she'd come to view. She moved to the kitchen door, and from there through to the dining room. Her stomach twitched; her throat was suddenly so dry she could barely swallow.

From dining room to lounge, and thence into the hallway. Still nothing, no whisper or sigh. Julia and her companion could only be upstairs, which suggested that she had been wrong, thinking she heard fear in the shouts. Perhaps it was pleasure that she'd heard. An orgasmic whoop, instead of the terror she'd taken it for. It was an easy mistake to make.

The front door was on her right, mere yards away. She could still slip out and away, the coward in her tempted, and no one be any the wiser. But a fierce curiosity had seized her, a desire to know (to *see*) the mysteries the house held, and be done with them. As she climbed the stairs the curiosity mounted to a kind of exhilaration.

She reached the top, and began to make her way along the landing. The thought occurred now that the birds had flown, that while she had been creeping through from the back of the house they had left via the front.

The first door on the left was the bedroom: if they were mating anywhere, Julia and her paramour, it would surely be here. But no. The door stood ajar; she peered in. The bedspread was uncreased.

Then, a misshapen cry. So near, so loud, her heart missed its rhythm.

She ducked out of the bedroom, to see a figure lurch from one of the rooms farther along the landing. It took her a moment to recognize the fretful man who had arrived with Julia—and only then by his clothes. The rest was changed, horribly changed. A wasting disease had seized him in the minutes since she'd seen him on the step, shrivelling his flesh on the bone.

Seeing Kirsty, he threw himself toward her, seeking what fragile protection she could offer. He had got no more than a pace from the door however, when a form spilled into sight behind him. It too seemed diseased, its body bandaged from head to foot—the bindings stained by issues of blood and pus. There was nothing in its speed, however, or the ferocity of its subsequent attack, that suggested sickness. Quite the reverse. It reached for the fleeing man and took hold of him by the neck. Kirsty let out a cry, as the captor drew its prey back into its embrace.

The victim made what little complaint his dislocated face was capable of. Then the antagonist tightened its embrace. The body trembled and twitched; its legs buckled. Blood spurted from eyes and nose and mouth. Spots of it filled the air like hot hail, breaking against her brow. The sensation snapped her from her inertia. This was no time to wait and watch. She *ran*.

The monster made no pursuit. She reached the top of the stairs without being overtaken. But as her foot descended, it addressed her.

Its voice was . . . familiar.

"There you are," it said.

It spoke with melting tones, as if it knew her. She stopped.

"Kirsty," it said. "Wait a while."

Her head told her to run. Her gut defied the wisdom, however. It wanted to remember whose voice this was, speaking from the binding. She could still make good her escape, she reasoned; she had an eight-yard start. She looked round at the figure. The body in its arms had curled up, fetally, legs against chest. The beast dropped it.

"You killed him . . ." she said.

The thing nodded. It had no apologies to make, apparently, to either victim or witness.

"We'll mourn him later," it told her and took a step toward her.

"Where's Julia?" Kirsty demanded.

"Don't you fret. All's well . . ." the voice said. She was so close to remembering who it was.

As she puzzled it took another step, one hand upon the wall, as if its balance was still uncertain.

"I saw you," it went on. "And I think you saw me. At the window . . ."

Her mystification increased. Had this thing been in the house that long? If so, surely Rory must—

And then she knew the voice.

"Yes. You do remember. I can see you remember . . ."

It was *Rory's* voice, or rather, a close approximation of it. More guttural, more self-regarding, but the resemblance was uncanny enough to keep her rooted to the spot while the beast shambled within snatching distance of her.

At the last she recanted her fascination, and turned to flee, but the cause was already lost. She heard its step a pace behind her, then felt its fingers at her neck. A cry came to her lips, but it was barely mounted before the thing had its corrugated palm across her face, cancelling both the shout and the breath it came upon.

It plucked her up, and took her back the way she'd come. In vain she struggled against its hold; the small wounds her fingers made upon its body—tearing at the bandages and digging into the rawness beneath—left it entirely unmoved, it seemed. For a horrid moment her heels snagged the corpse on the floor. Then she was being hauled into the room from which the living and the dead had emerged. It smelled of soured milk and fresh meat. When she was flung down the boards beneath her were wet and warm.

Her belly wanted to turn inside out. She didn't fight the instinct, but retched up all that her stomach held. In the confusion of present discomfort and anticipated terror she was not certain of what happened next. Did she glimpse somebody else (Julia) on the landing as the door was slammed, or was it shadow? One way or another it was too late for appeals. She was alone with the nightmare.

Wiping the bile from her mouth she got to her feet. Daylight pierced the newspaper at the window here and there, dappling the room like sunlight through branches. And through this pastoral, the thing came sniffing her.

"Come to Daddy," it said.

In her twenty-six years she had never heard an easier invitation to refuse.

"Don't touch me," she told it.

It cocked its head a little, as if charmed by this show of propriety. Then it closed in on her, all pus and laughter, and—God help her—*desire*.

She backed a few desperate inches into the corner, until there was nowhere else for her to go.

"Don't you remember me?" it said.

She shook her head.

"Frank," came the reply. "This is brother Frank . . ."

She had met Frank only once, at Alexandra Road. He'd come visiting one afternoon, just before the wedding, more she couldn't recall. Except that she'd hated him on sight.

"Leave me alone," she said as it reached for her. There was a vile finesse in the way his stained fingers touched her breast.

"*Don't*," she shrieked, "or so help me—"

"What?" said Rory's voice. "What will you do?"

Nothing, was the answer of course. She was helpless, as only she had ever been in dreams, those dreams of pursuit and assault that her psyche had always staged on a ghetto street in some eternal night. Never—not even in her most witless fantasies—had she anticipated that the arena would be a room she had walked past a dozen times, in a house where she had been happy, while outside the day went on as ever, gray on gray.

In a futile gesture of disgust, she pushed the investigating hand away.

"Don't be cruel," the thing said, and his fingers found her skin again, as unshooable as October wasps. "What's to be frightened of?"

"Outside . . ." she began, thinking of the horror on the landing.

"A man has to eat," Frank replied. "Surely you can forgive me that?"

Why did she even feel his touch, she wondered? Why didn't her nerves share her disgust and die beneath his caress?

"This isn't happening," she told herself aloud, but the beast only laughed.

"I used to tell myself that," he said. "Day in, day out. Used to try and dream the agonies away. But you can't. Take it from me. You can't. They have to be endured."

She knew he was telling the truth, the kind of unsavory truth that only monsters were at liberty to tell. He had no need to flatter or cajole; he had no philosophy to debate, or sermon to deliver. His awful nakedness was a kind of sophistication. Past the lies of faith, and into purer realms.

She knew too that she would *not* endure. That when her pleadings faltered, and Frank claimed her for whatever vileness he had in mind, she would loose such a scream that she would shatter.

Her very sanity was at stake here; she had no choice but to fight back, and quickly.

Before Frank had a chance to press his suit any harder, her hands went up to his face, fingers gouging at his eye holes and mouth. The flesh beneath the bandage had the consistency of jelly; it came away in globs, and with it, a wet heat.

The beast shouted out, his grip on her relaxing. Seizing the moment, she threw herself out from under him, the momentum carrying her against the wall with enough force to badly wind her.

Again, Frank roared. She didn't waste time enjoying his discomfort, but slid along the wall—not trusting her legs sufficiently to move into open territory—toward the door. As she advanced, her feet sent an unlidded jar of preserved ginger rolling across the room, spilling syrup and fruit alike.

Frank turned towards her, the bandaging about his face

hanging in scarlet loops where she'd torn it away. In several places the bone was exposed. Even now, he ran his hands over the wounds, roars of horror coming as he sought to measure the degree of his maiming. Had she blinded him? She wasn't sure. Even if she had it was only a matter of time before he located her in this small room, and when he did his rage would know no bounds. She had to reach the door before he reoriented himself.

Faint hope! She hadn't a moment to take a step before he dropped his hands from his face and scanned the room. He saw her, no doubt of that. A beat later, he was bearing down upon her with renewed violence.

At her feet lay a litter of domestic items. The heaviest item amongst them was a plain box. She reached down and picked it up. As she stood upright, he was upon her. She loosed a cry of defiance and swung the box-bearing fist at his head. It connected heavily; bone splintered. The beast tottered backwards, and she launched herself toward the door, but before she reached it the shadow swamped her once more, and she was flung backward across the room. It came in a raging pursuit.

This time he had no intention beyond the murderous. His lashes were intended to kill; that they did not was testament less to her speed than to the imprecision of his fury. Nevertheless, one out of every three blows caught her. Gashes opened in her face and upper chest; it was all she could do to prevent herself from fainting.

As she sank beneath his assault, again she remembered the weapon she'd found. The box was still in her hand. She raised it to deliver another blow, but as Frank's eyes came to rest on the box his assault abruptly ceased.

There was a panting respite, in which Kirsty had a chance to wonder if death might not be easier than further flight. Then Frank raised his arm toward her, unfurled his fist and said: "Give it to me."

He wanted his keepsake, it seemed. But she had no intention of relinquishing her only weapon.

"No," she said.

He made the demand a second time, and there was a distinct anxiety in his tone. It seemed the box was too precious for him to risk taking it by force.

"One last time," he said to her. "Then I'll kill you. Give me the box."

She weighed the chances. What had she left to lose?

"Say please," she said.

He regarded her quizzically, a soft growl in his throat. Then, polite as a calculating child, he said, "Please."

The word was her cue. She threw the box at the window with all the strength her trembling arm possessed. It sailed past Frank's head, shattering the glass, and disappeared from sight.

"*No!*" he shrieked, and was at the window in a heartbeat. "*No! No! No!*"

She raced to the door, her legs threatening to fail her with every step. Then she was out onto the landing. The stairs almost defeated her, but she clung to the bannister like a geriatric, and made it to the hallway without falling.

Above, there was further din. He was calling after her again. But this time she would not be caught. She fled along the hallway to the front door, and flung it open.

The day had brightened since she'd first entered the house—a defiant burst of sunlight before evening fell. Squinting against the glare she started down the pathway. There was glass underfoot, and amongst the shards, her weapon. She picked it up, a souvenir of her defiance, and ran. As she reached the street proper, words began to come—a hopeless babble, fragments of things seen and felt. But Lodovico Street was deserted, so she began to run, and kept running until she had put a good distance between her and the bandaged beast.

Eventually, wandering on some street she didn't recognize, somebody asked her if she needed help. The little kindness defeated her, for the effort of making some coherent reply to the enquiry was too much, and her exhausted mind lost its hold on the light.

TEN

1

She woke in a blizzard, or such was her first impression. Above her, a perfect whiteness, snow on snow. She was tucked up in snow, pillowed in snow. The blankness was sickening. It seemed to fill up her throat and eyes.

She raised her hands in front of her face; they smelled of an unfamiliar soap, whose perfume was harsh. Now she began to focus: the walls, the pristine sheets, the medication beside the bed. A hospital.

She called out for help. Hours or minutes later, she wasn't sure which, it came, in the form of a nurse who simply said, "You're awake," and went to fetch her superiors.

She told them nothing when they came. She had decided in the time between the nurse's disappearance and reappearance with the doctors that this was not a story she was ready to tell. Tomorrow (maybe) she might find the words to convince them of what she'd seen. But today? If she tried to explain, they would stroke her brow and tell her to hush her nonsense, condescend to her and try to persuade her she was hallucinating. If she pressed the point, they'd probably sedate her, which would make matters worse. What she needed was time to think.

All of this she'd worked out before they arrived, so that when they asked her what had happened she had her lies ready. It was all a fog, she told them; she could barely remember her own name. It will come back in time, they reassured her, and she replied meekly that she supposed it would. Sleep now, they said, and she told them she'd be happy to do just that, and yawned. They withdrew then.

"Oh, yes . . . ." said one of them as he was about to go. "I forgot . . . ."

He brought Frank's box from his pocket.

"You were holding on to this," he said, "when you were found. We had the Devil's own job getting it out of your hand. Does it mean anything to you?"

She said it didn't.

"The police have looked at it. There was blood on it, you see. Maybe yours. Maybe not."

He approached the bed.

"Do you want it?" he asked her. Then added, "It has been cleaned."

"Yes," she replied. "Yes, please."

"It may jog your memory," he told her, and put it down on the bedside table.

2

"What are we going to do?" Julia demanded for the hundredth time. The man in the corner said nothing; nor was there any interpretable sign on his ruin of a face. "What did you want with her anyway?" she asked him. "You've spoiled everything."

"Spoiled?" said the monster. "You don't know the meaning of *spoiled*."

She swallowed her anger. His brooding unnerved her.

"We have to leave, Frank," she said, softening her tone.

He threw a look across at her, white-hot ice.

"They'll come looking," she said. "She'll tell them everything."

"Maybe . . ."

"Don't you *care*?" she demanded.

The bandaged lump shrugged. "Yes," he said. "Of course. But we can't leave, sweetheart." *Sweetheart*. The word mocked them both, a breath of sentiment in a room that had known only pain. "I can't face the world like this." He gestured to his face. "Can I?" he said, staring up at her. "Look at me." She looked. "*Can I*?"

"No."

"No." He went back to perusing the floor. "I need a skin, Julia."

"A skin?"

"Then, maybe . . . maybe we can go dancing together. Isn't that what you want?"

He spoke of both dancing and death with equal nonchalance, as though one carried as little significance as the other. It calmed her, hearing him talk that way.

"How?" she said at last. Meaning, how can a skin be stolen, but also, how will our sanity survive?

"There are ways," said the flayed face, and blew her a kiss.

3

Had it not been for the white walls she might never have picked up the box. Had there been a picture to look at—a vase of sunflowers, or a view of pyramids—anything to break the monotony of the room, she would have been content to stare at it, and think. But the blankness was too much; it gave her no handhold on sanity. So she reached across to the table beside the bed and picked up the box.

It was heavier than she remembered. She had to sit up in bed to examine it. There was little enough to see. No lid that she could find. No keyhole. No hinges. If she turned it over once she turned it half a hundred times, finding no clue to how it might be opened. It was not solid, she was certain of that. So logic demanded that there be a way into it. But where?

She tapped it, shook it, pulled and pressed it, all without result. It was not until she rolled over in bed and examined it in the full glare of the lamp that she discovered some clue as to how the box was constructed. There were infinitesimal cracks in the sides of the box, where one piece of the puzzle abutted the next. They would have been invisible, but that a residue of blood remained in them, tracing the complex relation of the parts.

Systematically, she began to feel her way over the sides, testing her hypothesis by pushing and pulling once more. The cracks offered her a general geography of the toy; without them she might have wandered the six sides forever. But the options were significantly reduced by the clues she'd found; there were only so many ways the box could be made to come apart.

After a time, her patience was rewarded. A click, and suddenly one of the compartments was sliding out from beside its lacquered neighbors. Within, there was beauty. Polished surfaces which scintillated like the finest mother-of-pearl, colored shadows seeming to move in the gloss.

And there was music too; a simple tune emerged from the box, played on a mechanism that she could not yet see. Enchanted, she delved further. Though one piece had been removed, the rest did not come readily. Each segment presented a fresh challenge to fingers and mind, the victories rewarded with a further filigree added to the tune.

She was coaxing the fourth section out by an elaborate series of turns and counter turns, when she heard the bell. She stopped working, and looked up.

Something was wrong. Either her weary eyes were playing tricks or the blizzard-white walls had moved subtly out of true. She put down the box, and slipped out of bed to go to the window. The bell still rang, a solemn tolling. She drew back the curtain a few inches. It was night, and windy. Leaves migrated across the hospital lawn; moths congregated in the lamplight. Unlikely as it seemed, the sound of the bell wasn't coming from outside. It was behind her. She let the curtain drop and turned back into the room.

As she did so, the bulb in the bedside light guttered like a living flame. Instinctively, she reached for the pieces of the box: they and these strange events were intertwined somehow. As her hand found the fragments, the light blew out.

She was not left in darkness however; nor was she alone. There was a soft phosphorescence at the end of the bed, and in its folds, a figure. The condition of its flesh beggared her imagination—the hooks, the scars. Yet its voice, when it spoke, was not that of a creature in pain.

"It's called the Lemarchand Configuration," it said, pointing at the box. She looked down; the pieces were no longer in her hand, but floating inches above her palm. Miraculously, the box was reassembling itself without visible aid, the pieces sliding back together as the whole construction turned over and over. As it did so she caught fresh glimpses of the polished interior, and seemed to see ghosts' faces—twisted as if by grief or bad glass—howling back at her. Then all but one of the segments was sealed up, and the visitor was claiming her attention afresh.

"The box is a means to break the surface of the real," it said. "A kind of invocation by which we Cenobites can be notified—"

"Who?" she said.

"You did it in ignorance," the visitor said. "Am I right?"

"Yes."

"It's happened before," came the reply. "But there's no help for it. No way to seal the Schism, until we take what's ours . . ."

"This is a mistake," she said.

"Don't try to fight. It's quite beyond your control. You have to accompany me."

She shook her head. She'd had enough of bullying nightmares to last her a lifetime.

"I won't go with you," she said. "Damn you, I won't—"

As she spoke, the door opened. A nurse she didn't recognize—a member of the night shift presumably—was standing there.

"Did you call out?" she asked.

Kirsty looked at the Cenobite, then back at the nurse. They stood no more than a yard apart.

"She doesn't see me," it told her. "Nor hear me. I belong to you, Kirsty. And you to me."

"No," she said.

"Are you sure?" said the nurse. "I thought I heard—"

Kirsty shook her head. It was lunacy, all lunacy.

"You should be in bed," the nurse chided. "You'll catch your death."

The Cenobite tittered.

"I'll be back in five minutes," said the nurse. "Please go back to sleep."

And she was gone again.

"We'd better go," it said. "Leave them to their patchwork, eh? Such depressing places."

"You can't do this," she insisted.

It moved towards her nevertheless. A row of tiny bells, depending from the scraggy flesh of its neck, tinkled as it approached. The stink it gave off made her want to heave.

"Wait," she said.

"No tears, please. It's a waste of good suffering."

"The box," she said in desperation. "Don't you want to know where I got the box?"

"Not particularly."

"Frank Cotton," she said. "Does the name mean anything to you? Frank Cotton."

The Cenobite smiled.

"Oh yes. We know Frank."

"He solved the box too, am I right?"

"He wanted pleasure, until we gave it to him. Then he squirmed."

"If I took you to him . . ."

"He's alive then?"

"Very much alive."

"And you're proposing what? That I take him back instead of you?"

"Yes. Yes. Why not? Yes."

The Cenobite moved away from her. The room sighed.

"I'm tempted," it said. Then: "But perhaps you're cheating me. Perhaps this is a lie, to buy you time."

"I know where he *is*, for God's sake," she said. "He

did this to me!'' She presented her slashed arms for its perusal.

''If you're lying''—it said—''if you're trying to squirm your way out of this—''

''I'm not.''

''Deliver him alive to us then . . .''

She wanted to weep with relief.

''. . . make him confess himself. And maybe we won't tear your soul apart.''

ELEVEN

1

Rory stood in the hallway and stared at Julia, *his* Julia, the woman he had once sworn to have and to hold 'til death did them part. It had not seemed such a difficult promise to keep at the time. He had idolized her for as long as he could remember, dreaming of her by night and spending the days composing love poems of wild ineptitude to her. But things had changed, and he had learned, as he watched them change, that the greatest torments were often the subtlest. There had been times of late when he would have preferred a death by wild horses to the itch of suspicion that had so degraded his joy.

Now, as he looked at her standing at the bottom of the stairs, it was impossible for him to even remember how good things had once been. All was doubt and dirt.

One thing he was glad of: she looked troubled. Maybe that meant there was a confession in the air, indiscretions that she would pour out and that he would forgive her for in a welter of tears and understanding.

''You look sad,'' he said.

She hesitated, then said: ''It's difficult, Rory.''

''What is?''

She seemed to want to give up before she began.

''What is?'' he pressed.

"I've so much to tell you."

Her hand, he saw, was grasping the bannister so tightly
the knuckles burned white. "I'm listening," he said. He
could love her again, if she'd just be honest with him.
"Tell me," he said.

"I think maybe . . . maybe it would be easier if I
showed you . . ." she told him, and so saying, led him
upstairs.

2

The wind that harried the streets was not warm, to judge
by the way the pedestrians drew their collars up and their
faces down. But Kirsty didn't feel the chill. Was it her
invisible companion who kept the cold from her, cloaking
her with that fire the Ancients had conjured to burn sinners
in? Either that, or she was too frightened to feel anything.

But then that wasn't how she felt; she *wasn't* frightened.
The feeling in her gut was far more ambiguous. She had
opened a door—the same door Rory's brother had opened—
and now she was walking with demons. And at the end of
her travels, she would have her revenge. She would find
the thing that had torn her and tormented her, and make
him feel the powerlessness that she had suffered. She
would watch him squirm. More, she would enjoy it. Pain
had made a sadist of her.

As she made her way along Lodovico Street, she looked
round for a sign of the Cenobite, but he was nowhere to be
seen. Undaunted, she approached the house. She had no
plan in mind: there were too many variables to be juggled.
For one, would Julia be there? And if so, how involved in
all of this was she? Impossible to believe that she could be
an innocent bystander, but perhaps she had acted out of
terror of Frank; the next few minutes might furnish the
answers. She rang the bell, and waited.

The door was answered by Julia. In her hand, a length
of white lace.

"Kirsty," she said, apparently unfazed by her appearance. "It's late . . ."

"Where's Rory?" were Kirsty's first words. They hadn't been quite what she'd intended, but they came out unbidden.

"He's here," Julia replied calmly, as if seeking to soothe a manic child. "Is there something wrong?"

"I'd like to see him," Kirsty answered.

"Rory?"

"Yes . . ."

She stepped over the threshold without waiting for an invitation. Julia made no objection, but closed the door behind her.

Only now did Kirsty feel the chill. She stood in the hallway and shivered.

"You look terrible," said Julia plainly.

"I was here this afternoon," she blurted. "I saw what happened, Julia. I *saw*."

"What was there to see?" came the reply; her poise was unassailed.

"You know."

"Truly I don't."

"I want to speak to Rory . . ."

"Of course," came the reply. "But take care with him, will you? He's not feeling very well."

She led Kirsty through to the dining room. Rory was sitting at the table; there was a glass of spirits at his hand, a bottle beside it. Laid across an adjacent chair was Julia's wedding dress. The sight of it prompted recognition of the lace swathe in her hand: it was the bride's veil.

Rory looked much the worse for wear. There was dried blood on his face, and at his hairline. The smile he offered was warm, but fatigued.

"What happened . . . ?" she asked him.

"It's all right now, Kirsty," he said. His voice barely aspired to a whisper. "Julia told me everything . . . and it's all right."

"No," she said, knowing that he couldn't possibly have the whole story.

"You came here this afternoon."

"That's right."

"That was unfortunate."

"You . . . you asked me . . ." She glanced at Julia, who was standing at the door, then back at Rory. "I did what I thought you wanted."

"Yes. I know. I know. I'm only sorry you were dragged into this terrible business."

"You know what your brother's done?" she said. "You know what he summoned?"

"I know enough," Rory replied. "The point is, it's over now."

"What do you mean?"

"Whatever he did to you, I'll make amends—"

"What do you mean, *over*?"

"He's dead, Kirsty."

(". . . *deliver him alive, and maybe we won't tear your soul apart.*")

"Dead?"

"We destroyed him, Julia and I. It wasn't so difficult. He thought he could trust me, you see, thought that blood was thicker than water. Well it isn't. I wouldn't suffer a man like that to live . . ."

She felt something twitch in her belly. Had the Cenobites got their hooks in her already, snagging the carpet of her bowels? "You've been so kind, Kirsty. Risking so much, coming back here . . ."

(There was something at her shoulder. "*Give me your soul,*" it said.)

"I'll go to the authorities, when I feel a little stronger. Try and find a way to make them understand . . ."

"You killed him?" she said.

"Yes."

"I don't believe it . . ." she muttered.

"Take her upstairs," Rory said to Julia. "Show her."

"Do you want to see?" Julia enquired.

Kirsty nodded and followed.

It was warmer on the landing than below, and the air greasy and gray, like filthy dishwater. The door to Frank's room was ajar. The thing that lay on the bare boards, in a tangle of torn bandaging, still steamed. His neck was clearly broken, head set askew on his shoulders. He was devoid of skin from head to foot.

Kirsty looked away, nauseated.

"Satisfied?" Julia asked.

Kirsty didn't reply, but left the room and stepped onto the landing. At her shoulder, the air was restless.

(*"You lost,"* something said, close by her.

"I know" she murmured.)

The bell had begun to ring, tolling for her, surely; and a turmoil of wings nearby, a carnival of carrion birds. She hurried down the stairs, praying that she wouldn't be overtaken before she reached the door. If they tore her heart out, let Rory be spared the sight. Let him remember her strong, with laughter on her lips, not pleas.

Behind her, Julia said, "Where are you going?" When there was no reply forthcoming, she went on talking. "Don't say anything to anybody, Kirsty," she insisted. "We can deal with this, Rory and me—"

Her voice had stirred Rory from his drink. He appeared in the hallway. The wounds Frank had inflicted looked more severe than Kirsty had first thought. His face was bruised in a dozen places, and the skin at his neck plowed up. As she came abreast of him, he reached out and took her arm.

"Julia's right," he said. "Leave it to us to report, will you?"

There were so many things she wanted to tell him at that moment, but time left room for none. The bell was getting louder in her head. Someone had looped their entrails around her neck, and was pulling the knot tight.

"It's too late . . ." she murmured to Rory, and pressed his hand away.

"What do you mean?" he said to her, as she covered

the yards to the door. "Don't go, Kirsty. Not yet. Tell me what you mean."

She couldn't help but offer him a backward glance, hoping that he would find in her face all the regrets she felt.

"It's all right," he said sweetly, still hoping to heal her. "Really it is." He opened his arms. "*Come to Daddy*," he said.

The phrase didn't sound right out of Rory's mouth. Some boys never grew to be daddies, however many children they sired.

Kirsty put out a hand to the wall to steady herself.

It wasn't Rory who was speaking to her. It was Frank. Somehow, it was Frank—

She held on to the thought through the mounting din of bells, so loud now that her skull seemed ready to crack open. Rory was still smiling at her, arms extended. He was talking too, but she could no longer hear what he said. The tender flesh of his face shaped the words, but the bells drowned them out. She was thankful for the fact; it made it easier to defy the evidence of her eyes.

"I know who you are . . ." she said suddenly, not certain of whether her words were audible or not, but unquenchably sure that they were true. Rory's corpse was upstairs, left to lie in Frank's shunned bandaging. The usurped skin was now wed to his brother's body, the marriage sealed with the letting of blood. Yes! That was it.

The coils around her throat were tightening; it could only be moments before they dragged her off. In desperation, she started back along the hallway toward the thing in Rory's face.

"It's you—" she said.

The face smiled at her, undismayed.

She reached out, and snatched at him. Startled, he took a step backward to avoid her touch, moving with graceful sloth, but somehow still managing to avoid her touch. The bells were intolerable; they were pulping her thoughts, tolling her brain tissue to dust. At the rim of her sanity, she reached again for him, and this time he did not quite avoid her. Her nails raked the flesh of his cheek, and the skin, so recently grafted, slid away like silk. The blood-buttered meat beneath came into horrid view.

Behind her, Julia screamed.

And suddenly the bells weren't in Kirsty's head any longer. They were in the house, in the world.

The hallway lights burned dazzlingly bright, and then—their filaments overloading—went out. There was a short period of total darkness, during which time she heard a whimpering that may or may not have come from her own lips. Then it was as if fireworks were spluttering into life in the walls and floor. The hallway danced. One moment an abattoir (the walls running scarlet); the next, a boudoir (powder blue, canary yellow); the moment following that, a ghost-train tunnel—all speed and sudden fire.

By one flaring light she saw Frank moving toward her, Rory's discarded face hanging from his jaw. She avoided his outstretched arm and ducked through into the front room. The hold on her throat had relaxed, she realized; the Cenobites had apparently seen the error of their ways. Soon they would intervene, surely, and bring an end to this farce of mistaken identities. She would not wait to see Frank claimed as she'd thought of doing; she'd had enough. Instead she'd flee the house by the back door and leave them to it.

Her optimism was short-lived. The fireworks in the hall threw some light ahead of her into the dining room, enough to see that it was already bewitched. There was something moving over the floor, like ash before wind, and chains cavorting in the air. Innocent she might be, but the forces loose here were indifferent to such trivialities; she sensed that to take another step would invite atrocities.

Her hesitation put her back within Frank's reach, but as he snatched at her the fireworks in the hallway faltered, and she slipped away from him under cover of darkness.

The respite was all too brief. New lights were already blooming in the hall—and he was after her afresh, blocking her route to the front door.

Why didn't they claim him, for God's sake? Hadn't she brought them here as she'd promised, and unmasked him?

Frank opened his jacket. In his belt was a bloodied knife—doubtless the flaying edge. He pulled it out, and pointed it at Kirsty.

"From now on," he said, as he stalked her, "I'm Rory." She had no choice but to back away from him, the door (escape, sanity) receding with every step. "Understand me? I'm Rory now. And nobody's ever going to know any better."

Her heel hit the bottom of the stair, and suddenly there were other hands on her, reaching through the bannisters and seizing fistfuls of her hair. She twisted her head round and looked up. It was Julia, of course, face slack, all passion consumed. She wrenched Kirsty's head back, exposing her throat as Frank's knife gleamed toward it.

At the last moment Kirsty reached up above her head and snatched hold of Julia's arm, wrenching her from her perch on the third or fourth stair. Losing both her balance and her grip on her victim, Julia let out a shout and fell, her body coming between Kirsty and Frank's thrust. The blade was too close to be averted; it entered Julia's side to the hilt. She moaned, then she reeled away down the hall, the knife buried in her.

Frank scarcely seemed to notice. His eyes were on Kirsty once again, and they shone with horrendous appetite. She had nowhere to go but *up*. The fireworks still exploding, the bells still ringing, she started to mount the stairs.

Her tormentor was not coming in immediate pursuit, she saw. Julia's appeals for help had diverted him to where she lay, halfway between stairs and front door. He drew the knife from her side. She cried out in pain, and, as if to assist her, he went down on his haunches beside her body.

She raised her arm to him, looking for tenderness. In response, he cupped his hand beneath her head, and drew her up toward him. As their faces came within inches of each other, Julia seemed to realize that Frank's intentions were far from honorable. She opened her mouth to scream, but he sealed her lips with his and began to feed. She kicked and scratched the air. All in vain.

Tearing her eyes from the sight of this depravity, Kirsty crawled up to the head of the stairs.

The second floor offered no real hiding place, of course, nor was there any escape route, except to leap from one of the windows. But having seen the cold comfort Frank had just offered his mistress, jumping was clearly the preferable option. The fall might break every bone in her body, but it would at least deprive the monster of further sustenance.

The fireworks were fizzling out, it seemed; the landing was in smoky darkness. She stumbled along it rather than walked, her fingertips moving along the wall.

Downstairs, she heard Frank on the move again. He was finished with Julia.

Now he spoke as he began up the stairs, the same incestuous invitation:

"Come to Daddy."

It occurred to her that the Cenobites were probably viewing this chase with no little amusement, and would not act until there was only one player left: Frank. She was forfeit to their pleasure.

"Bastards . . ." she breathed, and hoped they heard.

She had almost reached the end of the landing. Ahead lay the junk room. Did it have a window sizable enough for her to climb through? If so, she would jump, and curse them as she fell—curse them all, God and the Devil and whatever lay between, curse them and as she dropped, hope for nothing but that the concrete be quick with her.

Frank was calling her again, and almost at the top of the

stairs. She turned the key in the lock, opened the junk room door, and slipped through.

Yes, there was a window. It was uncurtained, and moonlight fell through it in shafts of indecent beauty, illuminating a chaos of furniture and boxes. She made her way through the confusion to the window. It was wedged open an inch or two to air the room. She put her fingers under the frame, and tried to heave it up far enough for her to climb out, but the sash in the window had rotted, and her arms were not the equal of the task.

She quickly hunted for a makeshift lever, a part of her mind coolly calculating the number of steps it would take her pursuer to cover the length of the landing. Less than twenty, she concluded, as she pulled a sheet off one of the tea chests, only to find a dead man staring up at her from the chest, eyes wild. He was broken in a dozen places, arms smashed and bent back upon themselves, legs tucked up to his chin. As she went to cry out, she heard Frank at the door.

"Where are you?" he enquired.

She clamped her hand over her face to stop the cry of revulsion from coming. As she did so, the door handle turned. She ducked out of sight behind a felled armchair, swallowing her scream.

The door opened. She heard Frank's breath, slightly labored, heard the hollow pad of his feet on the boards. Then the sound of the door being pulled to again. It clicked. Silence.

She waited for a count of thirteen, then peeped out of hiding, half expecting him to still be in the room with her, waiting for her to break cover. But no, he'd gone.

Swallowing the breath her cry had been mounting upon had brought an unwelcome side effect: hiccups. The first of them, so unexpected she had no time to subdue it, sounded gun-crack loud. But there was no returning step from the landing. Frank, it seemed, was already out of earshot. As she returned to the window, skirting the tea-chest coffin, a second hiccup startled her. She silently reprimanded her belly, but in vain. A third and fourth came unbidden while she wrestled once more to lift the window. That too was a fruitless effort; it had no intention of compliance.

Briefly, she contemplated breaking the glass and yelling for help, but rapidly discarded the idea. Frank would be eating out her eyes before the neighbors had even shaken off sleep. Instead she retraced her steps to the door, and opened it a creaking fraction. There was no sign of Frank, so far as her eyes were able to interpret the shadows. Cautiously, she opened the door a little wider, and stepped onto the landing once again.

The gloom was like a living thing; it smothered her with murky kisses. She advanced three paces without incident, then a fourth. On the fifth (her lucky number) her body took a turn for the suicidal. She hiccuped, her hand too tardy to reach her mouth before the din was out.

This time it did not go unheard.

"There you are," said a shadow, and Frank slipped from the bedroom to block her path. He was vaster for his meal— he seemed as wide as the landing—and he stank of meat.

With nothing to lose, she screamed blue murder as he came at her. He was unshamed by her terror. With inches between her flesh and his knife she threw herself sideways and found that the fifth step had brought her abreast of Frank's room. She stumbled through the open door. He was after her in a flash, crowing his delight.

There was a window in this room, she knew; she'd broken it herself, mere hours before. But the darkness was so profound she might have been blindfolded, not even a glimmer of moonlight to feed her sight. Frank was equally lost, it seemed. He called after her in this pitch; the whine of his knife accompanying his call as he slit the air. Back and forth, back and forth. Stepping away from the sound, her foot caught in the tangle of the bandaging on the floor. Next moment she was toppling. It wasn't the boards she fell heavily upon, however, but the greasy bulk of Rory's corpse. It won a howl of horror from her.

"There you are," said Frank. The knife slices were suddenly closer, inches from her head. But she was deaf to them. She had her arms about the body beneath her, and approaching death was nothing beside the pain she felt now, touching him.

"Rory," she moaned, content that his name be on her lips when the cut came.

"That's right," said Frank, "Rory."

Somehow the theft of Rory's name was as unforgivable as stealing his skin; or so her grief told her. A skin was nothing. Pigs had skins; snakes had skins. They were knitted of dead cells, shed and grown and shed again. But a name? That was a spell, which summoned memories. She would not let Frank usurp it.

"Rory's dead," she said. The words stung her, and with the sting, the ghost of a thought—

"Hush, baby . . ." he told her.

—suppose the Cenobites were waiting for Frank to name himself. Hadn't the visitor in the hospital said something about Frank *confessing*?

"You're not Rory . . ." she said.

"*We* know that," came the reply, "but nobody else does . . ."

"Who are you then?"

"Poor baby. Losing your mind, are you? Good thing too . . ."

"Who, though?"

". . . it's safer that way."

"*Who*?"

"Hush, baby," he said. He was stooping to her in the darkness, his face within inches of hers. "Everything's going to be as right as rain . . ."

"Yes?"

"Yes. Frank's here, baby."

"Frank?"

"That's right. I'm *Frank*."

So saying, he delivered the killing blow, but she heard it coming in the darkness and dodged its benediction. A second later the bell began again, and the bare bulb in the middle of the room flickered into life. By it she saw Frank beside his brother, the knife buried in the dead man's buttock. As he worked it out of the wound he set his eyes on her afresh.

Another chime, and he was up, and would have been at her . . . but for the voice.

It said his name, lightly, as if calling a child out to play.

"Frank."

His face dropped for the second time that night. A look of puzzlement flitted across it, and on its heels, horror.

Slowly, he turned his head round to look at the speaker. It was the Cenobite, its hooks sparkling. Behind it, Kirsty saw three other figures, their anatomies catalogues of disfigurement.

Frank threw a glance back at Kirsty.

"You did this," he said.

She nodded.

"Get out of here," said one of the newcomers. "This isn't your business now."

"Whore!" Frank screeched at her. "Bitch! *Cheating, fucking bitch!*"

The hail of rage followed her across the room to the door. As her palm closed around the door handle, she heard him coming after her, and turned to find that he was standing less than a foot from her, the knife a hair's breadth from her body. But there he was fixed, unable to advance another millimeter.

They had their hooks in him, the flesh of his arms and legs, and curled through the meat of his face. Attached to the hooks, chains, which they held taut. There was a soft sound, as his resistance drew the barbs through his muscle. His mouth was dragged wide, his neck and chest plowed open.

The knife dropped from his fingers. He expelled a last, incoherent curse at her, his body shuddering now as he lost his battle with their claim upon him. Inch by inch he was drawn back toward the middle of the room.

"*Go,*" said the voice of the Cenobite. She could see them no longer; they were already lost behind the blood-flecked air. Accepting their invitation, she opened the door, while behind her Frank began to scream.

As she stepped onto the landing plaster dust cascaded from the ceiling; the house was growling from basement to eaves. She had to go quickly, she knew, before whatever demons were loose here shook the place apart.

But, though time was short, she could not prevent herself from snatching one look at Frank, to be certain that he would come after her no longer.

He was *in extremis*, hooked through in a dozen or more places, fresh wounds gouged in him even as she watched. Spread-eagled beneath the solitary bulb, body hauled to the limits of its endurance and beyond, he gave vent to shrieks that would have won pity from her, had she not learned better.

Suddenly, his cries stopped. There was a pause. And then, in one last act of defiance, he cranked up his heavy head and stared at her, meeting her gaze with eyes from which all bafflement and all malice had fled. They glittered as they rested on her, pearls in offal.

In response, the chains were drawn an inch tighter, but the Cenobites gained no further cry from him. Instead he put his tongue out at Kirsty, and flicked it back and forth across his teeth in a gesture of unrepentant lewdness.

Then he came unsewn.

His limbs separated from his torso, and his head from his shoulders, in a welter of bone shards and heat. She threw the door closed, as something thudded against it from the other side. His head, she guessed.

Then she was staggering downstairs, with wolves howling in the walls, and the bells in turmoil, and everywhere—thickening the air like smoke—the ghosts of wounded birds, sewn wing tip to wing tip, and lost to flight.

She reached the bottom of the stairs, and began along

the hallway to the front door, but as she came within spitting distance of freedom she heard somebody call her name.

It was Julia. There was blood on the hall floor, marking a trail from the spot where Frank had abandoned her, through into the dining room.

"Kirsty . . ." she called again. It was a pitiable sound, and despite the wing-choked air, she could not help but go in pursuit of it, stepping through into the dining room.

The furniture was smoldering charcoal; the ash that she'd glimpsed was a foul-smelling carpet. And there, in the middle of this domestic wasteland, sat a bride.

By some extraordinary act of will, Julia had managed to put her wedding dress on, and secure her veil upon her head. Now she sat in the dirt, the dress besmirched. But she looked radiant nevertheless, more beautiful, indeed, for the fact of the ruin that surrounded her.

"Help me," she said, and only now did Kirsty realize that the voice she heard was not coming from beneath the lush veil, but from the bride's lap.

And now the copious folds of the dress were parting, and there was Julia's head—set on a pillow of scarletted silk and framed with a fall of auburn hair. Bereft of lungs, how could it speak? It spoke nevertheless—

"Kirsty . . ." it said, it begged—and sighed, and rolled back and forth in the bride's lap as if it hoped to unlodge its reason.

Kirsty might have aided it—might have snatched the head up and dashed out its brains—but that the bride's veil had started to twitch, and was rising now, as if plucked at by invisible fingers. Beneath it, a light flickered and grew brighter, and brighter yet, and with the light, a voice.

"*I am the Engineer*," it sighed. No more that that.

Then the fluted folds rose higher, and the head beneath gained the brilliance of a minor sun.

She did not wait for the blaze to blind her. Instead she backed out into the hallway—the birds almost solid now, the wolves insane—and flung herself at the front door even as the hallway ceiling began to give way.

The night came to meet her—a clean darkness. She breathed it in greedy gulps as she departed the house at a run. It was her second such departure. God help her, her sanity that there ever be a third.

At the corner of Lodovico Street, she looked back. The house had not capitulated to the forces unleashed within. It stood now as quiet as a grave. No, quieter.

As she turned away somebody collided with her. She yelped with surprise, but the huddled pedestrian was already hurrying away into the anxious murk that preceded morning. As the figure hovered on the outskirts of solidity, it glanced back, and its head flared in the gloom, a cone of white fire. It was the Engineer. She had no time to look away; it was gone again in one instant, leaving its glamour in her eye.

Only then did she realize the purpose of the collision. Lemarchand's box had been passed back to her, and sat in her hand.

Its surfaces had been immaculately resealed, and polished to a high gloss. Though she did not examine it, she was certain there would be no clue to its solution left. The next discoverer would voyage its faces without a chart. And until such time, was she elected its keeper? Apparently so.

She turned it over in her hand. For the frailest of moments she seemed to see ghosts in the lacquer. Julia's face, and that of Frank. She turned it over again, looking to see if Rory was held here: but no. Wherever he was, it wasn't here. There were other puzzles, perhaps, that if solved gave access to the place where he lodged. A crossword maybe, whose solution would lift the latch of the paradise garden, or a jigsaw in the completion of which lay access to Wonderland.

She would wait and watch, as she had always watched and waited, hoping that such a puzzle would one day come to her. But if it failed to show itself she would not grieve too deeply, for fear that the mending of broken hearts be a puzzle neither wit nor time had the skill to solve.